Erector Set
Erected
Hammered
Nailed

Galaxy
Retrograde
Critical Density

Anthologies
Night of the Senses: Carnal Caresses
Christmas Goes Camo: Melting the Ice
Treble: Trouble at the Treble T
Subspace: Head Games
Bound to the Billionaire: Made for Him
Three's a Charm: Double Entry

Collections
Heatwave: Summer Spice
Feral: Black Cat Fever
Clandestine Classics: Northanger Abbey
A Little Bit Cupid: Hot Pants and Valentines

Galaxy

CRITICAL DENSITY

DESIREE HOLT

Critical Density
ISBN # 978-1-83943-955-1
©Copyright Desiree Holt 2021
Cover Art by Claire Siemaszkiewicz ©Copyright March 2021
Interior text design by Claire Siemaszkiewicz
Totally Bound Publishing

CRITICAL DENSITY

Dedication

Although there are so many people who help me as each books gets life, this one is dedicated to my wonderful team, who is with me from start to finish: Maria Connor, the very best PA in the world and incredible friend; Margie Hager, beta reader par excellence and incredible friend — Margie, it's been a wonderful journey since it stated more than right years ago; Kate Richards, another wizard who knows what friendship means; Rebecca Fairfax, whose editing skills make my books sing; and to all of my readers, without whom there would be no Desiree Holt.

The *critical density* is the precise density that marks the transition between eternal expansion and eventual contraction. The analogy to the critical density is the escape speed, which is the speed necessary for an object to escape the gravity of another body.

If the expansion of your life has suddenly contracted and movement has halted or turned, you have reached your critical density.

If the speed of your life is less than the escape speed it will settle to earth. In a Universe full of matter, both its overall geometry and its fate are controlled by the density of the matter within it.

Chapter One

How fucking long can they keep me here?

Hannah Modell looked out of the window of her hotel suite to the esthetic view of...the parking lot. Beyond it, she could see other buildings in downtown Houston, accented by the sparkle of the evening lights just coming on. Traffic filled the streets as people came and went, punctuated by the impatient honking of horns. She'd be happy to be in that irritated crowd. She'd be happy to be anyplace except this hotel. *Scratch that.* Anyplace except for Houston.

How in hell had this happened? One minute, she'd been doing her dream job. The next, she'd been one step away from being arrested and tried for murder. Or whatever they decided to call it.

Fourteen days since it happened, and she was still shocked by the whole thing. She and the rest of her GO-Team had been in a remote location, delivering explosives via drone to take out a key terrorist figure. They'd been told the man was hiding out in a house on Chesapeake Bay. The word was that he'd planned a strike on a major United States city and their assignment was to take him out first.

Her GO-Team had been flown to an isolated location to launch the drone, which had been outfitted with special equipment because of the explosives and had a long-range capacity. This was a black ops assignment, so only the top brass at Lowden and Hannah and her team had the details. It was only the third time she'd been tasked with doing something this enormous and she'd spent hours checking and double checking everything to make sure nothing would go wrong. She knew she'd probably driven her team nuts, but she didn't care. There was no room for error in a situation like this.

She'd been stunned when the helicopter carrying Greg Kingsley, Lowden's executive vice president, had shown up at their site. He never came out to remotes. Jumping out of the chopper, he'd told them they had to shut down the job. Right. Now. Right that minute. Finish packing everything up so they could get the hell out of there.

For a moment, she'd just stood there, shocked.

"But — why?"

"There's a situation, Hannah. Something went wrong big time with the drone delivery. A fuckup and we have a tragedy on our hands."

"A tragedy?" She'd stared at him like he was speaking a foreign language.

"Worse than that. A disaster of epic proportions. No, bigger than epic."

Fingers of panic had curled in her stomach. "Greg. Please, please tell me what happened. You know how carefully I check everything before we even leave the campus."

"Okay, but right now we have to get everyone out of here while we sort this out. Especially you."

"But—"

"No buts, Hannah." His voice had had a hard edge to it. "Lowden needs to see you ASAP, since this is your baby. He'll go over everything with you. I'm just the delivery guy."

What the hell?

On the flight back, she'd pestered him for details, but he'd had little to say beyond what he'd already told her. He'd just kept repeating that she should wait until they were back at Lowden. She'd been baffled at how this had happened. *Misdirect a drone to dump its payload in a different place? Me? Hell, no.* She was committed to her job, her country, her patriotism. That was why working for a paramilitary company that—among other things—did black jobs for the government had been so satisfying. Because she got to serve her country in a way a lot of people never could. She didn't even have friends outside of the job, and those she could only categorize as acquaintances. How disgusting was that?

The moment they'd landed at the complex, Kingsley had hustled her right to Eric Lowden's office, where he'd told her she was off the job until the situation was resolved.

"Situation?" She'd repeated the word. This was a hell of a lot more than that.

"Your drone flew off course." Lowden hadn't minced any words with her. "I don't know if the programming got screwed up or something else did. The fact remains that somehow, instead of taking out the terrorist, which was your assignment, that drone ended up at Senator Mark Hegman's summer house and blew it all to shit. Including the senator. We're just damn lucky his wife wasn't there at the time."

"What?" Her stomach had cramped and a chill had slithered down her spine. "I don't understand. How did this happen?"

"That's what we have to find out. Right now. There's a shitstorm you wouldn't believe."

"But I double and triple checked all my settings," she'd assured him, "and we tested it several times before leaving the campus. I always do. You know that."

"Like I said, we're being bombarded with questions," he'd told her. "From all sides, including the fucking government that contracted this. We can't let them near you until we have answers. I'm doing my best at the moment to avoid everyone, including the media, and juggle everything else. I managed to get the story out that the drone veered off course, which is how this terrible tragedy occurred."

"But we have to figure out what really happened," she'd kept insisting. "*I* want to know what happened. I should be involved."

"We'll do that, of course, Hannah," he'd assured her, "but we have to keep you tucked away."

"Do *you* think it was my fault?" she'd demanded. "Mr. Lowden, you know my work. It's always impeccable."

"Yes, but that doesn't matter to the outside world. And for the sake of Lowden Tactical, I have to get answers without you in the middle of a media frenzy."

At least they weren't throwing her to the wolves. She supposed she should be grateful for that.

"We'll probably have eighteen kinds of federal agencies crawling up our butts," he'd continued. "It's important for you not to be available to them while we manage this."

"But—"

Lowden had shaken his head. "We can't chance it that somehow they'll trap you. It's for your own good as well as ours. Better it be the story that the drone malfunctioned than that you made a mistake or someone sabotaged the flight. That works the best."

The word *sabotage* had made her feel physically ill. Was it even possible?

"But it didn't," she'd insisted again. "It was programmed perfectly. I want to know what happened, too." She could hear her voice in her head now, edged with desperation.

"I understand you, but listen to what I'm saying. I'm trying to keep everyone off your ass. That's why you're on leave for the moment. With you being the pilot and engineer, they'll look to you first. And nothing you say will mean a thing to them. That drone killed the chairman of the Senate Armed Services Committee, for Christ's sake. We have to keep you out of sight."

She remembered the feeling of nausea choking her as he'd continued talking to her in a low voice, but underneath his quiet tone was hard anger at what a disaster this was for Lowden Tactical. *Of course*. To him, that came first.

"Eric's on top of it," Greg had assured her. "He just told you that. But to make this work, we need to keep you away from the media. Nothing good can come of you being interviewed."

She'd certainly agreed with that. And now, as she stood in her hotel room, his words kept replaying in her head.

'Don't worry, Hannah. We're planning to keep you hidden away for your own good, until we get a public

13

relations handle on this. And get some answers. We've got nice accommodations ready for you, Hannah. You'll be very comfortable while we sort this out. We just need to keep you away from the media while we figure out how it went wrong. You understand. If you're not guilty, you have nothing to worry about. Besides, you might not be safe at home.'

Not safe? Who would she be in danger from? Did they know? Or was the evidence not that conclusive? It was, after all, as Lowden had pointed out, her drone, her controls that had supposedly misdirected the drone to dump its payload on the vacationing chairman of the Senate Armed Services Committee.

Now, as she paced the living room of the suite, she went over it again and again in her mind, trying to make sense of it. The stated target was supposed to have been an ISIS leader. That was what they had been told. The government had received word that he was hiding out on the estate of a known sympathizer, plotting an attack of some kind on the United States. Lowden had been tasked with delivering the payload because the government was afraid of leaks in its own system.

Mistake! This has to be a mistake.

Except...she'd never made a mistake. *Ever.* The drones were her life. Was it something with the equipment? Something she'd somehow missed? Except that was verified and calibrated regularly. And all the questions. So many questions. And cooped up in this hotel, that was all she'd been able to think of.

They knew her. They had to know someone else had done this, had committed what could actually be classified as espionage. *Espionage.* Just the word made her sick to her stomach, as she had been almost every day she'd been tucked away in this upscale jail.

'You'll be safe. We have people guarding you.'

Guarding. *Right.* Private security sitting outside her door at all times. She snorted. *Bodyguard, my ass.* Despite what they said, they were more like jailers, and the comfortable suite, the cable television with streaming channel and anything she wanted from room service, didn't make up for the fact that she knew she was a prisoner. The windows might have drapes on them instead of bars, but the result was the same.

She wondered what Lowden had even told the rest of its employees, and what they thought. Had he brought up the espionage possibility with them? She considered them her friends, sort of, but would they buy into it or swear she couldn't have done it? It occurred to her that she didn't have any kind of social life beyond Lowden, but until now that hadn't bothered her...but it meant there was no one to deny the charges or defend her.

When they'd taken her to her apartment to pack up what she'd need for what they'd called 'a possible extended stay' elsewhere, she'd loaded everything she could. Of course, her unsmiling guards had checked everything including her undies before letting her fill her suitcases. *What the hell did they think I was hiding in them? Secret plans? A payoff?* If she'd taken one, for the love of god, she'd have it in a secret offshore bank account where no one could find it.

Wait...that—that *wasn't* what they thought, was it? That someone had been paid to drop the load on a non-target and she was the most likely candidate? Supposedly she wasn't under suspicion. If she hadn't done this—big *if*—then she was possibly in danger from whoever the guilty person was. *Or persons. Oh, yeah?* She guessed that was why they were hesitant to dump her in a jail cell. If everything pointing to her didn't stick, Lowden could be in for a huge lawsuit. Maybe the company would be shut down.

And no one seemed to want to give her any information. Three times a day, when one of the 'guards' wheeled in her food, she badgered them with questions, but they might as well have been mute for all the info she got from them. She asked to please meet with Greg Kingsley, and each time was told he was busy doing damage control. *What about the damage to me?*

With each passing day, she became more nervous. More desperate. More convinced she was being set up to take the blame for everything.

Her life, like the movement of the planets, had reached critical density. What had she read when studying the mathematics of space? *If the expansion of your life has suddenly contracted and movement has halted or turned, you have reached your critical density.* Yeah, that was her all right. *Stuck in time with no answers and no way forward.*

She turned from the window and paced the room, hands shoved into the pockets of her jeans. *How in the everlovin' hell did this even happen?*

She had been so excited to get the job interview with Lowden Tactical and it had gone well. She knew she had an unusually high aptitude for spatial awareness and action that made her an expert in the field of drones. Eric Lowden had seemed impressed with her and soon, from the air-conditioned comfort of her control room, she'd been able to kick butt all over the world.

When Lowden had assigned her to one of their GO-Teams, she'd hardly been able to contain her excitement and pride. These were the highly trained covert teams that took drones into enemy territory to surveil or deliver payloads in places where the government politically could not. Positions on the teams were considered highly restricted. She'd made it through the rigorous training and managed to earn the respect of the others. She was one of only two women assigned to the teams and she wore the selection like a badge of honor. She would *never* do anything to bring shame on it. Ever.

Someone had done this and manipulated things to place the blame on her. Someone who was going to make a lot of money for getting the payload dumped on a different target. She was discovering in a most painful way there was a big difference between having brains and being smart.

One thing she did figure out was how precarious her situation really was. After all the hours she'd spent taking everything apart bit by bit, starting with when she'd been hired by Lowden, she'd come to some frightening conclusions. They'd wanted her brain and her skills, which were the best in the company. They had planned this well in advance. And they could not afford to let her talk to anyone. She had no idea why they hadn't just gotten rid of her to begin with, but she figured they had some use for her. After that, she was now convinced not even her body would be found.

The story of Hegman's death was front and center on the news every day. She'd watched for a while on television, but she reached a point where she couldn't stand it anymore. Although her name had not been mentioned specifically, reporters continued to refer to "a member of the Lowden GO-Team responsible for the drone."

She had to get out of here and try to figure things out, but how? She was never allowed out of the suite and both doors were guarded twenty-four-seven. All her food came from room service, the trays minutely examined before she was allowed to receive them, and even then, one of her keepers wheeled in the table. The waiters weren't allowed to enter. When housekeeping came to clean the rooms, one of the men dogged her every footstep. She was surprised they didn't follow her into the bathroom, for god's sake.

She had her laptop, but she wasn't allowed an internet connection. No cell phone, and the desk had been told not to accept any phone calls from this room. She was completely shut off from the outside world. And she had become so immersed in her job that the only people in her life were those on her GO-Team and others at Lowden. *How sad is that?* And frightening. No one would be banging on doors asking where she was and what was going on.

She stopped pacing for a moment to look out of the window again. It was darker now, the outside lights brighter, more people moving in the area filled with hotels and restaurants and shops. She might try to climb out of a window, except the windows were sealed and she was on the fifteenth floor. But there had to be a way out of here. No one was going to try to prove her innocence except her. *Can I just catch a break here, please?*

A knock sounded on the door, breaking into her train of thought, not that it was much of a train.

"It's Santos. Your dinner is here."

She opened the door, something that was just a formality. She was told—ordered—not to put the chain on the door in case she had a problem and they needed immediate access. It was for her safety.

Right. She'd almost snorted when they told her that. It wasn't her safety they were worried about. They just wanted to make sure she couldn't disappear on them.

She opened the door and found Paul Santos standing there with the room service table bearing her meal.

"If you wouldn't mind stepping back from the door," he told her in the even, measured voice she'd gotten used to, "I'll just wheel this into the room."

Step back. In other words, don't try to make a run for it. Everything they did made her feel more and more like a criminal and gave the situation an increasingly hopeless slant. She had to figure this out. She couldn't just wait here in this hotel while incorrect evidence was gathered about her to frame her and the person who was really behind this got away with it.

Chapter Two

But for the moment, she stepped away while Santos wheeled the table in.

"Enjoy your meal, Miss Modell."

Santos backed out of the room and closed the door. Hannah had to restrain herself from throwing the safety lock. The lack of it left her feeling exposed and vulnerable, and she hated it.

As she'd done every night for the past two weeks that she'd been locked away here, she lifted the lids on the dishes. Food had begun to lose its appeal to her, but she needed to keep up her strength. She never knew when an opportunity would present itself. Tonight it was sliced steak and mashed potatoes with gravy — simple food, but nourishing.

When she'd eaten as much as she could force down, she rose from the little wheeled table and pushed it toward the door. And as she did so, an idea came to her as to how she could get out of here and to the bottom of this.

She still had her purse, so she grabbed her money, a nice secret stash she always kept with her. She added identification and anything else she could fit into the pockets of her jeans. No cell phone. They could track her. And certainly no laptop for the same reason, and also because she didn't want to have to carry it. Next, she dug out the hoodie she'd taken when she'd packed, pulled it on and filled those pockets, too.

Finally she found what she needed on a little table in the living room of the suite. She had been told to knock before she opened the door, to give whoever was outside warning, but for this to work she needed the element of surprise. She yanked the door open, startling Santos. He jerked in surprise and stepped into the suite. Hannah slammed the door shut and immediately swung the solid statue she'd picked up and smashed it into the side of his head.

All that training for the GO-Teams paid off and he went down like a dead fish.

"Sorry," she whispered.

She slipped out into the hallway, thankful that after two weeks, they'd reduced the number of guards from two to one. Then she took off, racing down toward the door to the stairs. *No elevator.* If he woke up right away, he could have it stopped. She hurtled down fourteen fights until she reached the main floor. She had no idea where the door she came to led, so she opened it slowly, praying Santos wasn't conscious again and waiting for her.

She eased the door open, realized she was at the side of the lobby and spotted a door to the outside at the end of a short corridor. Rushing but still doing her best not to call attention to herself, she blended into the crowd moving along the sidewalk and moved away from the hotel. Once, when she looked back, she saw her guard standing outside with a cell phone to his ear, looking both ways. Okay, she needed to get off the street.

A little group of people hurried out of the business she was standing next to, swallowing her up, and she moved toward the door they'd just come through. She pushed inside without even checking what kind of business it was and discovered she was in a Texas-themed bar. It was dark, or as the ads would say, intimately lit, so she had to blink twice before she could focus and take in the scene. There were high-backed booths along the walls, all of them occupied, plus a few high-tops, also full, and a polished bar where every stool but one was taken.

What to do, what to do?

If she went out, her guard dog might be on the sidewalk looking for her. Worse yet, he might be trying every business near the hotel. For sure, he'd already called for reinforcements.

She maneuvered past the people standing close to the bar until she got to the one empty stool. Fortunately, it was at the far end. She wriggled into it and pulled back her hood, knowing if she kept it up, she'd call attention to herself. Then she undid the holder that kept her hair in its usual high, tight ponytail and finger-combed it so it was loose. Not her usual style, so hopefully the guard dogs might not be looking for it.

The bartender slapped a napkin down in front of her, startling her.

"What's your pleasure?"

Oh. Right. She'd taken the only empty seat, so she'd better order something.

"Beer. Whatever's on draft."

She wasn't a huge beer drinker, but it was the first thing she could think of. When he set the frosty mug down in front of her, she took a sip, thankful that her hands were not shaking. She tried her best not to keep checking the entrance, but her glance kept sliding in that direction.

"Whoever you're looking for is sure to show up if you keep staring at the door."

The deep, rusty voice stabbed her like a spear, except the sensation was a pleasant one, not painful. She wanted to fall into that voice and wrap it around her like a blanket, only right then she couldn't afford it. Nor could she afford even a second to inhale the light pine scent that drifted across her nose and sent out a call to her nearly dead hormones.

What in the everlovin' hell? Her entire life was in crisis, killers were tracking her and the sexiest man she'd ever laid eyes on popped into it? *Right now?* Doing her best to ignore him, she took another sip of her beer, which at the moment tasted like spoiled vinegar, and tried to pretend the person next to her was totally unappealing. Except it wasn't quite working.

"It does help if you try to blend in with the crowd."

He was talking to her again, only this time there was a hint of humor in his tone.

Hannah slid a sideways glance at him, taking a better look, and nearly fell off her stool. *Ignore him?* It might take all her discipline. He was wearing a Henley that molded to the muscles of his arms and back. His dark blond hair was just a little longer than a military cut, leading her to think he was either in some branch of the service or had been until recently. The scruff on his cheeks and strong-looking jaw was at least three shades darker. It was his eyes, however, that captured her, even in the soft lighting of the bar. Deep blue, with flecks of gold, that looked out from beneath thick lashes.

Don't look, don't look, don't look.

A tiny shiver raced through her body, and it wasn't fear. Her nipples tightened and the long-suppressed pulse between her thighs chose that moment to spring to life. And speaking of life, she'd better figure out what to do with hers and the situation she was in. She tried to drag her gaze away from his.

It had been such a long time since she'd had a reaction like this to a man. *Any man.* Of necessity, she'd mentally turned all the men she worked with into androids with no sex appeal. Getting involved at work would have compromised her self-respect and her job. And since her social life was less than that of an ant, she hadn't had a relationship in forever. *Scratch that.* Forget relationship—she hadn't had a date in two years. She just couldn't handle the complexities of it along with the demands of her job.

Maybe that was why the guy sitting next to her made her hormones take off like a jet engine. She did her best to ignore him, wondering what terrible twist of fate had brought them together at the worst possible time.

"It's none of my business," he went on in that low, sensual tone, "but you look like someone packing a trunk full of trouble."

"Oh, and I suppose you can help me with that."

Why was she even talking to him? The last thing she needed was to hook up with a sex god—her life and her future were on the line and he was probably just looking for a quick roll in the hay. She needed a savior, if one even existed. And at the moment, she needed to figure out how to get the hell away from here and where to go. She had a limited amount of cash, couldn't use credit cards and didn't even have a cell phone. Worst of all was the way she'd isolated herself from everyone she used to hang out with. Calling someone out of the blue might not be the best move.

So now what?

She looked away from the sizzling stranger next to her and took another sip of beer, then slid a glance toward the door again. The agents would start checking every business up and down the street, especially when they discovered she hadn't taken a cab. She'd started to drag her gaze away from the entrance when the doors swung open and two men in suits strode in. Neither of them was her guard dog, but they immediately began to scan the room. Hannah wondered if it would look too obvious if she tried to hide below the bar.

The bartender, who had been watching them along with other customers and was now drying a glass, slid a glance to the door and back to them. "Don't look now, guys, but I think one of you has unwanted company. You guys good at playacting?" he asked.

While she was trying to make herself as invisible as possible, a strong male arm came around her and pulled her against that hard, masculine body. A hand cupped her face and turned it toward him.

"Just follow my lead." His voice was low, barely above a whisper.

Her entire body tensed. *What the hell?*

"Pay attention to what the bartender said. If you don't want those guys who came in to focus on you, put on a good act. I'm pretty sure you can do it."

She had two choices. Play along with this or push him away and let the suits grab her. *Not much choice there.* But his lethally quiet air of power and containment gave her unexpected assurance, so she decided to follow his lead. She leaned into him, turning her body so she could bury her face against his chest. But he, apparently, had other ideas. Cupping her cheek, he tilted her face just enough to take her mouth in a hot, steaming kiss, one that almost melted her into the bar stool. She was so shocked she couldn't even move, which was probably a good idea.

The kiss seemed to go on forever. She vaguely heard the man on the other side of her chuckle and say to the bartender, "I want whatever he's drinking."

Then, just as she was sure she'd used up all her breath and the traitorous parts of her body were starting to send unwanted messages to her brain, he lightened the pressure of the kiss and eased her back to her position on the bar stool.

"They just left," he told her in a low voice, "but they didn't look like they were giving up."

"Who just left?" She did her best to pretend she had no idea what he was talking about.

"You know who. Just follow my lead. When we get outside, you can kick me in the balls and run if you want, but I get the feeling you're in real trouble. And that's my specialty."

For all she knew, he was a killer and a rapist, but he'd just saved her from disaster when he didn't have to, and she did need to get out of here. She didn't argue when he slapped money on the bar for both their bills and slid off his stool. Standing, he was a good head taller than she was. His long legs were encased in jeans that outlined muscular thighs and a really nice ass.

Nice ass? Was she crazy? People were trying to dump a load of trouble on her and she was admiring some guy's ass? She really *was* going crazy.

He eased her gently toward the end of the bar, one arm keeping her body glued to his. He guided her out through the back door and into the rear parking lot, where a tricked-out pickup sat.

"I can take you wherever you want to go," he told her, unlocking the doors.

Where would that be, exactly? Home was out of the question, and she'd left herself with no alternatives. *God.* What could she tell him? Something visceral made her trust him, which was unusual considering her situation and the fact that she hardly trusted anyone. Maybe it was because her life had turned upside down?

She caught her bottom lip between her teeth. "I, uh, have no idea where to go. And yes, I'm in trouble."

He looked over at her and smiled, and her insides tried to do a jig. *Crap, Hannah. This is no time for fun and games.*

"Then you've found just the person to help you. Let's get out of here."

He pulled out onto the main drag, blending into the traffic.

"Where are we going?" she wanted to know.

"For a plane ride." He took out his cell phone and pressed a number. "Saint? Fire up the plane. We have a new passenger."

All Hannah could think was, *Oh, god, what have I gotten myself into?*

Chapter Three

Matt 'Viper' Roman slid a quick glance at the woman sitting next to him. He couldn't figure out what it was that had made him step into what was obviously a problem for her. It wasn't hard to tell she was in trouble. He could smell the fear radiating from her, and it wasn't caused by him. She was so tense, he was afraid that if she bent over, she might snap in half. Then there was his assessment of what had happened back at the bar. Her weak attempt to disguise her appearance, her furtive looks at the door and the fear that had been a living thing when the two men in suits had walked in.

Feds, corporate hired guns or well-dressed crooks, his brain told him. None of them boded well for her. Call him crazy, but he didn't think the woman next to him was a criminal. She was, however, in trouble, and that reached out to his protective nature. He couldn't wait to find out if his antennae were working properly.

He tried telling himself it wasn't the kiss that had shot heat straight to his balls that was prompting him to do this. Jesus, she kissed like a dream, even under stress. *And tastes like magic.* But he tried not to think with his dick. Okay, so maybe he had a protective gene, but that was what had made him a good SEAL. *Right?* His partners might tell him he was crazy, but he knew that in the same circumstances they'd probably have done the same thing. This was the kind of stuff Galaxy had been created for. If his judgment turned out to be wrong, well, he'd just be out a few hours of his time and a few gallons of airplane fuel.

He tried to figure out what she'd been doing in that bar, where she'd been that men in suits were looking for her. She wore jeans that looked expensive, but she'd paired them with a dark T-shirt and a hoodie. *Is she staying at the hotel? Did she have a fight with whoever she was with?* The guys in suits hadn't looked as if they were trying to patch up a lovers' quarrel. He didn't think she'd killed anybody, although he could be wrong. Beyond that it was anyone's guess, but whatever it was, it looked like he was going to find out.

They had driven for about five minutes before she spoke.

"Did I hear you say something about a plane?"

Was that tension he heard in her voice? Did she not like planes?

"Yeah, it's where we like to have all our meetings. You afraid of flying?"

"No. No, not at all. Just...surprised." She paused. "But intrigued."

"Gives us total privacy," he explained. "No chance for eavesdropping."

"Oh. Well, yes. That makes sense."

The silence stretched out again. He figured he'd just keep his mouth shut and not answer questions until they were on the Gulfstream 550.

"Do you live in Houston?" she asked

"As a matter of fact, no. But I just finished a...project here and the pilot and I decided to stay over until morning."

"So I'm screwing up your plans." Her words were more a question than a statement.

He knew she was still wondering what the hell he was all about, and if she was safe with a guy she'd just met in a bar. Who was taking her on a flight to nowhere, for god's sake. She had to be in pretty big trouble to have taken this step.

"Nope. Nothing interesting going on in that bar, as I'm sure you saw."

She gave a short little laugh. "You didn't look like you were trying too hard. Or do you just have to sit there, and the women just crawl all over you?"

He laughed. "That's some image you have of me. No, I'm very particular about my women, as a matter of fact. There wasn't anyone in there who interested me..." He paused. "...until you popped in."

"Oh. So crazy strange ladies are your specialty?"

He was glad to see she still had a sense of humor.

"I guess we'll find out."

They drove in silence for a while, leaving the busy downtown behind them and heading out of town. Viper decided that whatever she was thinking, she needed time to let it rattle around in her mind. They'd have plenty of time to talk once they were airborne.

She broke the silence first.

"I didn't even ask you your name."

"No, you didn't." He grinned to himself. "I didn't ask yours, either." He'd learned a long time ago that he got more out of people waiting for them to speak than he did bombarding them with questions.

There came another long silence. She broke it first.

"Okay, tell me yours."

"Matt Roman. But everyone calls me Viper."

She turned in her seat to face him. "Because you're a snake?"

He laughed again. "No, because I can strike without warning and my aim is deadly. It was my call sign with the SEALs. My partners have their own."

"You were a SEAL?" She sat up straighter and there was a slight change in her tone of voice, as if being a SEAL took the curse off a lot of things.

"Sure was. All of us were."

He could almost see her frown.

"All of you? How many are there?"

"Five. Including our pilot."

More silence. Was she starting to feel overwhelmed?

"It's just us on the plane, though," he added. "And Saint, our pilot. Can't fly without him."

"Right, right, right."

She was almost vibrating with the tension that rolled off her in waves. Whatever she was into, it had to be pretty bad juju, and something obviously foreign to her. He knew he couldn't tell a lot about a woman in a short amount of time, even if she did kiss like a scorching dream. What he could tell, however, was that something had scared the shit out of her, and if he could help her, he would.

"Mine's Hannah." The words broke the silence.

"Hannah?"

"My name." She blew out a breath. "Hannah. I'm Hannah."

"Nice name." And it was. Traditional. He realized suddenly he really liked traditional things. *Well, well.* A surprising revelation, because he'd always thought of himself as a rebel. "Is there a last name that goes with it?"

She gave one brief nod. "Modell. Hannah Modell."

Okay. Now he had what he needed to check her out. They'd reached the airport where Saint was waiting for him in front of the terminal building. He pulled into one of the parking spots for leased vehicles and turned off the engine. Then he looked over at the woman next to him. She was so uptight that she nearly twanged. He walked around and opened her door to help her out. When she saw Saint walking toward them, she took a step back.

"That's just Saint, our pilot." He placed his hand gently on her arm, urging her forward. "He's harmless. See? He hardly bites."

She didn't smile, didn't relax at all, just nodded. Whatever her situation was, it had to be pretty bad. Of course, it was that way for most Galaxy clients.

"Hey, Viper." Saint had reached them by now. "Got us some company?"

He nodded. "Meet Hannah. I think she's got a little problem she might tell us about."

Saint dipped his head. "Hey, Hannah."

Saint was as tall as Viper and they towered over her. The two men exchanged a look then took a step back, so they weren't crowding her.

"Plane's all fueled," Saint told him, "and I filed our usual flight plan. Ready any time you are."

Viper put his hand on the small of Hannah's back, glad she was wearing a hoodie over her top. It gave him more of a barrier between his palm and her skin, because Jesus! Just that little touch made his balls twitch.

"We're right over this way," he told her, following Saint onto the tarmac where their Gulfstream 550 waited for them.

When she saw the plane up close, she stopped, so suddenly he nearly tripped over her.

"Problem?" he asked. "Afraid of flying? I'm sorry, I should have asked."

She shook her head. "No. No, it's not that. I guess, it's just, the last time I got on a plane like this..." Her voice drifted off.

"Bad flight?"

"You could say."

He hoped his smile was reassuring. "You can relax on this one. Saint's one of the best pilots in the world. Safest place to be."

"It wasn't the flight itself. It was... Never mind. You'll find out soon enough. So, what do you do? You and your friends? I mean, that you have a plane like this and take strangers for a ride."

"I'll tell you about it when we get on board. Come on. I promise we're not kidnapping you."

"Maybe it would help if you did," she muttered.

He chuckled. "I'll let you know on that after I hear your story."

He nudged her up the pulldown stairway, doing his level best not to focus on the curve of her very sweet ass in the jeans she was wearing. His hormones did not belong in this situation, but damn! It was taking every bit of his hard-earned discipline not to reach out and cup those sweet cheeks.

Hannah stepped into the cabin and again she stopped.

"Holy shit!"

Viper laughed, a low chuckle. "It is kinda sharp, isn't it?"

"Sharp?" She turned to him. "It's better than the hotel where I was staying."

He looked at the interior through her eyes. Configured in conversation groups, with comfortable seats and couches of plush leather and polished wood, it could also be rearranged for a conference if necessary. Concealed behind sliding doors was all the electronic equipment they would need to run an office. Which was a good thing, since that was what this plane was.

"Have a seat," he urged her, indicating a four-seat conversation group arrangement, "and I'll get us some coffee and pastries. Come on. You'll feel a lot better if you do." He winked at her. "I make the best coffee in the group."

"Don't let him fool you," Saint called from the cockpit. "The coffeemaker does it, and a damn good thing, too."

Viper continued his light chatter in a soothing tone while he got Hannah situated. While Saint was doing his preflight, he headed for the galley. Pulling out his cell, he dashed off a text to Rocket, with a brief outline of the situation and Hannah's name. John 'Rocket' Hardin was the best at digging stuff out about people and second to Viper in doing research. If he wasn't out somewhere tonight, he could get started on compiling Hannah's info. If this turned out to be a dud, they'd just erase the info and forget about tonight.

In seconds he had an answering text. *Sure, but I thought you were just hanging out tonight.*

Viper swallowed a grin.

Yeah, and sometimes you run into something.

Okay. I'll get on it.

No questions. That was one of the great things about the relationship between the four of them. Nobody ever had to explain themselves. Even adding Blaze Hamilton's newly minted fiancée, Peyton West, into the mix didn't change that.

Once he'd finished with that, he made coffee for them in the single server and carried it back to their seats, placing them in the special holders he'd had installed so they could use real mugs and not paper cups. Then he sat down across from her and buckled himself in.

She looked around the cabin, an expression that was a cross between surprised and inquisitive stamped on her face.

"Just as a matter of curiosity, what is it you and your friends do? I've flown in private planes before and this one has to cost ten fortunes."

He grinned. "Not ten, just a small part of one."

"What is this, anyway? What do you people do?"

He started to reach across and take her hands in his. *To reassure her*, he told himself. Except he really wanted to see if her skin was as smooth as it looked. *Yeah, asshole.*

But just then, Saint's voice came through the speakers. "Getting ready to taxi, folks. Buckle up."

He'd planned to wait until they were at cruising altitude to tell her, but she looked like she could use something now to distract her. "So," Viper said slowly as they rolled forward. "The plane."

Hannah nodded. "Yes. The plane. And everything else, because there's got to be a crazy story here."

Keep talking, he told himself. That way he'd be able to squelch the sudden insane urge he had to kiss the shit out of her again.

"Well. Here's how it started. There's four of us, friends from forever ago. We all went into the Navy together and we all became SEALs, although not on the same team. But we did leave the service on the same day and met to celebrate at dinner."

"And you decided to go into business together? Whatever this business is."

"Well, sort of." He took a swallow of coffee. "We decided, on the spur of the moment, after a few drinks, to buy lottery tickets. Figured if we won anything, it would be a sign of coming good luck."

"And did you?"

"Yeah, we did. It shocked the hell out of us when we hit the Powerball for a billion and a half bucks."

Hannah's jaw dropped and her eyes opened wide enough that he could see all the white surrounding her irises.

"Did you say billion? As in a thousand million?"

"And a half."

"That's unbelievable."

She seemed unable to stop staring at him, and her hands were shaking, so he took her coffee and placed it in the holder, figuring he'd make sure she didn't spill it all over herself and the plane.

He chuckled. "Yeah, we thought so, too. It was hard not to go crazy celebrating. But after we settled down, we realized we had the funds to do what we really wanted."

"Which was?"

"Start our own agency that took everything from hostage rescue to murder investigations to black ops. Stuff that no one else will take for a number of reasons. We could afford to operate well below the radar, plus our experience as SEALs gave us the skills to do it. We just cherry pick the cases we take." He chuckled. "We decided to call ourselves Galaxy, because we figured the sky is the limit."

"Intriguing. And the plane?"

"Yeah, the plane. We wanted to be someplace where no one could follow us or overhear and where electronic eavesdropping would be all but impossible. This is our office. We meet with clients on what we call a flight to nowhere. Saint cruises at thirty thousand feet until we tell him to land."

Hannah rubbed her face. "That's...unbelievable."

He could tell she was still trying to take it all in. "Maybe, but it works for us."

"You said you don't live in Houston, so where do you call home?" She shifted in her seat, and he did his best not to notice the way her jeans stretched across her thighs.

"Tampa. Florida. We all live there."

She sat in silence for so long he wondered if he'd just scared the shit out of her with his explanation. Did she think they were all nuts? That he was making it all up?

"I know it's a lot to take in," he added, "but..."

She held up a hand. "No, that's not it. Or, well, maybe it is, but on the other hand it may be what I need. I'm not sure where else to go."

"Someplace where the guys in suits aren't chasing you," he guessed.

Hannah snorted a little laugh. "That would definitely be preferable." She took a last sip of her coffee, made a face and set the cup in the holder.

"That's got to be cold. How about a fresh cup?"

"No, thanks. I'm jacked up enough as it is." She leaned back in the seat and closed her eyes.

He indulged himself for a few moments, just studying her. In the bar, she'd definitely been afraid, hiding from something or someone. *The gray suits? Whoever they represent?* He knew looks could be deceiving, but what the fuck could she have done to put her in this state? It was a good thing he had all that SEAL discipline, because what he really wanted to do was slide those clothes off her body, cup her breasts and squeeze the nipples, then lick that delicious place between her thighs.

But thank the lord he was able to throw mental cold water on his dick because, just as Saint announced they were at cruising altitude, she opened her eyes, let out a slow breath and began to talk.

"What do you know about drones?"

"Drones?" Well, that was one of the last things he'd expected to hear coming out of her mouth. "I know they're unmanned aerial vehicles that carry everything from cameras to explosives, depending on who's operating them. And they come in different sizes depending on the assignment. They were used in some of the missions my team was assigned."

"Right. Well." She drew in another breath and slowly let it out. "Have you ever heard of Lowden Tactical?"

"Not really," he admitted. "We never paid much attention to the manufacturers. All we cared about was the finished product and if it worked."

"Okay. Lowden is a little different than the four major companies that manufacture most of the drones. The company also handles some missions for good old Uncle Sam, missions that the government wants to keep as far off the books as possible. Assignments that they don't want any news coverage of."

Viper forced himself to sit still and listen. Was he going to hear something that could get him arrested and thrown in a military prison? Was that what she was afraid of?

"Hannah," he began.

She leaned forward and touched his knee. Good thing he had given his cock a stern lecture or her touch would have caused a disaster.

"If you don't want to hear the rest of this, please just say so. I'll find someone else to tell my story to."

Viper studied her face. "And do you have that someone else you can reach out to?"

After a moment, she shook her head. "No. And I'm not sure where I'd start to find one."

"Then how about telling me the rest of your story and let me decide how we can help you."

"Okay. All right." She twisted her hands together. "First I should tell you what I do at Lowden. I'm a drone engineer. I got the job because I have a very high degree of spatial awareness. That's understanding where your body is in relation to objects and responding to a change in position by those objects. And I trained specifically for this. I work with the engineers designing the controls for the drones, then manage them from the control room."

"Sounds like a highly technical job."

"It is." She nodded. "This is more than the mini-drones people fly around their yards or parks. These drones are what's called remotely piloted aircraft. I trained in the classroom and in the field in simulated combat situations. I love it. I eat that stuff up."

Excitement sparked in her eyes as she described what she did, despite the situation she was in right now. Viper had to admit he was impressed. He knew the training that those in the military who piloted these drones received. This wasn't just some ordinary techie who'd fucked up. She had to be a valuable part of Lowden's operation. Whatever had happened, it wasn't good on any front.

"And I did so well that I was plucked out of the main building and assigned to one of the GO-Teams."

"That's quite an honor."

"It is," she agreed. "I rocked all the physical training, and working with the remote-control center was a real trip. Knowing we had no limits to where we could go to take photos or video or deliver payloads was, well, exhilarating."

Her entire body language changed when she began talking about this and there was an animation about her that hadn't been there before. He liked it when someone was really into what they did.

"I'll bet it was," he agreed. "Been there myself."

"For your SEAL missions, right? But they were probably way above anything I've done."

He shook his head. "Not necessarily. Everything has a valuable place in the war we seem to be constantly fighting. So where do the gray suits come in?"

Color leached from her face and her hands curled so her fingers were digging into her palms.

"My team had an assignment from a black ops agency in the government. Orders came down that a high value target needed to be taken out. The guy was a major threat, a big player in the expressed intention of a terrorist group to make strategic strikes against this country."

"Good assignment," he agreed.

"We were excited to be chosen for it. Obviously, it had to be off the books. No government agency could claim ownership of it. The target was in a secluded home on the Maryland shore, at enough of a distance from the projected activity that if other people got killed, it wouldn't be one of them."

Viper snorted. "Nice guy."

"Yeah, well, none of them are, as I'm sure you know. Anyway, we were dropped about ten miles from it. We staged and the team formed a perimeter while I readied the drone. We were extra careful because of the amount of explosives we loaded onto it."

"What happened then?"

"I set the controls, made sure everything was correct and sent the drone off." She wet her lips as if they were suddenly dry. "Could I have a refill on the coffee?"

"Sure. Hold on."

Viper refilled her mug in the small galley and carried it back to her. She looked as if she was barely holding herself together and her hands shook when she took the mug from him. He thought it a minor miracle that she didn't dump it all over herself. He started to say something then thought better of it. Sometimes, if the wrong button was pushed accidentally, everything exploded. Instead, he just dropped back into his seat and waited while she got her shit together.

"So you set the controls," he prompted when he thought she was ready to continue.

"Yes. In the field I use an enhanced tablet to guide the route. Everything's already programmed in there..." She flapped a hand at him. "Never mind. You don't need all that right now. Just know that I checked the coordinates at least ten times before we kicked off the drone. Then I manipulated the controller following its path on the map."

"So what went wrong? I'm guessing something did and that was what set off whatever's going on with you."

A look of intense pain flashed over her face. "Somehow the coordinates got screwed up. Instead of dumping the load on the terrorist, we bombed a different villa." She paused then swallowed. "One where Mark Hegman, a high-ranking member of the Senate Committee on Armed Services, was having a vacation away from prying eyes. He's a good friend to the military and is rabid about the war on terrorism." She looked down at the mug she was holding. "Needless to say, it didn't make me a very popular person."

Well, fuck. She really was carrying a shitpile of trouble on her back. "How did you find out if you were that far away from the scene?"

Hannah frowned and rubbed her forehead.

"When the helicopter came to pick us up, the executive vice president of Lowden himself was on it. Pissed as hell and ready to kill someone. He gave us the happy news but wouldn't answer any of my questions."

"That must have been an unpleasant trip back."

Hannah clutched her mug as if it was a lifeline. "You don't know the half of it. The chopper took me to the Lowden campus. The other members of the team were ferried away somewhere and I was hustled into Lowden's office."

Viper kept his face impassive, something he was very good at. He needed to text Rocket, however, and get him started on a search for everything he could find on Lowden Tactical. He'd listen to Hannah's story, so he knew what they were stepping into, then send off the message. He knew already, though, that he wasn't walking away from this one. His sensors were working overtime even with the little Hannah had told him. He smelled something real bad here.

"Did they tell you anything on the way back to Houston?"

"No, nothing at all. No more details. They just kept repeating the same things over and over. This was a mess that had to be cleared up. Lowden had to be protected." She sighed. "Not me, of course. I figured out while I was stuck in that hotel that I was going to be the sacrificial lamb."

"Okay. Well, we've got a lot to discuss here."

Like the fact that these assholes are setting her up to take the fall then maybe, probably, making her disappear. For good. That kicks this up to the highest level of urgent.

"Yes." She nodded. "I hope I didn't dump too much on you."

"Darlin', you haven't even scratched the surface of what we can handle." He gestured at her mug. "More coffee?"

She shook her head. "My nerves are jittery enough already. As it is, I probably had too much."

"How about a glass of wine, then? Red or white?"

"White, please. And thank you."

She smiled, a weary uptick of the corners of her mouth, and his heart kicked over. It was the first smile of any kind he'd seen from her and suddenly he wanted to see many more of them. He thought about Blaze— Scott Hamilton—who'd fallen in love with a recent client and ended up engaged to her. He himself had no wedding plans of any kind—not even anyone in mind who might fit the bill—but apparently life changed course when a person least expected it. *Damn.* He gave his head a shake. *Forget that. At least for now.* He needed to keep his mind on business.

He fetched a glass from the galley but stuck with coffee for himself. He needed every one of his wits at their sharpest for this conversation.

"So what happened next?" he prompted as he dropped into his seat again.

"Eric Lowden was waiting for me in his office. They marched me into it like I was going to an execution, which turned out not to be too far wrong. He repeated what I already knew, that the payload had been dumped on Senator Hegman's vacation site instead of the target. That Hegman was chairman of the Senate Armed Services Committee and carried a lot of weight in Washington. This was just a huge fucking disaster. And on and on and on."

"Did he come right out and accuse you?" Maybe there was some ammunition there.

"He said they were investigating everything, checking every possibility. That in the meantime, they would put me up in a nice place while they created some kind of plan." She made a rude noise. "Put me up in a nice place. A polite way of saying an expensive prison where I couldn't see or talk to anyone."

"I'm surprised they didn't take you to some out-of-the-way place."

"Me, too. But the more I thought about it, the more I realized if they isolated me too much, I might be able to find a way out of it. The one thing they did have respect for was my brain."

"And they thought a hotel would be more secure?"

She shrugged. "Well, it turned out to be, at least for a couple of weeks. Special locks on the doors. Always at least one guard there. Even if I started to scream, they could just knock me on the head and tell people I was crazy. It also made it easy to change guards or add them if they felt they needed to. And there would have been a ton of ways to get me out of that hotel with no one seeing and just make me disappear."

She took another sip of wine and leaned back in the cushioned seat.

"I think that was their original plan. To dump it all on me, bury me and walk away clean. But during all those hours while I sat in that ugly gray room, imagining all sorts of punishment including destroying my future, something came up. Something. I just know it."

"Okay. Tell me what happened next."

Unlike a lot of people he'd known, Hannah Modell had the ability to stay on point, to relate facts in a coherent manner and not to let emotion color her presentation. He had to admire her for it. He also had to admit that it was sexy as hell, even as he realized that his dick had no place in this conversation.

"Two men in what looked like matching suits—I think they buy them in bulk online—finally came into the room. Eric had told me I was being 'comfortably housed' in a hotel while everything was being examined, and these men would take me there."

Viper's eyebrows spiked. "Comfortably housed?"

"Uh huh. Long story short, I had thirty minutes in my apartment to pack up everything I could before they stuck me in a hotel suite with a guard on the door. They set up the locks on the doors to the suite, sealing one of them so there was only one entrance and exit. They told me it was for my protection, so I'd be safe from the media and government agencies, and it would just be for a little while."

"Was it?"

"Depends how you measure time. It lasted just a little over two weeks. I had room service because I wasn't allowed in the restaurants." She made air quotes with her fingers. "For my own protection. I had my laptop but no internet service. They confiscated my cell phone, although I don't know who I would have contacted. I'd gotten so wrapped up in my work at Lowden that I lost contact with everyone else."

"What about a man in your life? Wasn't there someone you could reach out to?"

She made a disgusted sound. "I don't know if any of my coworkers tried to contact me since I had no phone accessibility and I'm sure anything left for me at the front desk was confiscated. They did *not* want me talking to anyone. My job had become my social life and I'd virtually cut myself off from everyone else."

Viper couldn't stop himself from reaching across the space between them, setting her wine glass in a holder and taking both her hands in his. They were chilled and had a fine tremor in them. He liked to think he had good instincts about people. That was one of the things that had made him so great as a SEAL. He was encouraged when she didn't try to pull away.

"We all do that at some time or other," he assured her.

"I was just so involved in everything," she explained, looking down at their joined hands. "My job at Lowden was an incredible opportunity."

"I agree. So what happened after that?"

"Nothing. I've been in that stupid hotel for more than two weeks, shut away from the world, while they 'handled' the situation. Nobody would tell me anything. Nobody would answer my questions. I was going nuts."

"My guess? And you won't like it. They were looking for a way to make sure the noose around your neck was good and tight. Their objective is to protect Lowden at all costs. I don't know who did this, but because you were the remote pilot, you were the most logical culprit. They couldn't afford to have you running around loose and didn't want you contacting other people, trying to clear yourself. Asking questions. Maybe finding out things they wanted hidden."

"They need a scapegoat," she agreed.

He nodded. "It sure can't be laid at the Lowden doorstep. We don't know yet if they were involved in this or something went fucking wrong. Either way, they need the blame on your shoulders. And you out of the way. Maybe permanently."

"That's what I keep coming back to."

"There's funny stuff going on here, Hannah, and you were set up to take the fall so the funny stuff could go on. Someone at Lowden went to a lot of trouble to arrange all this. It wasn't a spur-of-the-moment thing. Too complicated."

She sat up a little straighter, as if his words gave her sudden energy. "Yes. Absolutely. And I wasn't finding anything out while I was locked away in that hotel. I was going crazy confined to those two rooms and only being able to speak to whoever was guarding my door."

"How *did* you get out, anyway?" He was damn curious to find out.

"I pulled the door open so my keeper in the hallway could come in and take the room service table. Staff were not allowed in except to clean under strict supervision. I was told to always knock, but I needed to catch him off guard. I stepped back and as soon as he was in the room, I whacked him on the head with a heavy statue I found on one of the end tables." Her full lips stretched into the first grin he'd seen. "All that physical training with the GO-Team came in handy."

He couldn't help smiling back at her. "So it seems. Then what?"

"I'd grabbed what I could out of my purse and stuffed it into my pockets, so I got the hell out of there. I knew as soon as the guy I bashed on the head came to, he'd call for reinforcements and they'd come looking for me. Hell, he was probably already on the street while he was making the phone call. If I took a cab, they'd check that out, and where would I go, anyway? At that moment I just needed to get off the street and blend in someplace until they decided I'd left the area."

"Those two suits that came into the bar...was one of them the guy who'd been watching you?"

She shook her head. "No, but they all had pictures of me so they'd know for sure who they were guarding." She flashed the grin again. "By the way, thanks for helping me get out of there."

"Don't get offended if I tell you the pleasure was all mine. Besides, I can spot situations like that and you didn't look like a serial killer, so I was happy to help."

And by the way, I'd like more of those hot kisses.

Shut up, Viper.

"Well, okay. Thanks."

"The pleasure was mine. Anytime."

He hoped she knew he meant for the kisses and not for her to be in trouble.

They sat in silence for a long moment. She frowned as she fiddled with her wine glass.

"So," she said at last, "I guess I have to figure out what's next. Of course, I can't go home. Lowden's probably got a massive team on my trail." A tiny laugh escaped her lips. "Maybe I could just fly around in this plane until somehow the truth comes out."

"The truth doesn't usually come out unless you make it happen," he pointed out.

"I know, I know." She sighed. "I just have no idea where to start. Lowden Tactical is a highly respected, powerful corporation. I'm sure once they had the stage set, I'd have disappeared permanently. Getting out of there seemed the smartest thing to do. I just don't know where to go from here."

Viper had already made up his mind, even before he'd heard her entire story. He liked to think he was good at reading people, and right from the start tonight the only vibes he'd gotten from her were good. Each of the Galaxy partners had the authority to take on clients without consulting the others. Their strong bond of trust was one of the things that made the partnership work.

"I can help you with that. All of it."

"You can?" She studied him for a long moment. "But I'm not sure I fit into the kind of cases you said Galaxy takes on."

He leaned forward and took her ice-cold hands in his.

"We take on anything that hits us, any situation where we can help someone who can't get that help anywhere else. That definitely fits you. I can't imagine a lot of people would want to go head-to-head with a company like Lowden."

"But you didn't even tell me what you charge. What if I can't afford you?"

He grinned and gave her hands a little squeeze. "We can work all that out. Luckily, we have a sliding scale. So why don't we go back to the beginning. More wine?"

"Please. I think I'll need it."

Chapter Four

What do I do now?

Maybe the question should have been why she had gone off on a plane with a man she'd never met before and knew nothing about. The alternative, however, had been less appealing—locked up in that hotel room until they figured a way to lock her up in jail. And she'd had absolutely no one else to go to. Who would have believed her? She hardly believed it herself.

So she sat on the luxurious plane and talked until she was hoarse, spelling everything out for Viper, then going over it again. He had turned on a tablet to record it, so that, as he said, he didn't have to decipher his own miserable handwriting. He took her back to when she'd first been hired by Lowden Tactical, who had referred her, and everything since then, including how she'd been picked for the GO-Team.

By the time she was finished telling her story and answering questions, she was mentally and physically drained. The dinner she'd eaten hours ago sat like lead in her stomach, and the wine was making her head buzz. But she'd given Viper every bit of information she could dredge up from her exhausted brain. Now she just wanted to curl up in a ball someplace and sleep for the next twenty hours.

Sleep. Oh, right. Where will that be? She for sure could not go back to her hotel room or her apartment. She couldn't go to any place where she'd have to charge it, either. Lowden and the Feds probably had a watch on her credit cards and bank accounts. Maybe Viper could find a cheap motel for her someplace until she could access more money.

Damn! What the hell am I going to do?

"I'm going to give Saint the go ahead to turn back to the airport." He unbuckled his seat belt and stood. "Be right back. Why don't you close your eyes and try to get a little rest? It's been a grueling evening for you."

"Thank you. I might do that."

She was grateful that he seemed to know how drained she was. Leaning back in the chair, she shut her eyes and tried to relax. The problem was, she was so tense that relaxing didn't seem to be in her wheelhouse. She was too preoccupied going over what she'd told him and trying to figure out where she was going to sleep.

She sensed rather than saw him when he took his seat again and she heard the buckle on his seat belt click.

"We're about thirty minutes from touchdown," he told her. "You can try to catch a little more shuteye if you want."

"I wasn't sleeping. I don't think my brain will turn off enough for it."

"Been there too many times myself." His deep voice had a touch of humor. "But sometimes just being quiet is good, too."

"Yes, well, I've had two weeks of being quiet and by the time I broke loose tonight, I was done with it. Viper, if you're really going to help me with this, you have to tell me what your fee is. I have a healthy bank account. Comes from never doing anything to spend money. But still, I want to make sure I can afford this."

He leaned forward and took her hands again, like he'd done before. Their warmth and slight roughness were soothing to her jangled nerves, and the scent of outdoors that he carried was better than the most expensive men's cologne. Every time he touched her, it seemed that a hunger she'd thought had disappeared reared its hungry head.

Great, Hannah. You're in what might be the crisis of your life and you keep thinking about sex with this guy. Shouldn't you find out if you're going to stay out of prison first?

"Did I say that before? Money is never an issue. The Powerball set us up for life, plus we get hefty fees from the people who have hefty bank accounts. When we started Galaxy, we made a decision that if we believed in someone, were convinced they needed our kind of help, something they couldn't get anywhere else, money wouldn't be a factor. So drop that from your mind."

"I can't tell you..." She swallowed and started again, hoping he wouldn't let go of her hands. "I can't tell you what that means to me."

"If it helps you relax a little, then it's good." He squeezed her hands.

"Thank you."

She didn't know what else to say, so she tried to make herself relax for the rest of the trip, and not worry about where she'd end up after they landed. Viper was tapping into his phone as she closed her eyes. She must have dozed after all, because the next thing she knew was the wheels bumping on the tarmac. She opened her eyes and looked out of the window, watching as the plane taxied to the hangar in the private plane section of the airport. They rolled to a smooth stop. Viper unbuckled his seat belt and held out his hand to her. His grin was warming, as was his touch.

"Ride's over. Time to get off the plane."

Hannah swallowed and accepted his help. Now what? She'd better come up very fast with someplace for him to drop her off or she'd have to beg him to let her sleep on the plane. But before she could get a sentence together, he was nudging her forward to where Saint had opened the cabin door and lowered the stairs.

"Careful getting down," he told her.

When she stepped onto the tarmac, she stopped, still unsure of what came next. She felt like someone's poor relative begging for a handout. It wasn't a very good impression to make on the sexiest man she'd met in, well, probably forever.

"Hold on one sec while I talk to Saint."

Viper didn't wait for an answer, just strode over to the pilot, who was doing the post-flight check.

She looked around at other planes on the tarmac either finished with their flight or getting ready to taxi. People were coming and going from the building she knew was called the FBO—fixed base operation, or terminal, in layman's terms—that served the private planes. It was certainly a busy place, much busier than the smaller airport where Lowden kept its plane. Her brain was doing its usual thing, trying to calculate area and angles, when Viper was back beside her.

"He's all set. Come on." He cupped her elbow with his palm. "Let's get moving."

"Come on where? I have no place to go. I can't go back to the hotel. I don't have a lot of cash with me…"

"No worries. I'm taking you with me."

Taking me? With him?

"Um, are you at someplace special?"

"Not really. We're close to the airport. The only reason I was downtown was that I had to meet someone for dinner. Saint had the choice of coming along or not and he chose not. The good part about this is the people looking for you have no idea we've connected or where I'll be putting you up."

"Thank god for that."

But still, as they drove away, she couldn't help studying other cars on the road and wondering if any of them were following her.

No, dummy. Like he said, there's no way they can know where I am. This man whisked me away slick as rain.

But she also was aware that Lowden had all kinds of contacts and resources, so anything was possible.

They rode in silence for a while until Viper turned off the highway into the parking lot of a small hotel. Hannah noticed that no cars turned in behind them, which made her relax a tiny bit. She stared at the sign near the entrance.

"All suites? Isn't that expensive?"

He laughed. "When I say it doesn't matter, I'm just stating a fact, not bragging. But when I have to stay overnight someplace, I like my creature comforts and I also like being out of the mainstream of traffic."

"Oh." She didn't know what else to say...except, was she supposed to share his suite with him? How many beds were there? What would she sleep in? All she had were the clothes on her back.

Shut up. At least no one from Lowden knows where you are.

Instead of parking in the lot in front or to the side, Viper drove around to the back of the building and parked in the shadow of the main overhang.

"Here we are." He went around, opened her door for her and helped her out. "No one knows you're with me, but I'm not taking any chances."

He used a key card to open a back door that led into a corridor lined with doors to suites. Halfway down the hallway, he stopped, unlocked another door and gestured for her to go on in.

The living room was what she'd call quiet luxury. Thick carpeting on the floor and simple but elegantly styled furniture. A fireplace with a big flat screen television hung over it. To the left, French doors to the bedroom stood partially open, and she carefully restrained herself from staring in that direction.

"Okay." Viper closed the door and double locked it. "I'll feel a lot better in the morning when we get you the hell out of Houston. I told Saint we want to be wheels up by seven." He studied her face. "That okay with you? You haven't left any kind of trail, and at least at the moment, they don't know about me. But just in case they decide to get more manpower and do a sweep of the downtown areas, I don't want to take a chance on someone remembering you."

A shiver tiptoed the length of her spine. "I certainly don't."

What next? Who'd assign the sleeping places? Should she just curl up on the couch? She was getting to the point where even the floor looked good.

"I'll bunk on the couch out here, and you can take the bedroom."

His deep voice broke into her wandering thoughts.

She looked up at him. "Oh, no. That's not right. Besides, I think I'd fit on the couch better than you do. You'd be all cramped up on there."

He chuckled, a sound as warm as hot chocolate. "Believe me, I've slept in much worse places in conditions you wouldn't believe. It's not a problem. Come on. Let me show you where you'll sleep."

Lightly clasping her arm, he nudged her into the large master bedroom, which she noticed had… *Aha! Two large beds.* She had only met this man a few hours ago, and what did she really know about him? He was a great kisser and he said he could protect her while he took care of her situation. Well, that was more than she could say about anyone else in her life right now.

She wet her lips and dredged up her courage. "There are two beds in here. There's no reason for you to get crippled on that couch."

He turned her to face him, his eyes darkening almost to navy, the flecks of gold like tiny flames.

"I don't think I could ask you to do that."

"You didn't ask," she pointed out. "I suggested. That's different."

Again he pinned her with that electric gaze. "Aren't you afraid of what I might do?"

She let out a long sigh.

"If you had that in mind, you've had plenty time for it to happen." Her lips turned up in a small grin. "And truthfully, I'm so drained it would probably be like taking a wooden dummy to bed."

He slid his hands slowly up her arms to her head and cupped her cheeks.

"I'm not sure that would be even possible." He searched her face for a long moment. "I should be polite and stick to the couch, but you know what? No one ever accused me of being polite. If you're sure you're okay with it, I accept." His mouth slanted in that sexy grin again. "We'll be roommates."

Despite the late hour and a case of near exhaustion, her nipples tightened until they felt hard and the pulse between her thighs that had been dormant for so long began pounding away so strongly that she had to squeeze her legs together.

Great. Just great. Is this what happens when you haven't had sex in so long you almost forget how it works? Not to mention the fact that she couldn't give any of her partners more than a B minus. If she had sex with Viper, would he think her a loser in bed?

Hell, Hannah. Ge your head out of the gutter and back in the game.

"You can even choose which bed you want," he teased.

She turned away, hoping to conceal the blush of heat creeping up her cheeks. She took off her hoodie but then was stumped. How did she get ready for bed? She had no toothbrush or toothpaste, not even a comb for her hair. And what the hell was she supposed to sleep in? The bottom of her T-shirt barely covered the cheeks of her ass.

She stood there like an idiot, trying to figure out the sensible thing to do, or if there even was one.

But Viper seemed to get what was going through her now addled brain.

"One thing about staying at a classy joint like this. They have all kinds of amenities, including combs, extra toothbrushes and toothpaste."

"Uh, thank you. At least I won't have bad breath."

Wonderful line, stupid. Where did I leave my brain?

"They don't, however, provide extra sleeping stuff, but I think I've got that covered." He opened a small leather duffel and pulled out a black T-shirt. "I always bring a couple extra for when I spill coffee on myself." He winked.

And oh, god. That wink. Yup. She was definitely losing her mind.

She wanted to protest, but the alternative was either sleeping in her clothes or letting her bare ass hang out of her bikini panties. At least she wasn't wearing a thong.

"Thank you." She spoke as formally as possible. "I appreciate it."

"Hope you like Blake Shelton." He shook out the T-shirt, which had the singer's likeness on it.

"As a matter of fact I do. Thank you."

"No wonder we connected," he teased. "Listen, there's a second bathroom off the living room. I'll use that so you can have privacy in this one."

"Oh, but—"

He held up a hand. "It's no problem. Let's just get it done and get to bed. We're leaving early in the morning, and when we get to Tampa, we have a lot of work to do. I already texted one of my partners and I'm sure he told the others. That means they'll hit the road running, so sleep is important. Okay?"

"Okay. Yes. Thank you."

"Everything else you need is in the bathroom." He grabbed what he needed and headed out of the room.

Hannah closed the door to the bathroom and stripped out of everything but her bikinis. She looked at the shower longingly, started to pull on the black T-shirt, then thought, *The hell with it.* Especially when she found the upscale shampoo and conditioner next to the hair dryer.

She turned on the shower, yanked off her panties and stepped under the stream of hot water...and let out a long sigh. She couldn't remember the last time a shower had felt this good. She stood there, letting the water stream over her body, eyes closed, wishing it would wash away her desperate situation as easily as it washed away the sweat from the day. Lowden Tactical was a powerful company. They had a lot of money that could buy whatever they needed to have happen, and their tentacles reached everywhere.

The shower gel the hotel provided had a soothing floral fragrance to it that seeped into her muscles like a tranquilizer. The shampoo was even more relaxing. Finally, when she wondered if Viper would think she'd fallen asleep in there, she turned off the water and stepped out. She decided to give her panties a quick rinse, since she had none to change into, and hung them over a towel rack. She managed to dry her body and hair without falling asleep, but she was more than ready when she stepped out into the bedroom. She thanked god the T-shirt came halfway down her thighs so he couldn't see she was naked beneath it.

Viper was already back in the room, under the covers on the bed nearest the door. She couldn't help noticing the gun resting on the nightstand closest to him.

"My permanent companion," he told her when he saw her looking at it.

The sight of it actually made her feel safe. But how had she gotten herself into a situation where guns became a necessary part of things?

Viper had his arms folded behind his head, blankets covering him from the waist down. Hannah blinked, wondering if that was his cock pushing against the material. She immediately looked down at her own bed, but not soon enough, she was sure, for Viper to miss her staring at him.

His lips curved in a crooked grin. "Sorry. Not all of me goes to sleep at the same time. By the way, that shirt looks better on you than it ever did on me."

"I'm pretty sure I'll conk right out," she told him as she climbed into the other bed. She made sure the T-shirt was pulled down far enough and her rear end pointed away from where Viper was lying "No tossing and turning for me tonight." She hoped.

"We'll be up pretty early," he reminded her. "That okay?"

"Fine by me. If you're serious about helping me, the sooner we get started the better."

"Oh, I'm serious, Hannah. Trust me. I don't kid about things like this."

Good.

"Thank you."

She burrowed into the pillows and pulled the covers up to her chin. She heard Viper shut off the lamp on the nightstand and the room was plunged into darkness. Closing her eyes, she tried to forget the very sexy man sleeping in the other bed, but the faint outdoorsy scent that clung to him drifted through the room. She tried counting backwards from one hundred, usually a time-tested method for her. But that didn't seem to be working, either. Finally she dug deep for her shattered discipline and at some point, just fell into the darkness.

The chopper set down on the plateau where she and her team had staged. Greg Kingsley, Lowden's executive vice president, was hanging out of the door.

She turned, puzzled. What the hell was he doing here? Whatever it was had to be some kind of emergency. He never got involved in the actual operations.

"Get in the helicopter now. All of you."

They looked at each other, puzzled.

"What's going on?" she asked. "What's wrong?"

"Just get in the chopper. Someone will explain later."

Her hands shook as she set her controller down on the makeshift platform and, along with the others, packed up their equipment. As soon as everyone was boarded, the helo took off. The noise of the rotors precluded any conversation, but she was damn sure that everyone, like her, wanted to know why an officer of the company had personally come to fetch them.

She tried again to get answers when they landed someplace to offload the rest of her team, but Kingsley was more interested in taking off again and heading to the campus. By the time they got to Lowden and he took her silently to Lowden's office, she knew something was drastically wrong.

"Whatever it is, I didn't do it," were the first words out of her mouth.

She glanced at two men standing to the side wearing similar gray suits, and…

"What?" she cried. "I've done nothing wrong. What's going on here?"

"Hannah? Hannah, wake up."

A hand touched her shoulder, and she bolted upright, lashing out.

"I didn't do it." She couldn't seem to make them understand.

"Hannah? I know you didn't. Wake up. Come on." The deep male voice, sounding so far away, filtered into her dream. "Open your eyes."

She tried to push whoever it was away, but strong hands grasped hers, holding her in place.

"It's just me. Viper. Open your eyes, please."

She forced her eyes open. Maybe this would all go away if she did. When her eyelids lifted, she saw only total darkness, but someone was sitting beside her. A click, and the lamp on the bedside table popped on. She was shocked to see Viper, in a pair of boxer briefs, at her side, one hand on her shoulder, the other stroking her arm.

"What—?" She blinked. "What happened?"

"I think you had a bad dream." His voice was like warm syrup, his touch comforting as he brushed the hair back from her face then cupped her chin. "More like a nightmare. You okay?"

She blew out a breath, wishing she could hide under the bed. *How embarrassing.* She'd be lucky if he didn't decide she was a nut and change his mind about helping her.

"Yes. I'm fine. I'm sorry I disturbed you." She fiddled with the covers draped across her legs. "If you want to cancel our...agreement, I'll certainly understand."

"Because you had a bad dream?" He shook his head. "I'm surprised you don't have more of them, with the shit you've been through."

She hugged herself, rubbing her arms and trying to stop shaking. This was not her at all, but she was finally feeling the impact of her situation.

"You're shaking. Come here." Viper pulled her against his hard, warm, very masculine body and slowly stroked her back.

"I-I'm sorry." She buried her face against his shoulder. "I promise you, I never fall apart like this."

"Hannah, you have every right to. This situation would scare the shit out of anyone."

"I guess this is the first time I've let down my guard enough to let the full reality of it take over."

"Totally understandable. Come on now, lie down again."

Hannah felt as if she was twelve years old as he fluffed her pillows, leaned her back against them and pulled the covers up. She could not remember the last time anyone had given her this kind of comfort. Her family was scattered around the country and she'd made a career out of being self-contained. And of course she had no memory of a man like Matt 'Viper' Roman offering that comfort.

She was doing her best to ignore the way the boxer briefs molded to his thighs or the obvious bulge she had to work hard to draw her eyes away from. She really must be losing her mind if she was thinking about sex right now. Her relationships might not have been intense or lasting, but she made it a practice not to fall into bed with a guy the first night she met him.

But oh, god, just his touch sent shivers over her that had nothing to do with the nightmare. He smelled so good and his presence, unlike anyone else's ever, made her nerves settle just a little bit, but then a reaction of a different kind woke them up again.

"Just so you know," she told him, "I'm not a person easily given to nerves." She wet her lips, a habit that poked up whenever she was rattled. "I work with highly complicated equipment and I'm trained to be disciplined in all situations. Have to be. I can't figure out why I'm falling apart like this. I'm smarter than this."

"Not arguing there." Viper gave her a long, hard look, then turned and nudged her. "You are."

He studied her face for an intense moment, then was at the other side of the bed. Stretching out, he put his arm around her and pulled her against his side.

"Let's see if we can chase away the rest of that nightmare."

The thing that amazed her was that she didn't push him away. Any other man, she would have jabbed him in the balls, but with Viper she felt no threat, only a soothing calm.

"This okay?" His voice was soft. Deep. Soothing.

Oh, yes, she wanted to say. *Very okay.* The feel of his body with its hard, ridged muscles and male warmth was better than the finest glass of wine. She wondered what he'd think if she pressed against him just a little and had to swallow a chuckle. If the people at Lowden could see her now. The Ice Queen, they called her. Someone had once made the comment that she'd have sex with her drone equipment if she could, and she'd laughed out loud.

The hell with it.

Viper's arm around her made her muscles tighten with a different kind of tension and with his hard body pressed against hers, the crisis she was facing began to fade away. She leaned her head against his shoulder and let out a deep sigh as the remnants of the dream faded.

"Better?"

His deep voice was like a drug she wanted to keep taking.

"Yes. At least for the moment."

They lay in silence for a long moment, the warmth of his body seeping into hers, the feel of him against her settling her nerves for the first time since that helicopter had fetched her at the remote site.

"Just so you know," he said, his voice tinged with amusement, "I don't make a habit of ending up in bed with clients."

"Just so *you* know, I don't usually end up in bed with strange men."

He chuckled. "Strange, huh?"

She shifted her weight just a little. "You know what I mean."

"Uh huh. Consider it a rare part of my duties to a very special client." He rubbed his fingers lightly against her arm.

Pleasure sizzled through her body. She knew she should protest, move away, tell him she was fine. Except she wasn't. She was a hot mess, and she wanted to curl up against him and pretend none of this was happening.

"Here's another thing I don't do," Viper told her. "And please, feel free to object if you want to."

Before she could ask him what she would be objecting to, he cupped her chin with his free hand, turned her head toward him and brushed his lips over hers. The heat that consumed her even from that almost nothing touch was like a five-alarm fire, burning her everywhere. She couldn't believe a kiss so light scorched her from her nipples to her sex and everywhere in between. She melted into it, the gentle sweep of his tongue over her lips an invitation she didn't want to refuse—couldn't refuse—so she opened her mouth without thinking. His tongue licked over hers, touching, tasting.

I should stop this right now.

But she couldn't. Wouldn't. Had no desire to. And she was glad deep down that he didn't make a habit of this with clients. Not, she thought, that he didn't get his share elsewhere. She was sure getting women was not a problem for him.

Viper drew back just a little, grazed his lips over hers then scattered kisses along her jawline. Threading his hands through her hair, he held her head in place while he nibbled on the lobe of her ear, tugging it gently with his teeth. Hannah closed her eyes, letting his touch soothe her ragged nerves and ease her tension. She didn't remember the last time she'd been the recipient of such gentleness. *Such tenderness.* The men she'd been with had generally just gone for the sex and not given a shit about how she felt or what she wanted. Yet here was a man, one she probably had no business falling into this with, making her feel very feminine and desirable.

And suddenly it shocked her that she *wanted* him to let go. Wanted him to lose control. Wanted that rough sex. *What the hell?* But as she fell into the spell he was weaving, the tension created by both her situation and her dream began to fade slowly from her body.

"Making the bad dream go away?" His mouth slid from her ear and slid down to string kisses along her neck.

"Mm hmm. Yes, it is."

"Good. That's my plan."

He said the words as if they were the most natural thing in the world. His voice was so deep, the warmth of it blanketing her, coaxing her into a place where her nightmare disappeared. She stroked his cheek, loving the rough feel of the scruff on his face. Just the touching made her nipples tighten into hardened buds. She arched herself against him and tried to rub herself against his chest, but he had her held tightly against his very male body.

"Think you can go back to sleep now?" he asked.

Are you kidding? Sleep was the last thing on her mind now.

"Hannah," he began.

Oh, god, had she actually said that out loud? Way to embarrass herself. She dipped her head and tucked it against his shoulder. *Better reel it in, girl.*

"Sorry. I should never have said that."

The deep laugh rumbled softly to the surface again. "Only if you mean it." He locked his gaze with hers, something mysterious swirling in his eyes. "Listen, Hannah, just so you know. Cards on the table. You're a client and I don't expect this from clients. It's not part of the fee we charge."

"I…" She swallowed, tried again. "I don't think that at all." Heat crept up her cheeks. "And I don't usually fall into bed with a man five minutes after I meet him. Not ever."

"Just so you know, I didn't think so."

She tried to turn her face away. "I don't know what's wrong with me."

Except I haven't been with anyone for so long I'm not sure I know how to act.

"I'm hoping it's the same thing that's wrong with me. And I'm not sure wrong is the word." He brushed a strand of hair back from her face. "Last chance to stop me if this is not what you want."

This time there was nothing gentle or tentative about his kiss, as if he wanted to make sure she wasn't going to change her mind. Well, there was no chance of that now. His mouth was firm against hers, his tongue hot and hungry as he thrust it into her mouth and licked all the flesh. It was a flame igniting every place it touched. She thrust her fingers into his thick blond hair, cupping his head and holding it in place as if she never wanted to let it go. Everything exploded inside her, fear and anger merging into a hard ball of out-and-out lust.

She'd lost all sense of everything by the time he pulled his mouth away from hers and had barely drawn a breath before he trailed his lips down her neck.

"Let's get these out of the way," he murmured, throwing back the covers.

He moved his lips to the hollow of her throat to suck lightly on the tender flesh. Every one of her nerves was on high alert, her body screaming for him to run his hands over her everywhere. The pulse in her sex was throbbing with need and her breasts ached for his touch.

Viper tossed the covers aside and, as if reading her mind, slid slightly lower on her body. Rolling up the black T-shirt, he clamped his mouth around one sensitive nipple. When he sucked on it, hard, she arched up to him, swallowing a cry of pleasure. He tugged on it harder, scraping it with his teeth. Flame shot straight to her core, the pulse in the sensitive tissues pounding with hungry need.

Viper gave a last lick to the breast he'd been teasing and moved to the other one, biting that nipple then licking it to soothe it. Threading her fingers into his thick blond hair, she tugged his head even closer.

"More," she urged.

Heat flooded her body and set every pulse point thumping. Even as she pressed his head to her breast, she hitched her hips, managing to spread her legs apart so he fit in the cradle of her body. The thickness of his cock pressed into her thighs and she wanted to squeeze it between her legs. Could she make him come just by doing this?

Ohmigod! Who the hell am I?

Not that she didn't enjoy enthusiastic sex, but she had a feeling this could go beyond that.

By now she was so hot she was afraid she'd spontaneously combust, her body demanding his touch in every place. When he lifted his head to string kisses from the valley of her breasts down her body, fire stabbed at her everywhere. The feel of his tongue as it swirled through her belly button was so electric that her nerves sizzled and her body screamed, *More! More! More!*

Yes!

She tried to push his head lower on her body to the place she really wanted it, but apparently, he was determined to take his time and tease the hell out of her.

He lifted his head to look up at her, his firm mouth curved in a grin.

"In a hurry?"

"Yes! Please?" She hissed the words, gritting her teeth to keep from shouting them. She couldn't begin to remember when—if ever—she'd had this kind of reaction to a man. But she wanted more of it. She wanted all of it.

His laugh was a low, sexy rumble, thick with urgency.

"If I hurry, you might miss something," he teased, grasping her hips just before he trailed his tongue down over her mound to between her closed thighs.

She'd never known how good it would feel to have someone lick the insides of her thighs, and damn, did this man have an educated tongue. He used it for soft licks, for tracing little damp lines, for lapping her heated flesh. She squirmed in his grasp, afraid she might come just lying here like this.

Viper nipped each thigh once before shifting his position and spreading her legs wide. He looked up at her.

"No panties."

The heat of embarrassment crept up her cheeks — which, under the circumstances, was ridiculous, but there it was. She started to make an excuse, but then he looked up at her, his lips curved in a grin, hunger blazing in his eyes, and every thought fled.

"It's okay, Hannah. Believe me. It is very much okay. You have no idea the things I'd like to do to you. With you. I just don't want to scare you when we've only known each other for hours."

"Just do it." *Did I really say that?*

"Oh, honey, you have no idea how that tempts me, but one thing at a time."

He looked back down at her and with a light pressure of his thumbs spread the lips of her sex. Bracing himself on his elbows, he dipped his head and took a long, slow lick of the glistening pink flesh. The raspy feel of his tongue woke up every nerve in her body and her inner muscles began to throb.

Hannah fisted her hands in the sheet beneath her, pressing up against his very talented mouth. Each stroke sent shivers through her and woke up responses she'd thought long gone. Damn, the man was clever with his tongue. Knew just how to trace the sensitive flesh, when to lick and when to just press that tongue against her heated skin. But it was the sharp nip when he took her clit between his teeth and bit down gently that nearly sent her over the edge. His hum of satisfaction sent shivers through her.

The more he licked, the more intense the sensations shuddering through her. Her breathing accelerated and every inch of her felt as if it was on fire. When Viper moved one hand to slide two of his long fingers into her wet sheath, she nearly came off the bed. Her internal muscles clamped down on his fingers and she rode them as he worked them in and out.

"Yes. That's it." His voice was hoarse with need. "Like that."

He increased the speed, adding a third finger, driving back and forth. When he took her clit between his teeth again, she exploded, her entire body shaking with the force of the orgasm. She rode his hand, pushing as hard as she could as she came over and over again.

The tremors slowed, and Viper matched the speed of his fingers with that of her body until at last the final spasm died away. She lay there, limp, trying to catch her breath. She didn't think she'd ever come that hard in her life, and he hadn't even fucked her yet. When she glanced down the length of her body, Viper was looking up at her, his lips curved in a sensual smile. "You doing okay? Nerves not as jangled?"

A thready laugh escaped her mouth. "I'd say you took care of that. Is that part of your client obligation?"

"Not even a little." He moved up her body until he was lying between her legs and cupping her face in his palms. Then he brushed his mouth over hers.

She swiped her tongue over her lips, the taste of her liquid on him one of the most erotic sensations ever.

"Thank you," she whispered. "But you..." *Didn't come yet.*

"Oh, honey, we're not done yet. Don't move."

He levered himself off the bed and dug his wallet out of his jeans pocket. Hannah swallowed a sigh of relief. Thank the lord that like most men he carries the ever-present condoms there. In seconds he was back on the bed, kneeling between her legs, expertly rolling the latex onto his cock. He leaned forward and pressed his mouth to hers again, this time sliding his tongue inside and licking the slick flesh. She swept her tongue over his, brushing it back and forth, and the light vibrations created sent tremors through the sensitive walls of her sex. It shocked her that just like that, she was ready again.

This time there was no foreplay, no coaxing. He lifted her legs, bent them at the knees and pushed them wide. With the head of his shaft positioned at her opening, he inhaled a deep breath, let it out and thrust inside her.

"Fuck." The word slipped out of his mouth. "You are so damn tight. I think I've died and gone to heaven."

It was a good thing she was already so aroused, because there was no going slow this time. He drove into her like a jackhammer, pounding with deep, hard, fast thrusts, the thickness of his cock stretching her inner walls to their limit.

With shocking swiftness, her orgasm roared up within her, just as Viper's body stiffened and his cock pulsed inside her. She dug her heels into the small of his back and pulled herself as close to his body as she could, her muscles gripping him, milking him.

And then...

Like a rocket, the explosion went off. They came with such force that their bodies shook and they had to cling tight to each other, until the tremors faded and only the sounds of their heavy breathing remained. When he shifted his body to move away from her, she squeezed her legs around him, not wanting him to leave. If only they could have stayed that way forever and forget the hell that was waiting for her.

Viper brushed a kiss over her mouth.

"I need to get rid of this condom, but I'll be right back."

She closed her eyes for just an instant, reliving the last few moments, wondering what he'd say if he knew the erotic books she read. She'd wanted to try what she read in them herself but hadn't met anyone—until now—that she'd even dare mention it to. She'd known Viper for just a few short hours, but there was something between them— *God*. She hoped she wasn't blowing it all out of proportion.

True to his word, he was only gone for seconds. Then he was back, sliding in beside her and pulling her against his body, spoonlike.

"Think that chased away the demons for a while?" His voice was a soft rumble in her ear.

"Yes. I— Thank you."

"Oh, Hannah, the pleasure was all mine. I just don't want you to feel like I was taking advantage of you in a low spot."

She rested a hand on the forearm banded across her waist. "Maybe I was taking advantage of you."

"Then see how nice that works out?" He kissed her shoulder. "But bright and early tomorrow, we start digging into what really happened with that drone and who's behind it."

"And your partners will be okay with this?"

"I promise you they'll be all over it. Let's get some sleep so we can start kickin' shit bright and early."

She closed her eyes, settling against him. She was in big trouble here, and it had nothing to do with Lowden Tactical or the death of Senator Hegman. But for the first time since the helo had carted her off from the remote site, a sliver of hope that she'd get out of this situation wriggled through her.

Chapter Five

"Henry, sit down. You're making me dizzy."

The man seated in the armchair, known to his intimate friends as Diesel, made his voice as even and reassuring as possible. Shouting wouldn't help anything, and Henry Baumann's pacing was driving him nuts. He was having a hard enough time dealing with this shit show himself. There were some days he wished the man would just stay in his office and let the rest of them take care of everything.

The man stopped in front of the chair where Diesel was sitting and glared at him.

"I'll stop pacing when that stupid bitch is found and taken care of. You said you had it under control. Everything was planned. Everything was in place. She'd be labeled a traitor then quietly disappear. She couldn't stir up any kind of trouble that would derail what's up for me. You assured me. I wish I knew how the hell the so-called fucking security team let her slip through their fingers."

'*Slip through their fingers.*' That was an interesting way to put it. It was a little more than a slip, and no one knew it more than he did. Paul Santos, nursing a bad headache and a large lump on his head, might put it differently, but it meant the same thing. And the ten men who had scoured the entire downtown area where the hotel was also had a different opinion. Hannah Modell had somehow vaporized. Disappeared into thin air. She was gone, and no one knew where.

Fucking hell.

"Henry, it will be taken care of before it's time for the announcement. Nothing is going to change that."

"So you say. I'll feel better when she's exposed as a traitor then dumped six feet under."

She couldn't have called anyone, Diesel mused. That much he knew. They'd confiscated her cell phone and forbidden the hotel to put calls through on her room phone. One of the things that had made her ideal for this was her lack of social life, close friends or acquaintances, and — as far as they knew — no family. Her commitment to work and nothing beyond it pretty much isolated her, at least to their knowledge.

Her hotel location had been known only to a select few and no one had even tried to find her or see her. They had kept a careful watch on that. Lowden had put out a believable story and they'd been working toward the second part. *The part where she'd disappear forever.* Then, shockingly, she'd somehow disappeared from that hotel. *Pffttt! Gone!* She hadn't taken a cab or an Uber or Lyft, although he wasn't too surprised. She had no money, as far as they knew, and she was smart enough not to use her credit cards. She also wouldn't want to leave a trail for someone to follow.

So how had this happened? How had the asshole who was supposed to be guarding her room been so fucking stupid that she'd knocked him out?

Hannah Modell was smart enough to know if they made too much noise looking for her, they'd draw attention to things best kept hidden. Of course, she was thinking of their top-secret contracts and not the real reason behind the creation of Lowden Tactical. Only a select few were aware of that, not including her, and it had better stay that way.

"We have to find her," Henry insisted. "We've been building this since before Lowden Tactical opened. Since this first all came together that one weekend, as a matter of fact. When Hegman became a liability, we had all the pieces in place to get rid of him and keep moving forward. Millions — no, billions — are at stake, not to mention everyone involved in our private group. And my appointment as committee chair. If the top moneyman feels like it's falling apart, he'll pull the plug, take everyone with him and we'll be left holding the bag. Do you really want to walk away from that kind of money? And power? Or maybe end up in prison?"

"Of course not," Diesel assured him. "But while we're searching for her, we have to clean up any other loose ends so we don't get unexpectedly smacked. If everyone gets cold feet and bails after this, I'm not going to be the one left with my naked ass hanging out in the wind."

"Yeah?" Henry snorted. "You can cover it with the millions you're making from this. But I'm prime meat for the media. And there goes my future."

Diesel shifted in his chair, doing his best not to show his growing irritation. He'd only invited Henry because he provided a vital piece of the process. But even more than that, the man had focus. When there was a goal, a target, he never lost sight of it and never let anything deter him.

"We knew this would happen with a high-profile target," he reminded the other man. "We chose Modell to be the sacrificial lamb because she has no support system or anyone who would make a huge fuss. It's logical. It's doable. And the fact that she's disappeared is only a little blip on the screen. We'll find her. She has no resources and no place to go. Now tell me what's going on at the senator's? Are there still guards at the house?"

"Yes. There are guards all over the senator's estate in Kentucky. I don't think even the president could get in to see his widow or the family."

"I'm not sure his people would even let him try." Diesel grunted. "This is a very toxic situation for him right now."

Henry studied Diesel's face. "You don't think he knows anything about this, do you?"

"Hell, no. If he did, you and I would damn sure not be sitting here. We'd be in the basement of some federal building praying to god we could find some lawyer to save our asses. And he's not involved in the appointment process, so there's no problem there."

"How's Hegman's wife holding up?"

Henry shoved his hands in his pockets and stopped pacing, nervous energy rolling from him in waves.

"Devastated, as you'd expect. Their kids are with her. The whole family is in shock." He shook his head. "That's the only downside to this whole thing. The effect on them."

"Collateral damage is always a bitch," Diesel agreed. "I wish there was a way to avoid it, but mostly it can't be helped."

"I'm playing the role. I have to, especially right now." Henry sighed. "But it's hard, knowing what I do."

"That should be easy for you. Playing a part is what every politician does. Am I right?"

He rose from the big armchair, refilled his coffee mug from the silver pot on the sideboard and added a splash of Jim Beam for good measure. The alcohol warmed his blood and soothed his nerves. Henry was going to give him a goddamned heart attack if he didn't settle his shit.

"It's what we have to do."

"As long as our plans progress the way they should," Diesel told him, "it's a loss we'll have to deal with."

Henry slugged down a swallow of his drink. "I know I sound like a broken record, but I'll just feel a lot better about everything when we have the woman back and taken care of."

"Henry." Diesel gritted his teeth. "Listen to me. I'll repeat this all one more time. It's all logistics. Where can she go? She has no friends except at work, and it seems they're just acquaintances. No family. No one with the resources to help her. Calm down. There's a broader picture here that overrides everything else."

"And nobody better fuck with it," Henry growled. "You know what's at stake here."

"Power and money," Diesel growled. "Especially yours."

"Yours, too, and my appointment is critical to keeping it that way. And protecting a lot of our 'friends'. You know that."

"Yes." Diesel gritted his teeth. "It will cover a lot of people's asses."

"And your situation is at stake, too," Henry reminded him. "So don't act holier-than-thou. If we can't find her, we're all screwed. The president of the Senate is getting ready to appoint the next chairman of this committee and we've managed to get me at the top of his list. That's the key to moving our agenda forward. So pardon me for asking again, but are you sure we've looked everywhere?"

"We're working on it, looking for places in Houston where she could have gone to hide. Fucking damn. I'm telling you." Diesel wanted to punch someone—maybe Henry if he asked the question one more time. "Even though there's no sign of her, that could be a good thing. She hasn't gone to the media or the Feds."

"Yet," Henry snapped.

"You think I don't have a lot at stake here, too? Maybe more? We've had a good thing going here and it's about to get better once we get rid of this woman. We're still checking the area around the hotel, but I don't expect anyone to remember a woman who spends her life being invisible except at work."

"My point exactly." Henry glared at him. "A nobody like her can just fade into the woodwork until she reappears at the wrong time."

"I'll tell you this once more, then we're done." Diesel was sick of this. Henry just needed to suck it up and let the pros handle this.

"Done? Not until we find her and get rid of her."

"You'll have to take my word for it. I'm damned tired of repeating myself." Diesel took another swallow of his drink. "We'll get her. She has no network. That was checked out thoroughly before she was hired.

People on the GO-Teams don't need excess baggage distracting them from their jobs. Both parents are dead, and she seems to have no social life. Everything is focused on the drones. Studying them. Working with them. Learning more sophisticated ways of developing them."

"She's definitely the right person to have this tied to her," Henry agreed. "No loose ends. No one to care if the roof all falls on her."

"As long as it's done the right way," Diesel reminded him. "It can't look like a coverup. That's what's taking so long. There has to be a buildup. A detailed investigation, or at least a report of one so that we all look good. It's being handled."

"The way keeping a tight lock on her was being handled?" Henry snapped.

The other man glared at him. "Then answer this for me. If she's such an isolated individual, how in the hell could she just disappear like this? We should have made her disappear at once. Permanently."

"And ignite a gigantic investigation? You're kidding, right? We have to do this the right way. We have to make sure all the blame falls on her first. If everything falls apart and people learn what really happened, we might as well all figure out how to take the next spaceship to the moon." Diesel took another swallow of his spiked coffee. "For fuck's sake, Henry, we'll get it done. My group has good people on this. They'll find her. They'll stash her. And at the right time, we'll get rid of her."

"Your group?" Henry stared at him. "I thought we were all in this together. Now I'm on the outside looking in?"

"I'm talking about the people who handle stuff like this for me. We *are* all in this together, so calm down."

Diesel would have liked nothing better than to wrap his hands around Henry's throat and squeeze until his face turned red and he stopped breathing, but that wasn't possible. The man was a vital cog in their machinery. He couldn't afford to have him walk away, or worse, screw things up. His connections were vital to the execution of their plan, so he drank some more of his 'coffee' and forced a calmness he was far from feeling. He understood Henry's panic. He himself was goddamn pissed and a little scared that Hannah Modell had somehow found someone to believe her and help her.

It was okay to blame something on her if she was totally absent and no one could contact her. That had been the original plan. Sequester her until everything was in place, then cover her in irrefutable proof that the whole thing was her fault. Finally, at the right time, get rid of her if they had to.

What they could not afford was to have her just show up with proof of what had really happened. He just hoped that goddamn proof was being buried so deep it would never surface. Millions were riding on this, as well as a lot of people's futures.

"This is the last time I'll say this for now, but we have to find her," Henry said again. "We have other parts that have to fall into place. The critical point here is not knowing who might have helped her or who she's with now. She had to have help getting away from Paul Santos. He's done a lot of jobs for us. He's experienced and not easily fooled."

"She could have caught him off guard," Diesel pointed out. "If she hadn't done anything to put them on notice in two weeks, it could have happened."

"I agree. But we've checked everyone she's ever spoken to since she was six years old. I've had every source on it and they're good, and they've come up with nothing."

"Then get a new team on it. Go back to every business close to the hotel where she was purportedly sequestered and show her picture. Spend a little cash if you have to. You have the resources, Henry. Call them. And have a drink. The meeting's here in two hours. Maybe we'll be lucky, and someone will have news for us."

"They'd better," Henry snarled, and poured himself a drink. "Too much is riding on this."

Chapter Six

Hannah hadn't been sure how Viper would act in the morning. Would he pretend nothing had happened between them? Would he be resentful for losing control? Decide he didn't want to be bothered with her after all?

And what did she feel? More than she wanted, which shocked the hell out of her. Satisfying sex was… well…satisfying and last night's had been beyond that. But she was stunned to realize they'd made some connection beyond the physical. Did he feel it too? Was she getting herself in a bigger mess? *God, god, god.* She couldn't afford to do anything to antagonize him to the point where he just walked away. She truly had no place else to go. But this feeling, this unfamiliar feeling…

Suddenly, sitting in bed with him naked, she felt slightly embarrassed and completely defenseless. She'd had her share of meaningless sex, but she'd never, ever connected with a man the way she did with him, and she wasn't even sure how to act.

As if he read her mind, he wrapped his arms around her, pulling her tight against his body and telling her in a soft voice that everything was okay. He treated her as if they'd known each other forever, going out of his way to ease her nerves.

"It's all good," he murmured in her ear. "Relax. We're fine. Least I hope so. I hope I wasn't the only one into it all."

The tension eased from her muscles and she smiled, even though he couldn't see it.

"Not even a little. *I* was the one worried about *your* reaction. Some female picks you up in a bar and jumps into bed with you."

"Then we're good. More than good. Great, even. First of all, I believe I was the one who did the picking up, and the jumping was mutual. Right?"

"Um, yes, you're right." She swallowed a smile.

"Then there's nothing to worry about." He was quiet for a moment. "Listen to me, Hannah. Taking on your kind of problem? This is just what we do. If it looks impossible and no one else would touch it, it's made for us. Galaxy will be all over this today." He squeezed her gently. "And I'll be all over you personally."

"How much did you tell them in the texts you sent?"

"Enough to pique their interest and get them started on the list I put together."

She nibbled her lower lip. "Don't they want to meet me first?"

"*I* met you, and that's all it takes. Promise. And that means we'd better get up and out of here. I'm calling Saint to tell him to get ready for takeoff. Why don't you grab the first shower?"

Hannah hated to wash off the scent the man had imprinted on her body. She showered and washed her hair, taking advantage of the courtesy items the hotel stocked in the room. But then she had to put on the same clothes she'd been wearing. Somehow, she needed to acquire a limited wardrobe, so she wasn't living in the same undies forever.

Viper exited the bathroom with the fresh scent of pine soap clinging to him. He dressed quickly, then grabbed the gun and shoved it into his waistband at the small of his back.

"I've never been a big fan of guns," Hannah said, "but I have to admit they make me feel a lot better."

"Good. And just so you know, our first priority is always to avoid using them. But we never leave home without them. None of us."

"Thank you, for everything."

He nodded, then put his hands on her shoulders.

"Let me make this very clear, Hannah. Last night wasn't just burning off energy, or taking advantage of your situation. Truth to tell, I've been free and easy with relationships for the past several years. I had no desire to lock myself into one. The sex was great and I had fun." He shook his head, as if trying to puzzle this out. "Then you fell into my life."

"Viper, I—"

He held up a hand. "No. Let me say it. We've known each other, what, twelve hours? I've known women for twelve years I didn't feel this way about. I don't know about you, but I felt something that's been missing from my life for a long time. If I'm all alone in this, if you didn't get the same feeling, now's the time to tell me. No hard feelings, I promise. And you're still our client."

She blew out a breath, searching for words.

"I'm sure I don't have near the experience you do, but I do know when something works for me. It hasn't for a long time, but it did last night. It woke something inside me, and I want more. A lot more. Is it okay to say that?"

He grinned at her. "Damn right it is. You have no idea the things I want to do with you. I don't want this to be another short-term fling. Crazy to say it after a few hours, and my partners will think I'm nuts, I know. But I don't care. When this is over —"

"*If* it's over," she interrupted.

"It will be. That's a promise."

She stared up at him, searching his face for answers.

"Just so you know, I'm not...I don't..." She stopped and wet her lips. God, she sounded like the queen of idiots. "It's not my usual style."

His smile warmed her. "Just so *you* know, I didn't think so. I never mix business with pleasure, so this is not a regular thing for me." He brushed a strand of hair back from her face, a gesture so tender she wanted to cry. "So maybe something good comes out of this after all. But no matter what else, Hannah, count on this. My partners and I are going to take good care of you and keep you safe while we handle this situation. That's a promise."

As if to emphasize what he'd said, he brushed a soft kiss over her lips.

She sighed and leaned against him for a moment.

"This is new for me for a lot of reasons. But..." She managed an answering smile. "I'm good with it, too."

The smile was real, surprisingly. Go figure that with her life turned upside down, a man like Viper would walk into it, bringing the hint of a hot, exciting relationship. Even if it ultimately fizzled out, it was more than she'd had for too long a time.

Thankfully, Viper checked out electronically so they could just make their way out through one of the rear doors. Still, she couldn't help scanning everything in the area as they left the motel. She took note of everything and everyone around them as they pulled out of the lot and onto the highway.

"We're clear," Viper assured her. "I have a lot of years' experience evading the enemy. Trust me, darlin'. I don't catch even a smell of them."

"Okay. I trust you."

But she was still tense, constantly checking the rear-view and side-view mirrors.

When they reached the airport, Viper turned in the hot pickup then ushered her outside to where the Galaxy plane was waiting, Saint standing beside it.

"Morning, folks. Viper, we're cleared to take off in fifteen, so let's get shaking."

Viper nodded. "Got it. Hannah, after you." When she looked again around the area, he cupped her elbow with his hand, the touch reassuring.

"I know where you're at," he murmured, "but I promise you no one is here looking for you. I also had Saint on the alert for anything that smelled funny. It's all good, darlin'."

Saint nodded. "We're clean. Everything checks out." He smiled at Hannah. "And we're getting you out of here right now."

The Galaxy plane took off from Houston at seven a.m. Once they leveled off, Viper fetched coffee and pastries for them and set them on their tray tables.

"Eat up," he urged. "You'll need all your strength to fight this battle."

Isn't that just the damn truth? The coffee was hot and the breakfast rolls crusty, so she focused on eating and drinking while Viper ate his own breakfast and texted on his cell between bites. She was content just to sit quietly while he did whatever he was doing, trying to sort it all out in her head. Even two weeks alone in that damn hotel room hadn't answered any of the questions banging around in her brain.

The biggest one was, how had it all happened? Drones were like her alter egos. There was nothing about them she didn't know. They didn't just veer off course and drop their payload someplace by mistake. *Not when being handled by an expert.* Someone had to fiddle with the settings. Someone who knew what they were doing. But in that hotel room, she'd mentally gone over and over who would have done that, and only four names came to mind. Four people with the skills and knowledge to do it. The thought of each of them made her physically ill.

The second question she hadn't been able to answer was, why choose Senator Hegman? Assuming, she thought to herself, that the misfire was deliberate. What kind of powers did the chairman of the Armed Services Committee have that made someone want to get rid of him? She needed to talk to Viper about that more. Surely, he'd know more about it than she did.

He was still busy texting when she leaned her head back against the seat and closed her eyes. She hadn't expected to fall asleep, but the next thing she knew, Viper was nudging her knee.

"Wake up, Sleeping Beauty." He grinned. "It's nine-thirty and we're here."

"What?" She rubbed her eyes and looked out the window. "Oh. Oh, sorry."

"That's okay." A corner of his mouth hitched up. "I guess you didn't get a lot of sleep last night."

Heat crept up her cheeks in an unfamiliar blush. She smoothed a stray hair back from her face, not sure what she should say to that. Fortunately, the plane came to a stop at that moment, so she looked out of the window.

"Where are we? That doesn't look like any kind of airport out there."

Viper chuckled. "That's because it's not. Privacy is a big deal to us and for our clients, so we bought this huge tract of land outside the city and built a runway and hangar. We still have to clear with Tampa International for takeoff and landing, but we aren't exposed. And as I said, neither are our clients."

She wasn't sure what to say. She'd seen a lot of things since she'd started her work in aerodynamics, a lot of private situations, but not like this. The people she'd met who had hangars attached to their homes usually only housed planes like Beechcrafts or Cessnas.

They rolled to a smooth stop. As soon as the engines were silent, Viper was out of his seat and opening the door to let down the stairway. Then he helped her down onto the tarmac. This was, indeed, a large piece of land, with a double- sized hangar and a multicar garage.

"You good?" Viper asked Saint when he joined them on the tarmac.

Saint nodded. "All set. I've got some stuff to do at home. Call me if you want to take another trip."

The men shook hands, then Viper hitched the strap of his duffel over his shoulder and guided Hannah to the garage.

"No one here, either," he told her. "They wouldn't even know this place exists. Of course, before they could look for it, they'd have to know you were with me, and that didn't happen. We're good."

He opened the passenger door to a dark blue Lincoln Navigator and motioned her to climb in.

"Hmm. No pickup?" she teased.

He grinned as he started the engine. "I have one back at my place, so I can switch off when I want to. But sometimes I need a slightly different vehicle. Come on, let's get going so we can get to work on this. My partners are already dialed in and a couple have started looking into this."

He thumbed a quick text then put his cell phone in the cupholder and backed out of the garage.

We're really doing this. I didn't imagine the whole thing. These men are really going to take me on as a client and help me. But why? And this man is taking me to his home. I don't know whether to run and hide or rip off my clothes and attack him. And neither of those things is me.

Swallowing a sigh, she leaned back against the seat. This was the first time she'd taken a full breath since she'd made her escape from the hotel. Everything had been happening so fast and it all seemed like something out of a movie to her. Leaving a bar with a stranger, especially a very sexy one. Falling into bed with him. Putting her life in his hands. She hoped she wasn't making a mistake.

'In for a penny, in for a pound' as her avionics instructor, who'd loved cliches, used to say.

She was more curious to see where Viper lived, what kind of place it was. She wondered if, being a former SEAL, he'd be drawn to the water. As they drove through downtown Tampa, she realized the city was surrounded by a lot of it. And she wasn't surprised when they crossed over a short arched bridge into a separate community on an island. They passed shopping areas, apartments and restaurants before reaching a gate. Viper used a remote to operate it and waved at the guard on duty as they passed through.

"Nice area," she commented, taking it all in. "You all must be raking in the bucks."

Viper laughed, a warm sound.

"Not always. But the ones where we do make up for the ones where we don't. Besides, winning all that money allowed us each to buy the homes we wanted free and clear."

She didn't know what to say. She was used to being around people with lots of money. In addition to the military, Lowden had several clients with large bank accounts. But Viper seemed casual about his situation, his possessions like the plane, without wearing his money on his forehead. *More and more interesting.*

They drove by what looked like condo buildings, then some townhouses before passing through another gate into a section with single-family homes. Viper made a right turn onto a short, curved street, then turned into the driveway of a Spanish-style home with a decorative adobe fence surrounding the property. He used the same remote to open the wrought-iron gate before pulling into the garage, parking next to — sure enough — a tricked-out pickup.

"Here we are." He put the Navigator in park and turned off the engine. "Let's get inside."

He punched the button to close the garage door then led her inside through a side door, stopping for a moment to reset the security panel in the wall.

"This picks up anyone and anything outside. Sound and cameras." He grinned. "We're almost as tight as the president. First, they'd have to find you, which they won't. Then, they'd have to try to breach the security, which they can't. I even have a backup generator that kicks in if the first one gets taken out by a power failure or an EMP. Okay, this way."

She found herself in a kitchen. A very big kitchen, that looked like a cook's dream.

Viper turned into a short hallway, carrying his duffel and messenger bag,

"I'll be right back. Make yourself at home."

"Thank you."

A step down took her into a large family room furnished with comfortable-looking couches and chairs and a huge flat-screen television over the fireplace, and a wall of sliding doors that looked out onto a lawn, a dock and a large body of water.

"Wow!"

She stood, staring out at the scene, at the expanse of water with its gentle lapping waves, boats bobbing on its surface, and the dock that extended out from Viper's property, where a gleaming boat rested beneath a canopy. A peaceful scene if she had ever seen one, and something she needed right now.

"Like it?"

Viper had come up behind her so noiselessly she hadn't even heard him.

"Are you kidding? What's not to like? You must love coming home to all this."

He was silent for a long time, standing behind her, not saying a word until she wondered if she'd somehow insulted him.

"I spent a lot of years in the heat and sand of Iraq and the cold mountains of Afghanistan. Some missions, my team wasn't even sure we'd make it out alive. Some of them were killed. Others injured. All of us still have nightmares of that time occasionally. We all decided when we got the money that we'd buy homes that reflected what we needed and where we wanted to be for the rest of our lives."

She turned to him and looked up at his face, seeing the deep grooves that came with remembered misery and nightmares of days in hell.

"Oh, Viper, I'm so sorry. I was only trying to give you a compliment."

"No problem. And yes, I picked this lot and built a house that would make me feel good when I was home." He pointed to the dock. "Being out on the water when a stressor sets me off brings me peace unlike anything else."

"Well, you did a good job. And if it's safe, I'd love a boat ride, when we can."

"That's a deal." He dusted a light kiss over her forehead.

"But first I have to figure out how to get some clothes. I can order them online if I can use your name and address. Can't leave any electronic footprints. But" — she hurried to add — "I have some cash with me so I can pay you for them."

"I think I got the clothes thing taken care of. We'll worry about the cash later."

At that moment, a security panel on the wall by the front door buzzed and a woman's voice called out, "Viper? Open the gate. I'm here."

He had reached for the gun at his back, but at the sound of the voice, he left it where it was and grinned. "And that's why we don't have to worry about online orders right now."

"What —"

"I sent a text after we landed. There's someone I want you to meet." He pressed a button on the security panel, then another to speak. "Come on up."

He opened the front door, keeping his arm around her, as a silver Lexus pulled up and stopped at the stairs leading to the door. The woman who got out was about Hannah's height. She waved to them and smiled.

"Hey, Viper."

"Hey, Peyton. Come on in." He slid a glance at Hannah. "You'll love Peyton. She's really down to earth and doesn't take crap from anyone."

Hannah laughed. "That's some introduction."

"And I mean every word of it," Viper told her.

"Yes, he does." Peyton nodded, pulled some shopping bags from the back seat and trotted up the stairs. She gave Viper a one-armed hug. "At least he'd better, or Blaze will get after him. Anyway, I wasn't sure what all to pick up, but I think I bought enough for us to get started with." She turned to Hannah and held out her hand. "Peyton West."

"Hannah Modell." Hannah shook hands with the woman.

Peyton flashed a grin. "The super sexy drone engineer. Nice to meet you. Let's go on inside. I have some things for you."

Super sexy? Hannah didn't think anyone had ever applied that description to her. But she liked the woman instantly. She was natural, relaxed and friendly. Thick, shiny chestnut hair was pulled back with a clip, the few tendrils that escaped framing creamy cheeks and accenting warm, green eyes. She was about the same size as Hannah, although a little more endowed in the breast department and with slightly curvier hips. She had an air of self-confidence and happiness that Hannah found herself envying.

She also had the look of someone who was very satisfied with her life, something Hannah had thought she herself had until this disaster threatened to destroy it. *Shows just how wrong I was.*

Damn! What was the matter with her? She'd hardly met the woman and already she was jealous of her. No, not of her, of her situation. Of what she had, something Hannah hadn't even thought she was missing. *Freedom. Fun. Good friends.* But she managed a smile as they all moved into the family room. Peyton plunked the bags she was carrying onto the couch and turned to Hannah.

"Viper said we were about the same size. I can't believe how he nailed it."

Hannah frowned. "Nailed what? I don't understand."

"You didn't get to bring any clothes with you," Viper pointed out. "Right? I don't feel safe taking you into a store. I'm pretty sure Tampa's not on Lowden's radar at the moment, but there's no sense taking chances. So I called Peyton."

Peyton winked at her. "And it was fun."

Hannah was stunned that the man had even thought of it. She was definitely not used to anyone paying attention to the details of her life except her. All she could say was, "Wow."

"I love shopping with someone else's money, although I think Blaze would be happy if I never wore any clothes." She held out her hand and flashed a stunning engagement ring. "From Blaze. He's my hero. You'll meet him in a bit."

Hannah managed a smile. The woman's happiness was so obvious. "Congratulations."

"I feel as if he and I have known each other for six years instead of six months. Being with him is, well, exceptional."

Hannah drew in a slow breath. "And thank you for everything. I'm in your debt."

Then she embarrassed herself by bursting into tears. Her! Hannah Modell! The Ice Queen. She never, ever cried. All the tension from the past two weeks, especially the last twenty-four hours, just exploded. Eventually she managed to stop crying. She couldn't remember the last time she'd let anything get to her like this. She sniffed and wiped her eyes and cheeks with her palms, feeling like a prize idiot, and took in a deep breath.

"Sorry. Really. I feel like an idiot. I guess it's just the strain of everything. I apologize, especially after you've been so nice to do this."

Peyton crouched down in front of her.

"Hannah. I don't know what your specific deal is, but I've been in a place like that myself. That's how I met these big guys. Whatever it is, they'll fix it." She rose and gathered the shopping bags. "Come on, now. Let's go in the bedroom and play dress-up. That'll take your mind off things."

"Sorry I'm such a mess."

"Like I said, no worries." Peyton turned to Viper. "Blaze will be along shortly with his laptop and the food, and Rocket and Eagle soon after. Blaze is bringing subs for lunch and steaks and stuff for dinner, since we weren't sure how prepared you were to feed everyone."

Viper laughed. "I think I have stuff in the freezer, but thanks. This is better. Makes it easier."

Hannah tucked her hair behind her ears and let out a breath. She needed to get her shit together before Viper decided she wasn't worth the effort. She was already embarrassed at her breakdown. The last thing she wanted was to look like a melted tissue and have

Viper's partners wonder if he'd lost his mind in taking her on as a client.

She let out another deep breath and stood up.

Viper was there in an instant, cupping her face in his big hands. "You sure you're okay?"

She nodded and managed a smile. "Embarrassed as hell but otherwise fine."

The look he gave her was serious. "Like I said. Pressure. We all snap now and then. There's nothing wrong with it, Hannah."

She bit her lower lip. "But I—"

He touched a finger to her chin. "It's all good. Now go have fun with Peyton." He pointed at the hallway that ran from the big room. "Bedrooms are that way."

"Okay." Hannah nodded. "Yes. I'm good. Let's do this."

Blaze's eyes were on her as she walked out of the room and a warm feeling settled over her. She could hardly believe that a man she'd met less than twenty-four hours ago had somehow become such an integral part of her life. She just hoped she wasn't in for a big fall.

"Whatever these guys are doing for you," Peyton said as she began to unload the shopping bags, "I promise you they'll get it done. I know that for a fact."

"Is that how you met them?" Hannah was curious about the woman's connection to Galaxy. "Were you in trouble?"

Peyton shook her head. "Not exactly. I was trying to find out who killed my brother-in-law and put my sister in a coma."

Hannah stared at her. "You're kidding."

"Not even a little. My brother-in-law was dead, and the police were burying everything because strings were being pulled by some very powerful people.

Which, by the way, could easily be the case here. Anyway, when my sister's doctor, Ryan Hamilton, realized what was going on, he gave me the number for his brother, Blaze. Well, Scott, but no one calls him that. They agreed to help me. Galaxy dug out the truth and made sure everyone paid for it."

"Wow." Hannah dropped to the bed. "So they really can do it? Because this is very complicated and dangerous."

"Oh, yeah." Peyton grinned. "In spades. It's what they live for."

"What about your sister? How is she doing?"

"Good. Really good. She's still doing physical therapy and seeing a shrink, but she's back at work and piecing her life together." Peyton paused and let out a breath. "She still has a lot of bad days. And god knows, she misses Dane so much it's painful."

"I'm sure it is. I'm so sorry this happened to her." 'Sorry' seemed like such a weak thing to say. "But you say she's doing better now?"

"Every day. Brianne's a commercial photographer. She's very successful, so she can pick and choose her assignments, although it's taking her a while to get into the groove again. Blaze and I convinced her to stay in Tampa since her clients and her friends are here." Her lips tilted in a tiny grin. "And especially since we got engaged."

"You must be so excited."

"I am. Neither of us planned on it happening, but when it did, well, we knew it was perfect. I feel as if I won the jackpot."

Hannah studied the other woman. She hadn't really thought of Viper—or any of his partners—as having families or relationships, and wasn't that just too weird? But Peyton seemed happy in every inch of her body, so maybe… She gave herself a mental shake. There were a lot more questions she was dying to ask, but she figured she'd pried enough. If Peyton wanted to share anything else, she would.

"So how did you and Viper meet?" Peyton asked, emptying out the last bag and separating the items. "Sorry, I know I'm being really nosy, but these guys don't exactly advertise. Did someone refer you?"

Hannah shook her head. "No, nothing like that." She looked down at the blouse she was holding. "This is going to sound very weird. I—uh—met Viper in a bar. I'd been—how do they say it?—sequestered in a hotel for two weeks while people decided the best way to finish destroying my life. I managed to get away and I was trying to hide from some guys who didn't want me running around loose. I ducked into a bar and ended up on a stool next to Viper. He didn't ask any questions when the guys poked their heads in looking for me. He just got me out of there, asked me what it was all about and took me for a ride in their big plane."

Then into his bed. She could still feel the warmth and strength of his hands, the erotic movement of his lips, the thickness of him inside her. She hoped the flash of heat that swept over her didn't leave any telltale blush on her skin.

Peyton burst out laughing. "Sounds about right for them. They never get involved in anything ordinary."

"I kind of figured."

"Did he tell you the history of Galaxy?"

"Oh, yes. It still sounds like some wild tale."

"It does." Peyton nodded. "But it gave them their dream. Now they can take cases no one else wants or that are too dangerous."

Hannah hoped the woman didn't ask any more questions. She knew that, eventually, the details would come out. Especially when they were discussed over dinner that evening.

"Hey." Peyton put her hand on Hannah's arm. "These guys are something extra special. It's impossible not to fall for them. Ask me. It took me less than forty-eight hours."

"I know what you mean." Hannah sighed. "It's just so not me. I feel like I've been hit by a truck. No subtlety there."

Peyton burst out laughing. "Yeah, that's about right. But, Hannah? You couldn't find a better guy anywhere. I'm not kidding. And if you ever need to talk, I'm here. Okay?"

"Thanks."

Right now, however, she wanted to put them out of her mind for a while, if she could. And trying on the clothes Peyton had brought was a good way to distract herself.

* * * *

Viper had grabbed his laptop from his duffel, set it up on the island counter and had just finished making a pot of coffee in his new contraption when Blaze arrived. He handed over a grocery bag with dinner fixings in it and set his own laptop up next to Viper's. Hitching himself onto one of the bar stools, he opened the computer and booted it up, then took his weapon from his pocket and placed it next to the machine. Viper knew that, like all of them, he was always armed when he left the house and had his gun easily accessible. They all had a Concealed Carry license because, well, some habits should never be broken.

"I started searching for stuff when you texted me from the plane," Blaze told Viper, "although I think it's way too soon for anyone to even have a hint she's here. No one knows you're the one who grabbed her out of that bar last night, so they're probably still looking all over the Houston area. There's no way they can make a connection with us."

"I figured," Viper agreed, "but we need to keep on top of that. You never know what people like that can find out or what kind of network they have. And if somehow they find out she's involved with us, they can use one of their drones to search. The kind they build can have a range of up to sixty thousand feet."

"Got it. We'll all be digging deep to see if there's any way they could have made a connection. I told Eagle and Rocket I'd do the research on Lowden. I spent the past three hours on it. They've been in business for ten years. Eric Lowden was an engineer at a major facility. Had a good job. Then one day he up and quit and a year or so later opened Lowden Tactical. No one knows where the money came from. We're checking the source, but Viper? It's buried pretty deep, which makes me very suspicious."

"Okay. What else?"

"Greg Kingsley, his executive veep, was his first hire even before they opened the doors. Industry rumor has it that Kingsley helped him put together the top-notch crew he has now — designers, drone pilots, electrical engineers. Whatever."

"Anything not out in the open makes me suspicious," Blaze told him. "That's how we survived on our missions as long as we did. Any clues at all?"

"No. I put Rocket on it. He's got some sources he can reach out to."

Viper barked a short laugh. "Rocket's collecting sources just about everywhere."

"Yeah, he's always done that. A good habit to have. Meanwhile, let's see what's up with the situation at the heart of all this. You gave us the *Reader's Digest* version of her story. We bought in because that's how it works. We all get to bring in clients and we don't bring in some piece-of-shit situation that will blow up on us." Blaze shook his head. "But I gotta tell you, Viper. This one kind of has the makings of an explosive situation. If you pardon the pun."

"Your humor sucks, but yeah, it does have that. When you spend time with her today, you'll agree with me on that."

"Okay, I have an open mind. But she's trained specifically for this. People don't just get jobs handling drones in situations like this without specific training. Right?"

"Yeah," Viper agreed. "I thought about that, so I Googled her. She has a master's degree in Unmanned and Autonomous Systems from Embry-Riddle. They're considered the number-one school for that, so she knows her stuff."

Blaze refilled his coffee mug. "So someone like her would be thoroughly knowledgeable in how to misdirect a drone flight. Right?"

Viper nodded. "That person writes the programs for each drone flight then serves as the pilot, running it from their laptop. He or she wouldn't be prone to making mistakes of this magnitude. It would have to be deliberate, and, Blaze? I might have only known her for less than twenty-four hours, but I don't get the sense she's the kind of person who would do that."

"Rocket ran a check on her last night. Nothing unusual in her bank accounts, but of course for something like this, if she got paid, the money would be sent offshore. He's digging into that now."

"She didn't do this for money," Viper insisted. "In fact, I don't believe she did this at all."

"I hear you, but you know we have to check every angle." He tapped keys on his laptop. "We haven't really dug through all the layers yet, but so far nothing is ringing any bells. Honor student in college. Worked for another company before she got the job at Lowden, where she's been for ten years. Seems to have no friends except the people she works with." He glanced at Viper. "Have you checked to see what their reaction to all this is?"

"I did a little searching on my phone while we were on the plane. You'll love this. Lowden said it was a tragic malfunction of the drone. They're examining the blueprints and program carefully, and searching for the drone operator, who seems to have disappeared."

Blaze snorted. "That's the damn truth. Except they made her disappear to begin with."

"They did," Viper agreed. "My thoughts are that they planned to keep her locked in the hotel until they could spirit her out of town, kill her and make sure her body was never found."

"Why not do it right away?" Blaze wanted to know. "Why hang on to her like they did?"

"My guess? In case they needed her for something. In the meantime, they wanted her isolated, but in a place where they hoped she'd feel they were taking care of her. Otherwise, who knows what could have happened."

"No doubt," Blaze agreed. "We need to find people to reach out to. Quietly."

"I think Rocket needs to get with Tom Hernandez. He knows everyone in the whole damn universe. He also would know if Senator Mark Hegman was an accident as Hannah says—although she insisted someone had to monkey with the drone's programming without her knowledge—or the real target. And what would make him that target. Or at least he could make a guess. Either way, we want to know as much about Hegman as he can get for us."

Blaze scowled. "That opens the door to some very bad possibilities. Things I don't even want to think about."

"It does." Viper tapped his keyboard. "Meanwhile I also 'found' a list of Lowden personnel, but I think the first thing to do is ask Hannah the most likely people to be involved in something off kilter. Lowden has more than a hundred employees. I don't think she has a relationship with all of them."

Blaze nodded. "That would be unrealistic. Okay, the others will be here shortly. Let's get the ladies out here and see what's what."

Chapter Seven

"Hannah, meet two more of the partners."

Viper introduced Hannah to the team members who'd arrived shortly after Peyton and Blaze. She didn't think she'd ever been in a room so filled with testosterone, even at Lowden Tactical. She shook hands with each of them, sensing the same power and strength she found in Viper.

"This one's John 'Rocket' Hardin. Rocket, say hello to Hannah Modell, our client."

Rocket's hair was even darker than Blaze's, almost midnight black. But where Blaze's hair stopped at the nape of his neck, Rocket's was long enough that he tied it back with a leather thong.

"Don't you worry, Miss Hannah," Rocket told her in his soft drawl. "We'll get this taken care of."

"And this," Viper told her, "is Eagle. Vic Bodine."

He was the leanest of the partners, and possibly the shortest, although she judged that they all topped six feet. His hair was light brown but with an interesting white streak that ran from his forehead to the back of his head. He had piercing brown eyes and a hawk nose, and he reminded Hannah of something, but she couldn't think what.

"Like Rocket said, we'll take care of whatever this is. You can count on us." Eagle turned to Viper. "Rocket and I are all set to rock and roll. We did some looking last night, but it's always better when we're together and throw ideas out. Last night we sent some stuff to Blaze to put on his laundry list, too."

Blaze nodded. "I got it."

Hannah had wondered whether Viper's partners would think he'd lost his mind taking her in. She was prepared to give him an out, if it was a problem, although she had no idea what the hell she'd do after that. She was floored, however, when they just accepted her without question. The smiles they gave her, along with the relaxed atmosphere they created, eased most of her discomfort and uncertainty.

Damn! Luck had really been with her when she'd ducked into that particular bar. For the first time since the Lowden helicopter had fetched her back to the facility, she thought she might actually get out of this with her skin intact.

She smiled at each of them, more grateful than they could imagine. "Thank you. Really. Thank you so much. I know Viper just dumped this on you with no warning—"

"That's how we work," Eagle interrupted, holding up his hand. "We each have the ability to accept clients. When one of us does that, the rest of us buy into it. That's just the way we're set up."

"What if you already have a client you're working with?"

Eagle grinned. "We're big boys. We can handle more than one at a time."

She shook her head, still dazed. "I'm still floored at the way you all took me on as a client without any reservation at all"

"They were the same way with me," Peyton told her. "They have incredible trust in one another, so they don't question decisions like this. Someone brings in a client and everyone is all in for it."

Hannah blew out a breath. "Thank you for this. I don't know what I would have done if I hadn't met Viper."

"Well, then," Eagle drawled, "let's get to it."

They all moved to the big round table on the patio, since it could accommodate all of them comfortably. The two men set up their own laptops, then placed their cell phones and their personal weapons on the table next to them.

Hannah looked at Viper. "Are we going to be attacked on your patio?"

One corner of his mouth kicked up in a smile. "Hope not, but we always like to be prepared."

"Oh." She didn't know what to say.

"It's just a precaution," he assured her. "A habit we never break. Especially when we have a special package to protect."

Her throat tightened with emotion. Yes, she was paying them, but they were treating her as if she were someone special instead of just a business deal, accepting her because Viper vouched for her. Then there was the feeling of security that their presence gave her. She had breathed a sigh of relief when Viper had saved her bacon at the bar then unexpectedly turned out to be the answer to what she needed.

Not to mention the mind-blowing sex.

But somehow, all four of them together silently made her feel that her problem would be solved. They wore strength and commitment like a second skin. These men could have had *Hero* stamped on their foreheads and she'd believe it.

"It's so strange to see all of you with your laptops, even with the weapons," she whispered to Viper. "Not that I know much about SEALs, but I kind of figured you'd be all action."

"Oh, we have plenty of action in our mission," he assured her. "But one thing we learned with the SEALs is, don't set out on an operation until you have every single bit of information you can get. Otherwise, the enemy can blindside you. So the mental action always comes first."

Hannah helped distribute cold drinks or coffee to everyone, whichever they preferred. Then she sat down with her own mug, smiling a little when Viper made sure she was seated next to him.

Tension had gripped her all morning, lessening with Peyton's arrival. The clothes had created a bond between them. Now the anxiety eased even more when the woman sat down on Hannah's other side and gave her arm a quick squeeze. She wasn't sure what would happen with Viper going forward, or even if she'd still be around here. She hoped that somehow, she and Peyton could remain friends, because in just a few hours, she felt they'd really connected.

She thought it interesting that Peyton and Blaze had ended up engaged after her situation had been resolved. Hannah saw the strength of the connection between them. She didn't want to get ahead of herself here, not when her future hung in such a cloudy balance, but it gave her hope that maybe she and Viper might have a chance together.

She had at least two people now that she completely trusted. Especially Viper. That was two more than she'd had. And maybe there were more, if she could count on the other guys. She also felt better for having changed into some of the new clothes. Peyton had managed to pick out all the right sizes, even the lingerie. Now, showered again and dressed from the inside out in fresh new clothes, the feeling of optimism came sliding back. She'd never been one to believe in fate, but she couldn't deny that something had been in play, prompting her to pick that particular night to make a break for it and slide into that specific bar.

She folded her hands in her lap, and the tension still gripping her eased even more when Viper reached over and closed one of his big hands over both of hers, giving them a slight, encouraging squeeze. Just being near him settled her jittery nerves, a fact that amazed and stunned her.

Here she was, at the age of thirty-three, with what she considered to be a fairly low sex drive and a short list of what she called 'associations'. She'd long since accepted that men considered her little more than a quick fuck on a convenient basis. 'Lovers', in her mind, was too romantic a word for what had happened. She'd never connected like this with anyone at Lowden. She just went to work, did her job and got it done. Her work was the entire focus of her life, that and her team.

Yet suddenly, in the midst of all this, she'd met a man who was attracted to her and pushed her switch to fast forward. *How is that possible?*

Memories of the previous night flash-flooded her mind. She had definitely never had sex like that in her life or formed that kind of instant connection with any man. The feel of his hard body…hard everywhere. His sculptured muscles, the soft brush of the hair on his chest, his strong hands as they squeezed her breasts, his mouth on her nipples. His thick cock filling her. His—

Stop it!

There went her nipples again, hardening so much they were almost sore, and the pulse between her legs throbbed with an unfamiliar but insistent need. *Crap!* She slid a glance around the table to see if anyone was paying close attention to her, but luckily, they were all occupied. And they were working on *her* problem. Every so often, one of them would walk away from the table to make a call on his cell.

She wanted to pinch herself to make sure this was all real. These four wealthy, macho men who could pick and choose their clients had chosen her. She watched and listened to them, again enormously relieved it had only taken Viper's word for them to they'd do this. Whatever they ended up charging her, she'd find a way to pay it.

She leaned close to Viper so she could whisper. "What are they all doing?"

"Digging for information. Like I said, you learn in the SEALs that information is the key to everything. You'd better have it before you make a move. These guys know where to find a pebble under a rock in the middle of the earth, if there's even a smell of it out on the internet, dark web and all. We're going to take Lowden apart from the beginning and see just what there is about your latest project that has everyone getting their panties in a twist."

"Oh. Um, they can do that?"

"They can do anything." He winked and looked at everyone.

"We all set?" Blaze asked. "Everyone else ready?"

Viper glanced at Rocket. "Before we do that, Rocket, you need to get hold of Tom Hernandez. I tried to find out information on the fallout from Hannah's disappearance but there wasn't a sniff of it anywhere I looked. Of course, I pretty much figured there wouldn't be. We need Tom's connections."

"You want me to call him right now?"

Viper nodded. "Let's see what we can find out. The sooner the better, so we know what we're dealing with."

Rocket pulled out his cell and punched a contact number. "Hey, Tom. It's Rocket Man. Give me a call as soon as you get my message. Thanks."

"Not there?"

Rocket shook his head. "I called his private cell. That reaches him everywhere. When I get a voice mail message on that, it means he's really tied up. I'll keep trying, though."

"Good. Okay. Who goes first with what you've got?"

"I will." Rocket leaned back in his chair. "First of all, Hannah, I started with you since you're our client. Everything evolves from you and your situation. I did some research on your history, what there is of it, particularly your job, and I have to tell you, I am pretty much blown away. You have to be one of the smartest people I have ever met. That is some complicated job you have."

Her lips curved in a tentative smile. "I've been fascinated by electronics and avionics all my life, so it was a natural for me to study this. And I was lucky. I got a scholarship to Embry-Riddle." She hated talking about herself, but she'd do anything if it helped her to get out of this situation.

Rocket grinned. "Well, I'd take my hat off to you, if I wore one."

Viper took her hand and squeezed it, then looked around the table. "Can we get back to business, please?"

"Just letting you know how devilishly smart your girl is," Rocket teased. "Maybe too smart for you."

"Certainly more than too smart for you," Viper snapped, then let out a slow breath. "Sorry. So, work?"

Eagle tapped his keyboard. "Here's the public story on Senator Mark Hegman, the victim. When I got your message, I dug into what I could find about him. Which, by the way, is a lot."

Viper glanced at it. "Good. Can you give me the Cliff Notes version?"

"Mark Pruitt Hegman comes from a military family. Father, grandfather, two brothers. Father and grandfather both retired from the Army as generals. One brother was a Force Recon Marine, the other a SEAL. All highly decorated."

"And Mark is, what, the youngest? Not military? What's the deal?"

"He's the middle son. Went to Annapolis. Entered the Navy as soon as he graduated."

"And?" Viper made a 'come on' motion with his hand.

"And broke his leg the second week he was on active duty. In four places. Damage was so bad they gave him a medical discharge."

"Ouch." Viper frowned. "Bet that didn't sit too well with him."

"No doubt. Anyway, he got his shit together and went into politics. People love to vote for former military." He grinned. "We're all glamourous, didn't you know?"

Viper snorted. "I'll be sure to put it on my resume. So then what?"

"Well, it seems his major at Annapolis was political science, so he got himself a position at the Snellings Institute of Political Sciences."

"The think tank."

Blaze nodded. "He was theoretically researching political concepts, but I think he was being groomed to run for office. Two retired generals in the family carry a lot of weight out there. He also wrote a couple of books during this time that sold really well." He tapped the keyboard. "The senior senator from their home state was getting ready to retire. That makes the junior senator the—"

"Senior senator now." Viper waved his hand. "Yeah, yeah, yeah. I get it."

"Hey. You asked for the story? I'm telling it." Blaze looked back at the screen. "So Hegman makes a run for it and wins in a landslide, thanks to a lot of pressure from a lot of people. And before he starts his freshman term, he marries Trish McCallan. Her family tree includes members of a rich and powerful family. What more does a man need to have success, right?"

Viper frowned. "You saying Hegman bought his political positions?"

"Not at all." Blaze shrugged. "Just stating the facts. Like, here they are with an estate in Kentucky and a summer home on Chesapeake Bay. A fairytale marriage. Two perfect children. Worked his way up in a successful political career to chair the Senate Armed

Services Committee. The military thinks he's a god and half the population idolizes him because he holds hearings on people who may be skirting the law in some way with the military. He's death on contractors he becomes suspicious of."

"For god's sake. Has he also been nominated for sainthood?"

Blaze shrugged. "Maybe."

"Does it say if there was a particular hearing coming up? And who might be in the hot seat? Would that be reason enough for blowing him up? Here's another question. How did whoever it was know he'd be alone in his house? Because according to what I dug up after your text, no one was there but him. Not one member of the house staff in sight. I mean, not even a housekeeper? Doesn't that sound a little odd to you? If Senator Hegman was vacationing, would he do it alone?"

"Don't know." Blaze shrugged. "I'd say we have a lot more research to do."

Rocket tapped the keys on his laptop. "I managed to dig up a list of all the contracts Lowden has completed since the company opened. At least the ones that are public knowledge."

Hannah stared at him, open-mouthed.

"How did you do that? Eric Lowden is a fanatic about keeping everything secret, even the projects that have no confidentiality attached to them. There isn't anyone besides him that has all the details of any project. It's all on a need-to-know basis."

Viper grinned and winked at her. "Secrets of the black ops trade. But some of his contracts are government-related and those have to be open. And maybe some of his clients didn't know they were supposed to hide things." He nodded at Rocket. "Go on."

"So," Rocket continued, "I went back to the beginning. It seems Eric Lowden came out of nowhere. I mean, virtually. He had worked as a technician at Bright Star Avionics and from what I can find, he was a satisfactory employee. Did his job. Not outstanding but not a problem, either. Good routine worker. Period."

Eagle frowned. "Doesn't sound like the kind of guy to get involved in shady activities."

"Right. Only then, things changed." Rocket tapped a couple of keys on his laptop. "He quit his job at Bright Star and just disappeared off the face of the earth for a year. Literally. I couldn't find a trace of him anywhere." He paused and looked around the table. "Yet."

"A year?" Viper frowned. "Where did he go?"

"Still looking for that." Rocket clicked his keys again. "Then, suddenly, he opened Lowden Tactical in a top-notch facility, all the bells and whistles. He had a quality team and a stack of contracts. They've been going full tilt since then."

"How did he get the government contracts?" Viper asked. "They aren't so easy to come by unless you have the right connections."

"We all know there's a bidding process that's supposed to be open and aboveboard. But every single one of us is also aware that there's a lot more that goes on beneath the surface. He obviously has the connections, but no one knows who or what they are."

"I know about the government contracts," Hannah told them. "The one that literally exploded in my face was one, although it was part of a black op. The objective was to blow up a terrorist leader hiding in this country. So I'm not sure how open that one would be."

"Not much if at all," Rocket said. "How many times have you read online or heard in the news about funny business with government contracts that only came out because something fell apart? On the surface it looks smooth, but we don't know what went on behind closed doors or what money or favors changed hands."

"It's obvious," Eagle suggested, "that, accident or deliberate event, Hannah was targeted as the fall guy for this. If someone wanted Hegman out of the way, they'd have to figure out a way to get it done. A straight-out shooting would cause all kinds of stink and a shitload of cops, both state and federal, all over it, which is why they did it this way. Then, like we said before, stash her away until it's safe to get rid of her and hide the body so it's never found. Pass the rumor that she got a shitload of money for doing it and she's living incognito in some tropical paradise."

"But I'm telling you," Hannah insisted, "I check all the settings myself. I don't know how on earth a mistake could have happened. Someone would have to believe me."

"Assuming you ever got to talk to anyone," Blaze reminded her.

"Maybe Lowden's money man is behind it," Eagle added. "The one who's pulling the strings. Nobody gets as many lucrative contracts as he did without someone in a powerful position making it happen. There're too many possibilities here. We have to narrow it all down. I read drone companies get all kinds of contracts."

Hannah nodded. "You're right. We map property for real estate developers, do mineral surveys, check forest fires…you name it." She nibbled on her thumb nail. "We did other stuff, too, but after what happened I'm not sure they were actually legit. They seemed to be, but…" Her voice trailed off.

Blaze quirked an eyebrow. "What kind of other stuff?"

"Getting video footage of military establishments, especially overseas. We were told the Defense Department needed it to plan their strategy, but now I wonder. Another project is checking miles of border, supposedly for human traffickers. But we had footage in there, too, of vehicles that we were told were drug smugglers, although it was very hush-hush. And although I haunted the news sites, I never saw anything about big drug busts. There's usually a major story about it if there is one."

"You're right. That's a great way to track your own drug shipments and stay out of the line of fire." Viper typed something. "Guys, let's make a note to see how far we can check on this stuff."

Hannah frowned. "But if the media never covered it or it didn't make the business pages, how will you find out?"

Rocket chuckled. "Don't worry. We can find out anything."

"We also did a lot of military stuff." Hannah couldn't believe she was sharing all this, but these men—and Peyton, of course—gave her such a feeling of security and trust. Besides, if Lowden was skating the edge of legitimacy, they needed to be stopped. And her own situation cleared up. "Photographing facilities in other countries. Even getting video footage of some high-value targets. Twice we delivered explosives to terrorist camps. My group did, anyway. Maybe the others did, also." She rubbed her cheek. "I always thought we were taking out terrorists who the military were targeting. It was a lot easier than sending in people who might get killed. But now…"

"Now you're rethinking it," Viper finished for her.

She nodded.

"Did you get sent to a location off site for an operation very often?" Rocket asked.

"Once I became part of a GO-Team I did," Hannah answered. "Only the GO-Teams are sent off site. And it depended on what the situation was—if it was surveillance or carried a payload, and what the payload was. I did five off-site launches in the past two years. Otherwise, I worked from headquarters."

Viper exchanged glances with the others. "My guess," he said, "is that there were payloads or assignments Lowden didn't want broadcast company-wide. But I'd like to know why he didn't want to monitor them himself."

"Wouldn't it look suspicious if he handled any contracts himself?" Peyton asked. "Just sayin'."

"Probably," Rocket agreed. "And the real purpose of the mission could be disguised."

"He had a setup in his office," Hannah told him. "He was the only one with access to it. He could monitor there if he wanted to. And maybe he did, but we didn't know it. He was pretty closemouthed."

Eagle leaned back in his chair, hands behind his head. "Here's what I'm thinking. This guy had a lot of contracts that he got under the table, whether from a government contact or someone else. Jobs he did not want to expose to a lot of scrutiny. Hannah, did he ever act funny about them in any way?"

She shook her head. "He was kind of odd, anyway. He was always stressing how hush-hush the government and paramilitary contracts were, so I just figured they were mostly some kind of black ops jobs." She took a minute to sip her drink and settle her thoughts. She didn't at all like what was unraveling here as she took a close look at her job.

"A logical assumption," Viper agreed.

She sighed, wishing she hadn't been so trusting with this whole thing. "When I was hired, I got this big, long indoctrination on how everything at Lowden was confidential and it could cost me my job if I asked any questions except about the particular assignments." She rubbed her forehead. "And I did all kinds of drone assignments—taking video footage, mapping areas, mapping underwater areas. I got a feeling some of the missions I flew were not necessarily on the up and up, but there was nothing I could put my finger on. I even delivered explosives a few times. I was told, just like this last one, that these missions had to be off-book. They were for the government, but fully sanctioned."

No one said anything for a long moment. Hannah could almost hear the gears in their brains turning.

"Listen, guys. If I'd had the least suspicion things were even slightly off kilter I'd never have taken the job. I certainly wouldn't—"

"Ssh, ssh." Viper pressed a finger gently to her lips. "It's all good. You had no way of knowing anything. You got hired for a great job because you had the creds—"

"And was terminally unobservant," she interrupted, unable to keep the bitterness out of her voice.

"Hannah." Rocket leaned forward so he was closer to her. "Why would you even think there was something wrong to observe? No, please. Do not beat yourself up about this."

"He's right." Peyton smiled at her. "I don't know a lot about drone pilots, although I did a little research for one of my books. Hannah, I have to say, your knowledge and abilities blow my mind. That's a complicated job you have."

Hannah shrugged, even as she was warmed by Peyton's tone of voice. "That's very nice of you to say, but—"

"But nothing." Viper cut her off. "She's absolutely right. They were damn lucky to have you at Lowden. Brains like yours don't come along every day. Especially when they belong to someone who is really nice. Okay, guys, what's next?"

Eagle woke up his screen. "When something like this happens, it usually isn't out of the blue. The fallout has to be managed, and the nature of it makes me think there's something screwy about it. So I asked myself, what else is out of whack at Lowden? Do they have contracts that include funny business that they shovel under the table?"

"What did you get?" Blaze asked.

"I discounted the contracts Lowden's got that can stand up to scrutiny and ward off questions. So then I dug around in his past, looking for squirrelly friends and connections. People he'd been involved with in any way that are, uh, let's say, questionable. Jesus, the man's got a list long enough to fill a small phone book. And from a lot of different sources."

Hannah tugged her bottom lip between her teeth. "I know Lowden has many different types of clients. I never interacted with any of them, though. He kept his clients away from the staff. All the deals were handled in his attorney's office."

"So, you didn't have clients touring the facility?" Eagle wanted to know. "Getting a feel for how things worked?"

"No." She shook her head. "And to tell you the truth, I don't think any of us were concerned about it. We had our projects and those were what counted."

"I'm not surprised he kept his connections away from the facility," Eagle told them. "He's spent a lot of time with a strange mix of people. He's got Washington elite on the one hand and some not-too-savory uber-wealthy people on the other. His clients are both domestic and international. We need to do a lot more digging, but that takes time, even with all of us on it. Want my off-the-cuff assessment?"

Viper nodded. "I do."

"We can't tackle all of them," Eagle pointed out. "One of us has to focus on the Mark Hegman situation and the so-called contract for the drone to take out the terrorist."

"I'll do that," Viper said, "if Rocket will get whatever he can from Tom."

"No problem," the other man said.

"There's so much here," Eagle continued, "and each of them comes with complicated situations. We'd be at it until next year. The thing to do is identify some key figures out of these long lists, clients that have the most, shall we say, interesting needs for drones. Then we can start digging into everything, back to the day they were born."

"Okay." Viper nodded his agreement. "So which one do we start with?"

Eagle looked at his screen. "If I were making the choice, I'd pick one of the private security contractors. The first four I dug up do contracting work for the government, and we all know that's been a murky situation from day one."

Rocket nodded. "I don't think any of us will forget the Blackwater debacle."

"So I wanted to see what else might be skimming beneath the surface. I found four operations that need further digging, but they sure don't pass the smell test."

"Wait." Hannah couldn't seem to stop herself from interrupting. "If those companies have government contracts and they hire Lowden to do tactical surveys or whatever as part of that, doesn't it all have to be totally aboveboard?" She shook her head. "Never mind. How stupid does that sound? We read about shady stuff every day. I'm just stunned that Lowden would do anything that skirts the law at all. He seemed so…straightforward."

"If there's enough money involved," Rocket said, "some people will do anything. I say we drill down and find out where his seed money came from. See what the obligations were that he agreed to for a huge pile of cash. And who gave him his startup contracts, because you know they had to be rich. It could all be tied into Hegman's death."

"Meanwhile," Eagle interjected, "we need to start digging. Rocket, did Tom call you back yet?"

"Tell him we want him to get out his biggest shovel," Viper said, "and find every bit of dirt on Eric Lowden and the company. We need to be sure you have everything we've found so far, though, so he has the whole picture."

"No, but he'll call the minute he's free. If the rest of you will send me all the stuff you've got, I'll put it together in a doc for him."

As everyone hit their keyboards, Hannah looked around the table. Once again she gave thanks for the stroke of luck that had placed Viper min that particular bar at the time on the night she'd run from the hotel. And that for whatever reason, he'd chosen to help her instead of writing her off as a nut. That the attraction between them was so explosive, and that she'd connected at once with Peyton, was a double miracle to her. It made her realize how much she'd insulated herself with her job and how much she'd been missing out on.

She could feel the same type of intangible connection among the people at the table. Again, she gave a little silent prayer of thanks and focused on what everyone was saying.

"They can find out anything," Peyton promised, giving her hand a little squeeze. "You can't believe what they dug up when they were helping me."

"But you had your own source," Blaze reminded her. "And speaking of that, you've still got that connection to Senator Franz, right?"

Peyton nodded. "I'm happy to give him a call. Just tell me what you want me to ask him. I try to be specific where he's concerned."

"Ask him who's the most powerful man on the Senate Armed Services Committee right now," Viper told her. "Who's the most promising candidate to replace Hegman."

Eagle leaned back in his chair and nodded. "I was just thinking the same thing. With everything Rocket and I have dug up so far, there has to be funny stuff going on in that area. I don't trust most of those people further than the front door."

Viper turned to Hannah. "Do you recall if Lowden had many contracts from overseas clients? Foreign companies? Other countries? I wonder if we have foreign influence involved in this."

She scrunched up her forehead, wishing that she'd paid more attention now to the clients as well as the actual projects.

"I was always so caught up in my own assignments that I didn't pay a lot of mind to others. Plus, my team wasn't chosen for a lot of overseas assignments. Ours were usually in the States or Canada or sometimes Mexico. But if someone has a laptop or tablet I can use, I can dig around in the website and see if anything comes to mind. You never know."

"I have an extra one I use when I'm doing a deep search on this one." Viper pushed back from his chair. "Let me get it for you."

"And let me get you another cold drink." Peyton pushed her chair back and stood up, reaching for Hannah's glass.

"Oh, no. You don't have to wait on me."

"Are you kidding? After what you've been through, we should *all* be waiting on you."

For the first time in days, Hannah thought this nightmare might actually be resolved.

Chapter Eight

After lunch, Peyton made the phone call to the senator she knew, but he was in a meeting.

"It's supposed to last all day," she told everyone. "But I left a message for him to call me back. He's good about it. He won't dodge it." She grinned. "Besides, last time I turned him on to a situation that made him a hero." Then her grin disappeared. "Although I'm sure he would have been happier if it hadn't existed at all. A slimeball former senator was helping to cover up my brother-in-law's murder."

"But your friend came through," Blaze reminded her. "And told you to contact him anytime you needed something, so there you go."

Viper produced a slim laptop which he handed it to Hannah. "Password's 'buzzoff'."

Hannah looked at him, startled. "For real?"

"Uh huh." He winked. "That's what I say to anyone messing with my stuff. Well, actually the real term is a little rougher, but you never know who's going to see the screen."

Viper opened his own laptop again. "Meanwhile, let's divide up the chores and start digging again. Lowden's got such a funny smell to it I know we'll find more if we dig hard enough."

Hannah unlocked the computer in front of her and at once pulled up Lowden Tactical. She had a password to access material not made public, but Lowden monitored all activity on their site. If she used it, they could track it back to her, so she'd have to just do the best she could. While the guys worked, and Peyton sat cross-legged on the couch doing her own thing with a laptop, Hannah dug into all the public information on Lowden. Maybe she'd get lucky and something would ring a bell.

But at the end of two hours, she had to admit defeat, handing the laptop back to Viper.

"I made a list of likely projects you might want to do your dark web thing on," she told him, "but I can't really find out anything you can use. That site is locked up tighter than a vault."

"No less than I expect. But thanks for trying, anyway."

"I feel as if I should do something. Apparently, there's a whole list of things that went on there that I never noticed or paid attention to, which makes me feel like an idiot."

"And we'll find out what they are," he assured her. "Even having project names we might not have paid attention to is a big help. Something's hidden there, some kind of pattern, and we're going to find it." He leaned back in his chair. "We're going to be working away at this all afternoon, heavy time on our computers and cells. Think you could manage to relax a little? The last couple of weeks have been a bitch for you."

"I think that's a great idea," Peyton agreed. "I just turned in the manuscript I was working on to my editor and I need some time to air out my brain before I give any thought to what my next project will be. I've decided I'm going to play hooky for the afternoon. I think you should come hang out with me, Hannah."

She frowned. "You mean, like, go somewhere?"

Peyton shook her head. "Hell, no. I don't think Viper's letting you leave this house until he has everyone from Lowden—and everyone else involved in this—in a headlock. I'm thinking about hanging out on the dock. I love sitting there and watching the water." She shifted her glance to Viper. "Unless you think…"

He shook his head. "No chance they've located you this fast and are out on the water scouting. First, they have to make the connection between you and Galaxy, and that ain't happening. We'll know if they find out where you are. Go have a good time. You've had your life ripped apart and turned upside down. You need to catch your breath."

He smiled and heat flooded her. *Good lord!* When was the last time a man had that effect on her? She was just glad the blouse she was wearing was dark enough to hopefully hide her suddenly hard nipples.

Peyton nodded. "And I want some girl time with you, Hannah. Not that I don't love you guys, but I think I've overdosed on testosterone."

"Hope not." Blaze chuckled. "But I get your point. And Viper is right. Everything else aside, I bet Hannah can use some, too. She's had a wicked twenty-four hours."

Hannah wanted to say that not all of it had been wicked. Although of course that depended on a person's interpretation of the word.

Peyton turned to Hannah. "How about it? A little downtime hanging out on the dock? Water's great for relaxing you."

Hannah had to admit, she was glad Peyton had decided to hang around instead of having to leave. She felt comfortable with her, which surprised her. Now she nodded.

"I can do that. At least I'm going to try. I don't think I can remember the last time I just let go. At Lowden, you can't ease up for a second."

"Well, today we're changing all that. Think that'll work for you?"

"I do. At least I hope so. And thank you."

She took a last glance at the men concentrating on their laptops, on what she'd come to think of as her project. Eagle had just picked up his cell and walked away to make his call. She was totally amazed at the connection among all of them, the way they worked in a rhythm. The kind she knew came from being in Special Teams in the military. Sometimes they didn't even have to speak. It was as if they each knew what the others were thinking.

"Come on," Peyton urged. "Let's go sit down by the water and hang out while the guys do their thing."

Hannah couldn't remember the last time she'd done any hanging out, which was why this sounded so great. It underscored how she'd socially isolated herself since she'd gotten the job at Lowden. *Big mistake*, she thought now, but who'd have ever thought she'd find herself in this situation, where her entire life was compromised?

She followed Peyton down to the dock and allowed herself to be convinced to take off her shoes and sit with her feet hanging down into the water. This was so uncommon for her. Trusting a strange man enough to leave a bar with him. Jumping into bed with him in an erotic coupling. Flying off in a private plane with him. Now sitting here and actually making friends with a woman she hadn't known twelve hours ago. For the woman her co-workers and acquaintances also called Hard-assed Hannah, this was way out of her regular zone.

Looking around, she noticed that the adobe wall extended on both sides of the lawn down to the water itself.

"Viper's a fanatic about security and privacy," Peyton told her, seeing where she was looking. "The houses are really close together here, what with the property being so pricey, but he loved the location and the view. He just had to figure out how to shut out the neighbors."

"Are those mini lights along the top of the wall?" Hannah took a closer look at them.

"Uh huh, but they are also a sophisticated security system. The wall's too high to climb unless someone has a ladder, but Viper tried to think of all angles. If someone touches the top of the wall, those cute little lights emit an electrical charge. They also sound the alarm system up at the house."

"Wow! He really does take precautions."

"Yes, he does," Peyton agreed. "They all do. The only exposure is out on the dock itself, but people are really good at respecting privacy. And although it's possible someone could try to access this place from the water, again, there are sensors and triggers buried everywhere."

Hannah studied the boats out on the bay. Right now they were little dots against the horizon.

"What about people watching from out there?" She nodded toward the scene.

"Listen. Can someone sit out there on a boat with high-powered binocs and spy on this place? Of course. No place is entirely safe unless you isolate yourself in the woods or on a mountain. But the people who are after you? First, they'd have to find where you are. Then they'd have to do their snatch and grab, and these guys are the best at preventing stuff like that. Promise."

Hannah sighed. "I have to say, Viper got me out of that bar and out of Houston smooth as can be. I guess I'll just feel a lot safer when we find out who's really behind this fuckup and stop them."

"Amen to that. Meanwhile, you couldn't pick a better place to hide. Right?"

"Absolutely."

She settled herself down and realized with a start how many simple things were missing from her life, including a close friend. Her choice, but not necessarily a good one. Hannah considered herself damn lucky that she and Peyton had connected so easily and quickly. She had no idea what would happen when this was all over, or even where she'd end up, although she knew what she wished for. She hoped, however, that no matter what happened, the two of them could remain friends.

"Come sit here." Peyton patted the space next to her. "It's nice to have another female added to the group. I'm still trying to find a place in the social circle around here. I've only been here a few months and it's slow going. There's my sister, of course, and living in the same city with her is a real blessing. And I connected with a couple of authors who also write for my publisher, so I'm getting there." She chuckled. "And being around these guys does make the time pass. Plus, I was shoulder-deep in the book I just finished and sent to my editor. I wasn't lacking for something to do."

Hannah grinned. "I can't believe I'm hanging out with a famous bestselling author."

"And I can't believe I'm hanging out with a woman smarter than all of us together. So we're even there."

Hannah sighed. "I just hope these guys can fix this mess I'm in. I obviously can't spend my life hiding in Viper's house, wonderful though it is."

"And they're not sitting around waiting for anything to happen," Peyton pointed out. "If anyone can get to the bottom of this, it's them. Let me tell you how they saved my life and my sister's."

Hannah listened as Peyton told her the entire story of the death of her brother-in-law and the near death of her sister. Hannah was appalled at the trouble Owen Kendrick had gotten himself into, so extreme that his wife had been willing to kill Peyton's sister and brother-in-law to hide it. And that Owen's father, managing partner in the law firm, had then involved a disgraced senator to cover it up. Warren Sulzberger had been allowed to retire from the senate quietly to avoid a national scandal, but his participation in the aftermath of the crime, exposed by Peyton's sister, had ended all that.

"As it should," Hannah said.

Peyton nodded. "The whole thing made me sick. I nearly lost my sister and her recovery is still ongoing. If it weren't for Blaze, I don't know what would have happened." She smiled. "But Blaze and the rest of the Galaxy team found out everything and took care of it. You're so lucky to have them on your side."

"I know. I still can't believe how all this happened. I'm afraid it's a dream and if I pinch myself, I'll wake up."

Peyton shook her head. "I thought that at first, but they're the real deal. Granted, your introduction might have been a little, um, unorthodox, but so was mine. Hell! Their whole situation is unorthodox." She smiled at Hannah. "But I promise you this—once they commit to something, they are in one hundred percent."

Hannah wrinkled her forehead. "What do you mean?"

"Oh, honey, you can see it from miles away. He's definitely committed."

"After just a couple of days? How is that even possible?"

"I wondered the same thing, too, with Blaze. Didn't know if it was real or just happened because of the whole unreal situation. I was shocked that we connected so fast, but with them it doesn't take long. That's just the way they are. If anyone is shocked, I'm sure it's the guys. From what I gathered, Viper was one of their biggest playboys, but he certainly seems to have put his stamp on you."

"I just worry because it was so fast. Just a couple of days."

"Oh, it's obvious to anyone who looks at the two of you. Trust me. And I'm glad for both of you."

"I just need to get out of this disaster my life is in right now." Hannah rubbed her jaw. "I keep asking myself how I got into this spot. How I could have been so stupid. There were obviously things going on at Lowden that I never noticed or questioned."

"There was no reason for you to. Why should you?"

"She shouldn't."

Both women scrambled to their feet as Blaze and Viper come up behind them.

"Sorry." Peyton grinned at Blaze. "We were too busy talking about you guys."

"Feel free," Viper told them, "as long as it's about how wonderful we are. Hannah, on the surface, Lowden looks exactly like what you think it is. But if that were true, when this happened, they would have reacted differently. Sequestered you, sure, but gotten a whole platoon of lawyers for both the company and you. Hired avionics investigators. Maybe even shut down operations completely until answers could be found. The fact they didn't is one of the reasons we believe this was no surprise to them."

"The whole thing makes me feel sick. And betrayed."

"With good reason. But don't worry. We'll fix it. Anyway, I'm getting ready to put the steaks on the grill and thought you ladies would like to have a drink."

"Sounds great." Peyton slid her hand into one of Viper's, his touch grounding her.

As they reached the house, Rocket walked out to meet them.

"Tom Hernandez called back. He's caught up in a thorny situation, but I'm set to meet with him tomorrow afternoon. He apologized but said that's the best he can do. He understands it's important."

"We'll take him when we can get him," Viper said. "Okay, let's eat."

* * * *

Once dinner was over, everyone packed up their stuff, preparing to leave.

Viper walked them to the door. "So, let's just recap. We grabbed a lot of unorganized stuff out of thin air today."

Eagle patted his laptop. "And I took it and pulled it together so we'd know what to follow up on. After we went through it all, we discussed who should do what and I added that, too. We've all got copies of the file that includes all our notes and bits of information. I'm going to dig deeper into the Lowden contracts that look like they could be the most suspicious."

"Good. Let's get started early." Viper swallowed the last of his coffee. "I have a feeling Lowden isn't just going to hang around waiting to see if Hannah surfaces somewhere. They can mobilize an army to canvass the area around the hotel and show her picture. Give out some kind of sob story. Just our bad luck if someone remembers her, and recalls she left with Viper."

Blaze nodded his agreement. "You got that right. Of course, they'd have to trace who he is, and that wouldn't be so easy."

"They have unlimited resources," Eagle reminded them. "And they'll be persistent."

"Okay. First thing in the morning we'll get right back on it." He started to walk away, then stopped. "Wait a second. Houston. Don't we know someone there?"

Eagle nodded. "I do. I have a cousin there. He's a licensed investigator. Just opened his own office, as a matter of fact. And he'd be perfect for it. If anyone can blend into any environment, it's Ed. He could do some quiet scouting for us. Want me to call him?"

Viper nodded. "Give him the basics. Then have him give me a call in the morning."

"Will do. Talk to you later."

He reset the security system, and when he turned, he almost bumped into Hannah.

"Oops! Sorry." He put both hands on her arms to steady her. "And by the way, you have to be pretty damn good to sneak up on me."

Her mouth curved in a smile. "I'll remember that."

"I was preoccupied, anyway."

"Excuses?" she teased.

"Maybe." He told her about Eagle's cousin. "We'll all feel a lot better if we have someone on the ground sniffing things out. A direct line to what's going on there."

She turned pale. "They won't…" Then she shook her head. "Of course whoever it is won't give anything away. You wouldn't work with anyone who might do that." She blew out a breath. "Thank you."

"I think we need to try and forget about this for tonight. What do you think?"

"Absolutely."

"And I have just the way to do it."

He lifted her in his arms and carried her down the hall. She wondered which room he was taking her to, remembering the pile of new clothing she'd had fun trying on with Peyton. But he passed that door and went instead to one at the end of the short hall that was obviously his. He flipped a light switch with his elbow and the nightstand lamps came on, bathing the room in a warm glow. This room was twice as large as the one where she'd tried on clothes, glass doors opened onto the same patio where they'd had lunch, and beyond was an endless view of the bay. That alone could soothe her nerves.

Viper set her on her feet and cupped her face.

"Last night sort of happened. It was great. No. It was fantastic. Beyond that." He brushed his mouth over hers. "It made me want a lot more."

It had made her want a lot more, too. Things she'd only read about and never found anyone she could be that free with. Her pulse accelerated. "I know you've been with a lot of women, and —"

"Hush." He touched a finger to her lips, the heat in his eyes burning her to the center of her. "Forget them. I have already. You wiped it all from my mind. I want *you*. Right here, right now."

He pressed his mouth to hers again then traced the seam of her lips with his tongue. She opened for him and he slid his tongue inside, gliding it back and forth over hers. She tilted her head back and allowed him a better angle, her hands gripping the muscles of his upper arms to give herself balance.

He swirled his tongue inside her mouth, tasting every hot inch, scraping his teeth gently over her own delicate tongue before sucking it into his mouth. More shivers.

He slid his hands, which he'd been using to cradle her head, down her back to cup her nicely rounded ass and pull her tight against him. God, the things he wanted to do to this body, at the same time wondering if he'd scare her off. She'd been hot as hell the other night, but he also had the feeling she wasn't usually that unrestrained. He was well aware that a crisis would do that to people. He just wanted to make sure she knew how hot he was for her, how hungry, and not just for a quick fuck.

Take it slow, asshole.

But it was damn hard.

In his checkered life, Viper had had more than his share of woman, but none of them had ever affected him like Hannah Modell. Just looking at her made the desire to taste every inch of her consume him and made his cock painfully hard. He wanted to be inside her. *Now.* More than the intense physical connection, however, was an unexpected, instant emotional link, shocking in its intensity. How had this happened in just twenty-four hours? He'd tried to analyze it, but realized he couldn't pick apart something like this.

Her mouth tasted so hot and sexy. He thought he could drink from her forever, even as he imagined her lips wrapped around his cock, maybe with her on her knees before him, her hands squeezing his balls.

He broke the kiss to trail his lips along the soft curve of her jaw. Every place on her body tasted so good that he didn't know where to kiss her first. He nibbled at the lobe of her ear and licked the side of her neck on the way to placing a sucking kiss at the hollow of her throat. She moaned lightly, the sound vibrating against his mouth and sending electricity straight to his dick and his balls.

"Jesus, Hannah." He lifted his head to look at her. "Just...Jesus!"

The heat in her eyes dimmed a little at his words. "Is something wrong? I thought..."

"Nothing is wrong." Except that he was losing his mind over her. "Far from it. I just wish I could touch you everywhere at once." He grabbed her hand and placed it over his fly. "Feel what you do to me?"

He grabbed the hem of her blouse and tugged it upward. When she lifted her arms, he yanked the garment over her head and tossed it to the side. The upper swells of her breasts made his mouth water. Bending his head, he licked the curves, first one, then the other, before clamping his mouth over a nipple, bra and all. When he tugged on the hardened peak, she moaned, the sound inciting the lust boiling inside him even more. He bit down harder, and rather than pulling away from him, she thrust at him with even more force.

His balls ached and erotic thoughts of what he wanted to do to her filled his brain.

"Let's get this out of the way," he growled. "I don't want anything hiding those pretty breasts of yours."

He couldn't believe his hands were actually shaking as he unhooked her bra, slid the straps down and tossed the bit of silk and lace on top of her blouse. Rough-and-ready Viper felt like a high school kid about to lose his cherry. He'd had plenty of women, most of them with as much experience as he had and with similar tastes, but no one had ever affected him like this.

Cupping her breasts, he kneaded them as he sucked hard on first one rose-colored nipple then the other. The little moans that vibrated up from her throat were some of the sexiest sounds he'd ever heard, urging him on.

He'd worried that last night might have been an aberration for her. That in the light of day, past the stress of the moment, she might regret what happened, although he fervently hoped not. It was some of the best sex he'd ever had. Scratch that. *The* best. *Ever*. And they'd barely touched the surface. He had things he wanted to do to her, things he hoped wouldn't send her screaming into the night. Things that almost made him come just thinking about them.

He was stunned by it all, with no idea what the fuck was happening to him. Oh, he'd always had it in the back of his mind that once he was out of the SEALs, he'd think about settling down. *Maybe.* Find the right woman who pushed every one of his buttons. But at thirty-six, he hadn't been sure he was ready yet to think of life with just one person. Until Hannah had burst into his universe.

Stop thinking so much. Tomorrow you can think.

He blocked everything else from his mind and focused on the woman in his arms. Her soft flesh. Her warm body. The deliciously round breasts with their pebbled tips. He drew a line between those breasts down to the waistband of her new jeans, taking a little nip of the skin before kneeling in front of her.

"What—"

"Ssh. I have to see every bit of you. In the light, so I don't miss anything."

He undid the snap at her waistband and lowered the zipper, pushing them down past her hips to her ankles. Then, unable to resist the temptation, he drew his tongue across the lace band of her barely-there panties with his tongue, licking the skin as he did so. It was killing him to restrain himself, but he was determined to take it slow and bring her every ounce of pleasure he could.

Placing his hands on her hips, he lifted her and sat her on the edge of the bed. He eased off her shoes then slid her jeans and thong down her legs. The scent of her musk was driving him nuts, so much so that he had to bury his face between her thighs and inhale deeply.

God! Every nerve in his body leaped to attention, sending messages directly to his cock and his balls. He lapped the area, flattening his tongue to taste her delicious flavor.

"I could do this forever," he murmured, inhaling the scent of her flesh, and he meant every word. Except then he'd be neglecting the rest of her.

Easing her back until she was lying on the bed, half off, legs spread so she was naked before him, he took a minute to drink in all that sweet, mouthwatering flesh. Then he knelt in front of her, spread her thighs and draped her legs over his shoulder, and sucked in a breath at the sight of her sex with its nicely trimmed hair framing her oh-so-wet slit. He drew a finger between the pink folds, coating it with her warm juices, then licked the finger and slowly sucked it clean. The pulse beating at her throat accelerated, so he did it again.

God! He'd never tasted anything as sweet and intoxicating in his life.

He ran his tongue over his lips, pressed the pink flesh open and licked a long, slow path from top to bottom. Then he did it again, pausing along the way to move it in a swirling motion over her clit. Her moans grew louder, and she clenched her hands into fists and tried to lift her hips to be closer to his mouth. The more she made those delicious little sounds, the more he worked the slick pink flesh.

When he'd nibbled and licked, paying extra attention to her clit, he moved one hand to slide two fingers inside her. *Jesus!* She was soaked. His fingers glided right in, so smoothly that he added another one, working them to stretch the slick walls. The intense grip of her flesh excited him even more. He closed his eyes for a moment, centering himself and calling on all his discipline not to blow this.

"God!" The word burst from her mouth.

She dug her heels into his shoulder blades and squeezed him with her thighs, pushing herself to ride his hand. He tried to slow things down, but she wasn't having any of it. She pushed hard, moving her hips faster and faster. He clamped his teeth over her clit with a light touch and bit down, and she exploded. Her inner walls clenched tight around his fingers, squeezing them again and again. He worked her swollen nub, not easing up until the spasms subsided at last and her legs relaxed, falling to the side.

Viper rose, slid her body so it was completely on the bed, then lay on top of her, holding his weight on his forearms.

"You look so beautiful when you come." He touched his lips lightly to hers, smiling. "And you taste good, too."

"You... You're... That was amazing."

"You're the amazing one. How did I get so lucky for you to fall into my path?"

She searched his face, relaxing at whatever she saw there. "Maybe we were both due for a little good luck."

He lay there with her for a long moment, staring into her eyes, trying to read the expression that flickered. The pulse at the hollow of her throat was still stuttering and the heavy beat of her heart thrummed against his chest. He hoped he wasn't reading her wrongly, but he saw satisfaction, heat and desire. Hannah Modell was turning out to be a rare, undiscovered gem, and he silently gave thanks to whatever hand of fortune had sent her into that bar and onto the stool next to him.

He could hardly believe that less than forty-eight hours had passed since then, or that they had connected so instantly. It might not have been his style up to now, but he wasn't walking away from it. He was going to make sure they got her out of this so the two of them could look at a future together.

He shifted and his very swollen, very hard cock pressed against her thigh, a painful reminder that only one of them had come yet.

She smiled at the contact, half shy, half tease. "We should do something about that."

"When you catch your breath," he agreed.

"Maybe my breath is caught enough for this."

She moved so fast she startled him, pushing him to the side and rising to a kneeling position. Before he realized what she was doing, she had her slim fingers circling his throbbing dick and drew a line around the swollen head with the tip of her tongue.

"No, wait." He wound her hair around the fingers of one hand and tried to move her head. "Jesus, Hannah."

"I don't want to wait." She glanced sideways at him, a hungry, teasing look in her eyes. "I want to make you feel as good as you did for me."

She went to work on him and he reached for every bit of self-control he had. He did not want this to end too soon. While he'd really rather come inside her, her mouth was so hot and wet that he had no desire to pull away. She licked up one side of his cock and down the other before tracing the crown of flesh at the head. When she pressed the tip of her tongue into the tiny opening, electricity shot straight to his balls. She smiled against his cock, then opened her mouth and slid all the way down to the base. As she did so, she slipped one hand between his thighs and tightened her fingers around his balls. When she increased the pressure just a little bit, he sucked in his breath.

"Hannah! Jesus! Holy mother of god."

She squeezed again, a gentle pressure, and began moving her mouth up and down the length of his shaft. He kept his fingers twined in her hair, guiding her, although she sure didn't need it. Her lips were like velvet and her tongue like slick satin as it stroked him again and again. He needed her to go faster, then to slow down, then he didn't know what the fuck he wanted, except he sure didn't want her to stop.

He felt the orgasm gathering low in his body and for a brief moment he thought about telling her to stop. To let him shove his dick inside her right then. But it felt so damn good this way and he was past the point of no return. In an instant he exploded, his cock throbbing as he came in her mouth. She never let up on the rhythm of her hands and mouth until she'd sucked every single drop from him. Then she lifted her head and he saw a very satisfied look on her face.

It took him a moment to even out his breathing, but then he released his grip on her hair and smoothed it back, away from her face.

"Come here," he told her in soft tones, and pulled her so she was lying on top of him. "I want to feel you against me."

She smiled. "Was it good?"

He had to laugh. "Good is too weak a word for what happened. I hope you don't kill me before I get enough of you." He stroked her cheek. "Although I don't believe that's ever going to happen. I might never get to that point."

She lay against his chest, her head on his shoulder. "I hope not."

"Count on it." He tilted her chin up so he could look directly into her eyes. "Hannah, I know this has been fast. It's just been a couple of days since you tried to hide in that bar and luckily sat on the stool next to me. Maybe you think this is fast. I don't know. But for me? In our line of work, life can be a precarious thing. You hope that one right person will come into it. There are no guarantees, but people say you'll know it when it happens. I knew it five minutes after you sat down. I don't know if it's the same for you, and in this situation, I don't want to push you."

She pressed a finger to his lips. "I'm almost afraid to say yes, for fear I'm reading it wrong or it might go away. But I've never felt like this about anybody ever in my entire life. I just want to make sure you're..."

"Sure about it?" His voice was husky. "Oh, count on it. And I promise we're getting you out of this mess and taking care of the assholes who put you in it."

Hannah sighed. "I can't wait for that day. And, Viper? I know you and your partners can do it. I have faith."

He was pretty damn positive that was the most important thing anyone had ever said to him. He'd make sure Galaxy got her problem taken care of. But in the meantime, he planned to make good use of their nights together. He was already becoming addicted to Hannah Modell. He wanted to be sure it went both ways.

"Catch your breath, darlin', because I'm going to fuck you so hard you'll come like a maniac."

He waited for her to object, but instead she just licked her lips.

Chapter Nine

Diesel paced his den, on edge and trying to calm down, debating the merits of adding some bourbon to his morning orange juice. He could not figure out how things had gotten so incredibly fucked up. Hannah Modell was just a nothing female, her only skills having to do with drones. She had no close friends, no romantic relationships, and both of her parents were dead. Making her the fall guy should have been a slam dunk.

It wasn't as if they hadn't planned it out well, leaving markers for people to follow when they investigated. Grabbing her off the remote site, hauling her back to Lowden Tactical and stashing her in the hotel had been a seamless operation. So how had it blown up in their faces?

The people with the money behind this were less than happy, and that was putting it mildly. Henry would be showing up any moment, as frantic as an old lady. What a fucking pain in the ass he was. If he didn't have contacts that no one else could connect with, Diesel would have cut him loose. The people *he* reported to would chop off his head without blinking if he let Henry fuck things up. Except, short of killing him, he wasn't sure how he would do it. The man was a fucking ball of nerves.

He did have to admit, however, that having Hannah Modell literally vanish into thin air wasn't doing anyone's nerves any good.

Okay, he'd destroyed all the video of the flight. They often kept the discs of drone flights for their records in case they needed them, but some flights like this one needed to disappear into thin air. Everyone involved in the project had been fed the line that Hannah had fucked up big time and they were taking care of it. But if he didn't find her and resolve the problem soon, his ass was grass. No, he was a dead man. The people he owed everything to would eliminate him without blinking an eye and find someone else to replace him. He wouldn't even be a fond memory.

He finally gave in to the urge and poured a healthy shot of bourbon into his juice, then slugged back a mouthful. He had no plans to turn into a drunk over this, but he definitely needed the drink to deal with Henry. As the liquor slowly burned its way down his throat, he heard the sound of a car in the driveway. *Okay. Show time.*

He had the front door open before Henry could even ring the bell.

"Well?" Henry demanded. "Have you got her? I haven't heard a word from you since yesterday."

Diesel tamped down his temper. He hated to admit that he shared Henry's unease. They were on a specific timetable here. Step one had been executed correctly, the fallout was being manipulated and the plans were in place for step two. The one thing no one had expected and so hadn't planned for was that Hannah Modell would somehow manage to escape. Henry couldn't remember the last time anyone had gotten away from Paul Santos or caught him off guard. That was why they had chosen him for this particular assignment.

"I have people quietly scouring the area for blocks around the hotel," Diesel said. "How about a glass of orange juice, or some coffee?"

"How about a shot of that bourbon? I hope I don't become an alcoholic before this is all over."

"So do I," Diesel muttered under his breath. "I promise you these people are good. The Boss handpicked them. He's used them on other delicate assignments. They know what they're doing. Plus, he has an added ace in the hole."

"What?" Henry demanded.

Diesel shrugged. "You'll have to ask him. Meanwhile, I have people combing the records of her cell phone for the past eight years and reaching out to see if her contacts have heard from her."

"They'll get suspicious," Henry complained. "And what about the people in Houston? Aren't they going to think something's weird when people are questioned if they saw her?"

"Not the way they do it. They have a very believable cover story. I'm telling you. The Boss has a smooth black operation, second to none."

Henry studied him for a moment. "Doesn't it ever bother you calling him the Boss?"

"No. He is, and I'm damn grateful for him."

"Henry." Diesel took another swallow of his drink. If the man didn't calm down fast, he might have to drink the whole bottle. Or hit the man over the head with it. "It's barely been forty-eight hours. We have a cushion of time here."

"Not much of one," he objected. "You know as well as I do that the people satisfied with phase one of our plan are expecting the next one to happen within the next two weeks. If Hannah Modell is out there like a loose cannon, there's no telling who she's talking to and what the fallout will be."

"Her disappearance has complicated things."

"And whose fault is that? I don't want to hear excuses. Just find the damn woman and get rid of her before she ruins everything. We need to discuss that next step and our role in it. I've got a lot riding on the success of this whole thing."

Diesel wanted to point out that they all did, but he kept his mouth shut. After all, the man had some major financial situations that could fall apart unless there was a successful outcome to this situation.

"I want to know what you've heard in Washington," Diesel told him.

"I know our friends in the sandbox are pleased. A threat has been eliminated and a key principle is safe. The next step is a drastic one, but if it's done right, no one will connect the two incidents. Then we'll be on to number three."

"I remind you," Diesel said, "that there is going to be a lot of pushback when that happens."

"Not if we handle it right. The power of the opposition will have diminished, making it the right time to strike. That has to happen."

Diesel barked a humorless laugh. "The fact that you will be next to the seat of power has nothing to do with it, right? Or that a number of lucrative contracts will come your way?"

Henry narrowed his eyes. "We all have our reasons for doing this. I wouldn't be throwing mud at anyone if I were you."

"Fine." Diesel counted to ten in his head. "We all have our personal goals. And, I point out, the end result will be extremely rewarding for all of us."

Henry paced for a moment, hands shoved into his pockets, forehead wrinkled.

"I just wish we could find that fucking woman. She could blow up the whole thing. We've planned this for two years. This will be our only chance."

"Henry, get your shit together." Diesel was tired of the other man's whining. "Go home. Go to your office. You have things to get ready for. Go do them."

Henry glared at him. "I want regular updates."

"You will get them whenever I do. Now get the hell out of here."

"I'll get, but don't you forget whose money is funding a big part of this."

"And who will make millions after everything is in place," Diesel reminded him.

Henry looked like he was about to say something, then changed his mind. "I'll be calling you." He slammed the door behind him as he stomped out.

Diesel rubbed his forehead, hoping to ease the headache that was brewing back there. He was glad Henry and the others didn't know the other reason why they were all so panicked at Hannah Modell's disappearance. Not only had they lost their fall guy, but she had knowledge that, if she pieced the facts together, could destroy this complex project and land them all in prison forever. A drone accident could be explained away by incompetence or mistakes. What they were planning? There was no explanation but the real one, and they couldn't let that get out. Not until they reached their goal.

He'd never thought, when the Boss had come to him with this idea, that it could even work, but holy hell! They just might pull it off.

He refilled his coffee mug, took out his cell and pressed a speed dial number. After two rings, Ed Fletcher, the man in charge of the search, answered.

"Nothing yet," he snapped out. "That bitch has vaporized. That's all I can think of. But we're not finished yet. I never give up."

"And that's why the Boss keeps you around," Diesel pointed out. "But not even a sniff?"

"I'm giving it another hour. If we don't get any response, we're sending Caleb around with an enhanced sob story and a reward."

"But it's been three fucking days already."

"We're working the plane angle hard. We'll turn something up. Don't worry."

"We're running out of time," Diesel reminded him.

"I know. I'll get it done. I haven't failed yet, have I?"

"No, you haven't." Diesel had to agree that was true. Ed Fletcher could find a nail in a field of dirt. "Okay. Keep in touch."

He disconnected the call and shoved the phone into his pocket. *Fletcher better get results soon.* Zero Hour was approaching.

* * * *

Rocket always liked visiting Tom Hernandez. He had been recommended to them by their former SEAL team leader, which was as good a blessing as anyone could get. He had drawn up the legal papers for Galaxy and, in their meetings with the attorney, they had discovered that Tom was probably the most connected person in Florida, maybe in the entire southeast. Whatever a person might need or want to find out, Tom Hernandez was pretty sure to get it for them. He had given Galaxy a key piece of information when they'd been hunting for the killer of Peyton West's brother-in-law. They were hoping he could do the same for them now.

When Rocket had finally hooked up with him and told him what he wanted, Tom had said he'd see what he could do. The Galaxy partners had learned that when the man said that, it meant the attorney would turn over rocks others might not even know existed.

"You guys do get interesting clients." He grinned as he and Rocket shook hands.

Rocket nodded. "Wouldn't have it any other way. So. Got something for me?"

"Don't I always. Let's grab a cup of coffee."

They sat in two chairs in a comfortable conversation grouping. Tom took a sip from his mug then launched into what he'd found out.

"Background on Lowden Tactical first, which is very sketchy. Eric Lowden has a very thin public bio for a person in his position. He has a degree in Unmanned Systems Engineering from Lewis University in Romeoville, New York. Not a top school, but still rated very good."

"He'd have to have gone to one to acquire the skills to run an operation like his company. Right?"

Tom nodded. "Agreed. At least to know how things in his company work. I dug as deep as I could to see if I'd missed anything about his work at Bright Star or the time between when he left there and emerged as the head of Lowden Tactical."

Rocket frowned. "Just like that?"

"Just like that. Then, the next thing anyone knew, he was heading Lowden Technology and dealing with government contracts." He paused. "And not necessarily our government."

Rocket lifted an eyebrow. "Exactly what does that mean?"

Tom looked as if he was searching for words.

"Like what? Come on," Rocket urged. "This is me. You don't have to watch your words."

"Yeah, I know." The man sighed. "I'm just always very careful talking about shit like this. The stuff I learned — after practically taking a blood oath, I might mention — is unsettling. This is not speculated about except in very dark, soundproof rooms with the windows shuttered. But..."

"But?" Rocket urged.

"Dark gossip has it that a lot of Lowden's money comes from doing projects for foreign governments. That his seed money came from someone or some ones who don't pass the smell test. He did things for them that adversely affect the United States. Not necessarily within our borders either, for example, but those that ultimately disrupt our foreign policy."

"Like dropping the explosives on Senator Mark Hegman instead of who the real target was supposed to be."

Tom nodded and leaned forward, resting his elbows on his knees.

"Rumor has it that person is Hassan Atef, leader of the uber radical Sword of Allah."

"Fuck." Rocket raked his fingers through his hair. "They're everywhere. My SEAL team had to rescue prisoners from one of their camps in the Sudan. You can't believe the condition those people were in. And two of their group had been beheaded for propaganda videos."

"Makes me sick. And the dark word is that while Atef was the accepted target, Hegman was the real one."

"But why?" Rocket shook his head. "Who would want to get rid of a guy who's done so much good for this country?"

"That's what people want to know. There's something really screwy going on here, and beneath the surface, plenty of questions are being asked. Like, was Lowden getting something out of this? Was someone putting pressure on him, and how and why? Or was this something they did willingly and if so, why? What's their involvement?"

"Yeah, well." Rocket blew out a breath. "That's what Galaxy wants to know, also."

"Also, Hegman as chair of the Senate Armed Services Committee was fond of hearings targeting people he thought did not have the best interests of the country at heart. Could be he had his eye on someone that's a Lowden client that set this in motion. Or that Lowden itself is involved in funny stuff. There are a ton of possibilities, and I'm still quietly digging into them. When you called, you said you have a client. I'm guessing, based on what you guys do, that client is Hannah Modell."

Rocket nodded. "I know people always say their clients are innocent, or being framed, or both. It's part of the mantra. But in this case, it's true. Tom, I listened to every bit of her story and compared notes with what the others have dug up so far. The whole situation stinks to high heaven."

"Well." Tom leaned back in his chair and rested the ankle of one foot on the opposite knee. "I believe it because it's coming from you, someone I trust completely. And also because Eric Lowden is involved and something about him bugs me. His company is highly sought after, but from my end, after everything I've heard, something's wrong."

"I agree. That's why I'm here. Something smells. We need all the help we can get in this, Tom. Do you think you can dig any deeper and find out who the real players are? And where Lowden's money actually came from? Anything you can dig up, even the smallest fact, will be a help."

"Working on it," he said, "but I warn you, it could take some time, which I know your client doesn't have. I just have to be very careful digging into this. It could rattle some cages that could be disastrous."

"Listen." Rocket held up a hand. "I know how dicey political situations can be, but I also know you're the best at doing this. You're a very good friend, and I hope you know we all appreciate everything you do. However, the last thing we want is for you to get your dick caught in a wringer. If this is going to be too sticky—"

Tom laughed, a soft chuckle. "Don't worry. I'm an expert at keeping my dick safe. Let me see what I can do. I'll text you the minute I have anything at all."

* * * *

When Viper's cell rang, he looked at the screen to see Peyton trying to Facetime him. He hollered for Hannah to come into the kitchen so she could get in on the conversation, too.

"Go ahead, Peyton," he told her when he pushed the Answer button. "I've got Hannah here with me, too."

"Good. Hi, Hannah." Peyton smiled.

"Hey, Peyton. Thanks again for helping."

"Hey." She flipped her hand. "I know what it's like to be up against impossible odds, so I am truly glad to do whatever I can."

"We both thank you," Viper told her. "So what did you get?"

"First of all, I really thanked Senator Franz for taking the time to speak to me. He's a very busy guy but he still took my call."

"And you know we appreciate it," Viper told her. "Did you get anything? Was he able to help at all?"

"In a way. A lot of what he told me was veiled, because he can't put his foot in his mouth. But he gave me at least a place to start. Enough to point us in a direction that you guys will have to follow."

"Okay. Let's have it."

"So we know Mark Hegman was the chairman of the Armed Services Committee. They hold a number of hearings throughout the year on different contractors and their activities. The word he was death on anyone he thought was doing something to damage our country. He was apparently obsessed with maintaining our safety and security. Since Lowden Tactical does work for foreign interests as well as ours, they get checked every so often to make sure there's nothing shady going on."

"Do we know if they were on a list to be asked to testify at a hearing?" Viper asked.

"The word is they were—also, the list is not public yet. Which, by the way, it would be shortly."

"The drone flights we did never looked to be anything but normal," Hannah told them, "but then I wasn't suspicious of any of them. Why would I be? Besides, they'd keep that kind of stuff away from the employees, right?"

"Yup." Viper blew out a breath. "What next?"

"Franz says there's a very dark rumor that Hegman was right," Peyton went on. "That something hinky has been going on with Lowden and people are keeping their mouths shut tight. Those that he thinks might know something about whatever this is just aren't saying a word. About that or about Hegman's death. Just calling it a devastating accident caused by a drone pilot not paying attention."

"What else?"

"Some people want the committee to launch an investigation, but without a chairman, they can't seem to get a handle on things. They need to elect that new chairman first. It's very weird."

"No shit," Viper agreed.

"He's sure Hannah was set up as the fall guy but doesn't know why she in particular was targeted."

"Yes, why me?" Hannah echoed. "What did I ever do to them that they decided to make me the fall guy? I did my job—and damn well—and kept my nose clean."

"I can answer the last one," Viper told them. "Hannah, you spent all your time with your job. No family, no social life, and that is not a criticism. Just a fact."

"The senator said you were the perfect fall guy, Hannah," Peyton told her. "The word he used was…disposable. Ugly word. But you had no visible support system, so they figured they could dump it on you and get rid of you and no one would squeak."

Viper stared at Peyton's face on the screen. "Are you fucking kidding me? They thought they could just get away with killing off a US Senator and blame it on a drone operator, and get off scot-free? There must be a lot of power behind this whole thing if they think they can squash the kind of investigation a mess like this usually brings on. These people could be starting another world war if that's the case."

Peyton nodded. "You guys need to find out the reason behind all this. If Hegman was the real target, not the accidental one, something pretty evil is going on. Franz said there's a lot of money and power behind Lowden Tactical from sources not visible to the public eye. That always makes me suspicious."

"Me, too. Who's in line to replace Hegman as chairman?"

Peyton frowned. "That's the thing. According to Franz, there are three powerful senators on the committee who could be next up. I'm emailing you their names right now. We need to find out if any of them has a hidden connection to Lowden. And also what their political ideals are."

Viper saw Hannah's face lose all its color as a reality hit her.

"This was never about hitting the terrorist." She almost whispered the words. "Just like you said,

Hegman was always the target and they used me as the instrument to accomplish the task."

"Something like that."

Viper had to work to control himself. He was a SEAL who had fought honorably and bravely for his country, so something like this made him beyond angry. He didn't tolerate traitors, and it seemed to him that the label suited the people manipulating this situation. Not to mention their devastating plot to throw it all on an innocent woman.

"So what's our next move?" He looked at Hannah then back to Peyton.

"Well, obviously, Hannah needs to keep a low profile. Like invisible. We can't risk taking her out in public."

"That was always my thought, until we got this wrapped up."

"But—" She frowned. "As far as we know, they have no idea that I'm here. How could they? They have no idea what happened to me after I slipped out of the hotel."

"These people have money and resources," Viper reminded her. "Unlimited. We don't know for certain the extent of Lowden's reach to find out things, but you can bet it's damn wide. We want to keep them ignorant of where you are for as long as possible."

"You think he has people here searching for me? How would he even know where to look?"

"Under normal conditions, he wouldn't." Viper shook his head. "But you disappeared and left no trace. You're a walking disaster for them. They have to find out where you are and who you talked to and how much of a mess they have to clean up. They're actively looking for you and pulling out all the stops to find you."

"Yes." She shuddered at the thought.

"These are powerful people with the money, Hannah, and they have the connections to conduct a national search. It's the same way cartels find snitches. If they think you've figured out any part of the truth here, they'll find you and make you really disappear without a trace. And with a good cover story."

Hannah looked from the phone screen to Viper, then back to Peyton. "This is scaring the hell out of me."

"Good," Viper told her. "Being scared makes you alert. But you have an edge they don't know about. You have the four of us handling this, and these people have no idea what they stepped in." He took her hand and gave it a gentle squeeze. "And you have me personally. Your very own bodyguard."

Just that touch from him made her feel better.

"And me," Peyton called from the phone. "I'm an extra secret weapon." She lowered her voice. "I know a lot of people."

Viper barked a laugh. "That's the damn truth. And we may need some of them, before this is done."

"Blaze wanted to know if you guys are up for dinner again tonight?" Peyton asked. "Rocket met with Tom Hernandez and everyone's been doing some research. Based on what I learned from Senator Franz, I think the more the better."

"Absolutely," Viper agreed. "Let's make it seven o'clock. I'll do barbecue chicken on the grill."

Peyton nodded. "We'll all bring the rest of the stuff. See you later."

Viper disconnected the call and shoved his cell into his pocket. Then he pulled Hannah tight to his body, wrapping his arms around her. He could feel the tension running through her body.

"Nothing's going to happen to you, babe," he assured her. "You've got the best taking care of you. You have my word on that."

"But Lowden and his people have to be royally pissed that I disappeared. They have contacts everywhere. Their client base is worldwide, and after what Peyton said today—and what I've come to suspect—they could find me anywhere."

"And we're going to make sure that doesn't happen, to the best of our ability. But just remember, we can protect you, no matter what."

"Okay." She buried her face against his chest. "I'll keep that in mind."

Viper just wished he didn't sense the hesitation or insecurity in her. He'd have to have a talk with the others to take extra precautions.

Chapter Ten

Diesel was ready to kill someone, starting with Henry. The man was driving him fucking nuts. Conducting his business — the public one — had become a problem, because Henry never seemed to let more than two hours go by before he either returned to Diesel's house or called him on his cell.

"Henry," he ground out, clutching his cell, "if you don't fucking leave me alone, not only will I never find her, but the business will go to hell, which will create even more problems. Do you want to tell all our so-called friends that we're out of business?"

"Tell you-know-who to take care of it. He needs to earn his disgustingly fat salary."

"And he does," Diesel snapped. "We could do a lot better if you'd leave us the fuck alone."

"Leave you alone?" Henry snorted. "My life — my entire career — could hang in the balance if the truth about the drone strike gets out and you and your men are dinking around like we have all the time in the world. You have to find that bitch before she destroys us all."

"And I'm telling you she doesn't know shit. I made damn fucking sure of that."

"Then how come you had her all locked away like that? You said it was so she couldn't tell anyone anything."

"I set her up to take the fall, you stupid ass. That's why I had to keep her away from everyone. So I could arrange enough electronic and other evidence to make a charge stick. Then, when it was time to turn that all over to the government, we had it planned so she'd conveniently commit suicide. Or disappear permanently. How many times do I have to repeat myself?"

"As many times as I ask, until I get the answers I want."

If it wouldn't have brought hell raining down on them, he'd have killed Henry and tossed his body in the river. But he needed the man, too, in order to make sure the next part of the plan worked smoothly.

"We're checking everywhere." He tried to make his voice as soothing and confident as possible. "She had no resources with her in Houston. She was smart enough to leave her credit cards and I'm damn sure she had minimal cash with her. At least not a lot of it. She doesn't know anyone in Houston outside of work. She left her cell phone, although we put a tracker on it. I'm using every one of my connections and that gives us an army of people out there."

"But where are they looking?" Henry demanded. "I want details."

Diesel had to restrain himself from wrapping his fingers around the man's neck.

"We had to figure out a starting point. If she was still in Houston, we'd already have found her. We're checking all flights that left Houston within twenty-four hours of her disappearing, just in case she managed to get a ticket."

"She couldn't get on a commercial flight without identification. How do you suppose she handled that?"

Diesel gritted his teeth. "You yourself know there are several ways. We don't know if she had one available to her, but it's an option. But mostly we're focusing on getting a list of smaller aircraft, thinking she might have been able to hitch a ride with someone."

"Just like that?"

"She's not a stupid woman, Henry," he snapped. "If she found the right person and made up the right story, then yes, it's a good possibility. We're making a list of the cities where those planes were headed and working with contacts in each one of them. Hannah Modell is extremely smart and resourceful. If anyone could figure out a way, it's her."

"How the hell will you even sort it all out, though? Your people couldn't even find a trace of her in Houston in a ten-block area."

"Fuck, Henry. Will you keep your shit together? It's not like we can just walk up to people and show them her picture without a good excuse and without stirring up questions we can't answer. We've got a good cover story. Besides, as I said, there are lots of private planes that fly in and out of that airport. A resourceful person could figure out how to stow away on one of them or talk someone into giving them a ride."

"I want that list."

"You don't need it, Henry," Diesel snapped. "We're handling it. Get past this. Besides, you don't need to be connected to this in any way at all."

"What if she changes her appearance?" Henry demanded. "Women can do that easily, you know. Did you think about that?"

Diesel swallowed back the curse that wanted to explode from his mouth. If he could, he'd drug Henry up and lock him away in a room until this was all over.

"Yes, damn it. Am I stupid? Jesus fuck, Henry."

Henry blew out a breath. "No, you're not. It's just that there's so much at stake here."

"No one knows that better than me. Not to worry. There's a guy who does stuff for me who can adjust photos. I gave him different parameters, so everyone looking for her has a packet of four shots to use. Henry, for fuck's sake." He drew a calming breath. "You don't need to have every detail. I said it's being handled. We spent a long time setting up this structure. This operation. Do you think I want to fuck it up now?"

"It's more than the operation," he growled. "My goddamn career could be on the line here. I set everything up like we all discussed, and by next week the committee will be ready to move to elect a new chairman. We can move into phase two then, so we have to have this cleared away by then."

Diesel swore under his breath. The man was impossible. Maybe he wasn't worth all this trouble. Maybe they could find a way to do all this without Henry involved.

"You know, you aren't the only one who can give us what we need. Just keep that in mind. Now get the hell off the phone and let me get to work."

After he disconnected the call, he sat back in his chair, his cell in his hand, and stared out of the window. It had all seemed too simple to begin with. *Use people with clean backgrounds. Set them up to take the fall.* A new device allowed him to take full control of drones remotely, even the powerful, sophisticated ones, no matter what the distance, and send them to whatever location he chose. That was how the payload had been dumped on Hegman rather than the terrorist who'd supposedly been the original target.

Hannah Modell was the perfect fall guy. She had no connections to anyone and was a generally a pretty isolated person. As he'd expected. With her having no social support system, it had been easy enough to separate her from everyone else at the company and set her up in that hotel room. The big question was how the fuck she'd gotten away. Paul Santos was not an easy person to fool or sandbag.

Well, he wasn't going to accomplish anything just sitting here. He and his trusted lieutenants had set up a national search team. *Time to start reaching out again and ramp things up.*

* * * *

Hannah had listened quietly as the men talked during dinner, examining the situation from all aspects. She was doing her best to keep a lid on her fear and remain calm.

Viper will protect me. That's all I need to remember.

"We can't just sit here and wait for them to make a move," Viper pointed out.

Rocket wiped his mouth and threw down his napkin. "He's going to be looking everywhere for her. You know that."

Viper nodded. "And I imagine he can put an army together to do it. If Eric Lowden is in charge of this, he's had the chance to build the kind of structure he needs. Not to mention the fact that we don't know where he was before he popped up heading the company. He could have a system he's been setting up for years."

"I agree."

"That's why we asked Tom Hernandez and his crew to sniff around." As if he'd conjured the man out of thin air, Viper's cell rang. "And this is him." He pressed the Talk button. "Go."

He listened carefully, giving nothing away, although when he hung up he looked as if he wanted to kill someone.

"Well?" Eagle prompted.

"As we expected, they've got someone who's very good at this snooping around. He's checked the hotel and has been working the businesses for three blocks around it."

Hannah had to fold her hands together to keep them from shaking.

"Could he find out about us? That we left together?"

"Anything is possible." Viper put one of his large hands over both of hers. "But even if he does, he won't have a name or any idea where we went."

"If he has a large enough team working with him, he might get to it," Eagle told him. "Pretty soon they'll try to figure out if she left Houston, and how. No identification, so no commercial flights. They'll wonder if she managed to talk someone with a private plane into giving her a ride out of there."

"Oh, god." She was sure she was going to be sick.

Rocket took a swallow of beer. "What we need to do is create a false lead for him, someplace away from here. Hannah, do you have a contact anywhere at all that's someone you might go to if you were in trouble? Someone they could dig out?"

She was embarrassed that she didn't have people she could reach out to, but being social had always come hard to her. And ever since high school, her entire focus had been her education and her work. She didn't relate to people well anyway, as witnessed by her dismal sex life—never mind the absence of a love life. Until Viper had come along, she'd thought she was doomed to live in a social freezer forever.

Now she shook her head. "I'm sorry. I know you probably think I'm some kind of weirdo, but making friends was never that important to me."

Peyton, who was sitting on one side of her at the round patio table, reached over and squeezed her hand.

"Well, you have them now. You have all of us. Count on it."

Hannah's throat tightened, her eyes burned and for a moment she was afraid she would burst into tears. But Viper, on the other side of her, put his arm around her and pulled her tight against him, his hand stroking her arm, and she managed to swallow back the tears. Then she looked around the table.

"How did I get so lucky as to end up with all of you?"

Viper kissed the top of her head. "You picked me up in a bar. Remember?"

That put an end to her almost-crying jag. She jabbed him in the ribs.

"Oh, yeah? Who picked who up, buster?"

He chuckled. "Let's just say it was mutual. You had a problem and I was happy to help out."

"And we're all glad you did," Rocket assured him, then smiled at Hannah. "We have your back, Hannah. This is what we do."

"Tom Hernandez is checking all his sources," Rocket told them, "to see if he can pick anything up. These people are for sure conducting a search. We need to know how and where."

Hannah stared at him. "Can you do that?"

"Honey, we can do anything," he assured her. "Remember our motto, 'We are your last resort.'"

Eagle nodded. "And we need to get on with it. Normally I'd say the chances of them tracking Hannah here are almost nil, except this organization will have unlimited resources and contacts we don't even know about. We need to prepare for that, so put your brains to work."

"Yeah," Viper said. "I have a feeling we don't have any time to spare with this." He lifted one of Hannah's hands and kissed the back of it. "But don't worry, sugar. They won't get anywhere near you. That's a promise."

Hannah wished she felt as confident as they did. More and more, she was coming to realize Lowden could do anything.

"We're all going to head out," Peyton told her as they cleared the table. "It's been another long day and I can see you're riding a thin edge." She leaned close to Hannah and smiled. "You need to let Viper take that edge off."

Hannah wasn't sure what to say. Never having had any close girlfriends, she wasn't sure about making jokes about intimacy, but she managed a smile. Peyton West was certainly a good one to start with.

She realized with a start that by the time she and Peyton had finished storing the leftovers, the guys had cleaned up the grill and the dishes and wiped down the kitchen. Something else she wasn't used to.

"Thank you, everyone," she told them. "I really appreciate you doing this."

"No problem." Rocket grinned at her. "Viper would beat us bloody if we didn't."

"Damn right." Viper chuckled and came up behind her, giving her shoulders a soft squeeze. "Listen. Thanks for everything. Really. And not just the dishes."

"We're on it," Eagle told him. "Go take care of your lady."

His lady? Was that how they saw her? It hadn't even been three days, she reminded herself, yet somehow the title fit. *Comfortably.* It shocked her, since it was so out of her wheelhouse.

She watched while Viper ushered everyone out, and after the gate closed behind the last person, he set the locks and the alarm. Then he looked at Hannah, resting his hands on her arms.

"You look done in."

She sighed. "I feel totally drained."

"Sometimes stress can be the most tiring thing."

"I'm just so terrified they'll be able to find me."

"Listen to me." He cradled her face between his palms. "I know how you feel, but we are going to keep you safe. That's a promise."

She desperately wanted to believe him.

"Okay." But the word was a whisper.

"And now, I prescribe a nice hot shower to ease some of that tension that's practically making you vibrate with nerves. How about if I wash you and massage you all over your body? Think that'll help?"

Just the mental image of that sent shivers over her skin.

"Wow. All that? Absolutely. Whatever did I do to deserve it?"

"You showed up in my life. Never thought stopping into a bar to kill time would turn out so great." He brushed a light kiss over her lips. "Let's get to that shower."

He swept her up in his arms and carried her into his room then into the en suite bathroom. She ran her tongue over her lips, savoring the faint taste of him there. She took a moment to look at the surroundings. Last night, she had barely paid attention to it, but now she took a good look. *Talk about luxury.* The tile was all ivory and soft gray, a soothing combination, with double sinks, steel and crystal light fixtures, and towel warmers against one wall. A large, fluffy white rug covered a good bit of the floor. And the shower was surely the largest she'd ever seen.

Viper carefully removed her shoes before setting her on her feet and reaching in to turn on the shower. In slow motion, he eased her T-shirt up over her head, tossing it to the side and sprinkling kisses on the upper swell of her breasts as he removed her bra. At the sight of her rosy nipples, he sucked in a breath, then closed his lips over one pebbled tip. When he drew it into his mouth, she felt the tug clear to the center of her core. Her inner walls clenched, demanding to be filled. But he had already moved on to the other nipple, squeezing her breasts as he drew hard on the swollen bud.

Hannah arched her back, leaning with her hands pressed against the vanity counter to balance herself.

Viper unfastened her jeans and slowly drew them down her legs, lowering himself to his knees as he did so. One by one, he lifted each leg out of the garment, brushing soft kisses against the skin of her inner thighs and sending shivers down her spine. All that was left on her body was the tiny wisp of the bikini panties that had been part of Peyton's shopping trip for her. She felt totally exposed and hot all over, hungry for every bit of Viper's touch.

From the moment she'd fallen into bed with him the first night—a totally rare experience for her—every inhibition she'd had had seemed to vaporize. She had no rhyme or reason for it, just that there was some kind of chemistry between the two of them that consumed her.

Viper smoothed his thumbs over the tiny triangle of sheer fabric that covered her mound. Every touch, every caress, ratcheted up her heat. And when he pressed his lips to that soft curve of flesh and blew a tiny wisp of breath, she was shocked she didn't come just standing there.

"You have to take off your clothes, too," she urged, barely hanging on to her control.

"That's the plan. But first this."

He dragged the tiny bikini panties down her legs and tossed them to the side. Then he ran his thumb between the lips of her sex, feeling how wet for him she was.

"I need to tell you something." He punctuated his words with little kisses that sent electric shivers racing through her.

"What's that?" She was getting to the point where she could barely form a thought and they'd hardly done anything yet.

"Just so you know, I'm not a sex fiend. Not by any means. I don't want to give you that impression, although maybe it's too late. I just can't seem to get enough of you."

"It's only been two days," she pointed out. "Maybe it will wear off."

"When it's right, sometimes it only takes two minutes to know, and it never wears off." He coasted his glance over her body and up to her face. "Hannah, I want you to know this whole thing between us shocked the hell out of me. But truth to tell? I think I've probably been waiting for you all my life. So we have a lot of time to make up for. Starting now."

"I thought we started the other night?"

"Absolutely. But this is even better."

He gave a little pinch to her clit and she sucked in her breath then tried to push her hips toward him.

"Like that, do you?" he teased.

"Can't you tell?"

He placed an open-mouthed kiss on her sex. "Shower first," he reminded her. "Let's get the kinks out of your muscles and the knots out of your nerves. I promise you that you'll love it."

Heat sizzled through her at his words. It was all happening so fast. What was she doing? She'd known this man for less than seventy-two hours, and here she was, once again wrapped up with him in erotic sex. Maybe he was right. Maybe it was supposed to be. Maybe that was why he'd been sitting at the counter in that Houston bar.

He rose and shucked his clothing in seconds. When Hannah saw how his thick, swollen cock hung between his thighs, engorged with the blood pounding through the vein wrapped around it, her mouth actually watered.

"Okay. In we go."

One corner of his mouth kicked up in a smile as he lifted her as if she weighed nothing and placed her in the shower. He stepped in after her and adjusted the rain head spray. The water was warm enough without being hot. It was soothing, and Viper manipulated the shower head so it sprinkled soft droplets all over her body.

"Give me a minute," he told her, as he quickly soaped himself up and rinsed off. "This is for you and I plan to give you my full attention." When he was done, he brushed a kiss along her neck. "Just relax, Hannah. I'm going to make you feel so good."

The first thing he did was to take her mouth in a long, slow kiss, letting his tongue play with hers before he softly licked her lips. Then he braced her against the wall, poured body wash into his hand and began to spread it slowly over her body. His hands were like magic, stroking her skin and kneading her muscles that were tighter than she'd realized. She leaned her head back, closed her eyes and just let herself feel.

He massaged the body wash into her neck, down over her shoulders and arms, even paying attention to each of her fingers. Then more of the slick stuff, this time over the slope of her breasts, giving her nipples a light pinch before sliding his hands down over the slight curve of her stomach. Suddenly a different type of tension coursed through her. Deep inside, hunger and need rolled into a ball. The walls of her sex tightened and began a steady throb of need. She squeezed her thighs together to contain it, but the demand to feel Viper's dick inside her just continued to grow.

Suddenly he moved his hands away, making her cry out with need, and turned her so she faced the wall. Now he began the same slow, sensuous strokes, this time on her shoulders and back, easing his way down to her waist. When he rubbed his palms over the curve of her ass cheeks, she wanted to purr with satisfaction. But then he slipped two coated fingers into the crevice between those cheeks, and she realized satisfaction was a long way off. She wanted more. A lot more.

Her breath caught in her throat as he slid those fingers up and down. No one had ever taken her there before. To her, that was the ultimate indication of trust, and she hadn't ever trusted anyone that much. How was it that in just three short days she had connected so deeply with him, more than any other man she'd ever met? Any other person, for that matter. She'd never been a big believer in fate, but she had no other explanation for this.

Then her mind stopped working as the tip of one finger gently probed her opening. *Oh, god!* Heat blazed through her, scorching her nerve endings. Without thinking about it, she pressed backwards against his touch, silently urging him for more.

"Like that, do you?" His deep voice was right next to her ear, his warm breath caressing it.

"I... Uh..." His touch and the possibilities had robbed her of the power of speech.

"No worries. Talking can be overrated. But this will be special, darlin'. When I take you here, it will mean no other man will ever touch you again. I think it will be our celebration when we get this mess cleaned up."

She wanted to cry when he took his hand away, but then he turned her around to face him. In another moment, his mouth had taken hers in a scorching kiss. His tongue swiped across her lips before thrusting inside. When he scraped his teeth over her tongue, every nerve in her body sent signals directly to her sex. She had to squeeze her thighs together to try to control the little spasms vibrating there.

Viper gave her tongue one last little scrape before lifting his head. He went back to gently rubbing all her muscles, and when he reached her hips, he dropped to his knees and lifted one leg over his shoulder. The shower fell soft and light on them, not hard and intense as she was used to. She had to brace her hands against the wall as he stroked up the inside of one thigh and down the other, wanting to scream when he didn't put his hands where she most desired them.

Then, as if he'd read her mind, he separated the lips of her sex and took a long, slow lick of her flesh, dragging his tongue over her sensitive clit.

"Oh, god!" The words fell from her mouth.

Viper gave a long, low, rough laugh.

"Not god, just a man hungry for every inch of your body."

He repeated the caress with his tongue, the leisurely swipe that made every nerve in the area scream for more. When he slid one finger inside her, she pushed herself down on it as hard as she could, grabbing Viper's shoulders to brace herself. He stroked and stroked, slid one then two fingers in and out in a steady rhythm, then worked on her clit.

She tried to rock herself back and forth on his fingers, but he managed to keep her from pushing down all the way so he could stroke and tease every area of her sex. Her moans must have told him she was so close, so he thrust three fingers inside her and increased the speed of his rhythm. He stretched the walls of her sex, scraping them with his knuckles each time he pulled back.

She rode his hand, bracing herself by digging one heel into his back and pressing a hand against the shower wall. On and on he stroked, until she thought she would scream if he didn't let her come. He kept her right at the edge for so long, she thought for sure she'd lose her mind any minute. He increased the speed just a little more, bit down on her clit and...

And she exploded.

Oh, god!

The muscles of her sex spasmed so hard she squeezed the knuckles on Viper's fingers and the tips of the fingers touched the mouth of her womb. And still she pushed down harder. Her fingernails were making imprints on his skin as she shuddered again and again.

Light tremors still raced through her as he removed his hand and reached into the soap dish for a condom she hadn't even seen him put there. In seconds, he had sheathed himself, then, with both hands beneath the cheeks of her ass, he lifted her enough to slowly lower her onto his cock. She was amazed at the strength in his arms, that he could hold her so steady as they joined completely.

When he was fully seated, his thick shaft filling every inch of her, his hands cupping her ass to hold her in place, he began to move. She dug her fingers into his shoulders and moved with him, sliding easily into a rhythm that had quickly become familiar.

In and out, thrusting deep, her inner walls milking him, they moved as if they'd been doing this forever.

Everything fell away...the shower, her situation, the crisis about to boil over...as he drove into her hard, again and again. He would take her right to the brink, right to the edge of orgasm, then slow down and gradually build it up again until she thought she'd go crazy if she didn't come soon. She lost all sense of everything except the two of them on a wild journey to orgasm. And when it happened, when it swept over them, they shuddered together in huge spasms, his dick pulsing in her sex.

At last, when there was nothing left and the last tremor had faded, he lifted her enough that he could ease himself from the hot clasp of her body. When she lowered her legs and put her feet on the tile flooring, she was so weak she had to clutch Viper to hold herself steady. He braced her with one strong arm as he removed the condom and turned off the shower. Then he lifted her out, grabbed a towel from the heated rack and wrapped it around her, placing her on the bench at the counter.

"Don't move," he said, as he quickly dried himself off.

She wanted to tell him that she couldn't have moved if he'd begged her, but her vocal cords seemed to be as relaxed and limp as the rest of her. Instead, she just sat there and watched him dry her off with an efficiency that she knew came from his years with the military.

But there was nothing military about the way he slid the material over her breasts, between her thighs and down her back. Every place he touched ignited, making her grit her teeth and reach for control. How was this even possible? Was she turning into a sex maniac? Was she like one of these people who stayed on a perpetual diet but when given a box of chocolates just gorged themselves?

When he'd finished touching every inch of bare skin, he brushed his lips over hers.

"Be right back," he told her then hurried from the bathroom.

She didn't even have the energy to ask him where he was going, but she was shocked alert in surprise when he returned carrying her hair dryer and brush. This big, macho, ex-military man was going to dry and brush her hair? It was on the top ten list of things she'd least expected. Apparently so, however, since he plugged in the dryer then began to slowly brush her hair.

He bent to brush a kiss on her shoulder.

"Let's just hope I do this right. But, Hannah? I want to take care of you, and this is part of it." He looked in the mirror and caught her gaze. "And no, I've never done this with any other woman. Never had the urge to. But somehow, from the minute you slid onto the bar stool next to me, I've had all kinds of new feelings, and not just about sex. I know it's only been a couple of days and these are strange circumstances, but suddenly I understand what Blaze felt with Peyton. And I'll try not to make any mistakes."

"Oh!" She closed her eyes for a moment, enjoying the feel of the bristles against her scalp. "I thought I'd seen all your hidden talents."

"Darlin', you've just seen the tip of the iceberg." His grin was slow and sexy and full of erotic meaning.

A shiver rippled down her back, and despite the incredible orgasm he'd just treated her to, the pulse at the heart of her sex kicked into life. For just a little while, she could forget the situation she was in. *Lord!* If she didn't get a grip on herself, there'd be nothing left of her by the time they got this all sorted out.

But what a way to go.

She closed her eyes and gave herself over to the soothing sensation of the brush and the heat of the dryer. She only opened them when the motor shut off and the current of air disappeared. She was stunned when she looked in the mirror to see he hadn't done a bad job at all.

He grinned. "Can't go to bed with wet hair."

She was so drained she could barely move. It was a good thing Viper picked her up and carried her to his bed. He pulled the covers back then laid her down on the smooth sheets. She lifted one eyebrow in a questioning gesture.

"I'm not sleeping in my room?"

"Not even for a minute." He locked his gaze with hers. "You can keep your clothes and stuff in the other room if you want a place to have some privacy. But, Hannah? I want you in my bed every night." He studied her face, the blue in his eyes darkening almost to navy. "Listen, I don't want to force you into something that makes you uncomfortable."

A calm that had nothing to do with the incredible sex slid through her. "It doesn't. I want to be with you, Viper. Is it too forward of me to say that? But are you sure you wouldn't rather have a little break from me?"

"I don't want or need one." His mouth curved in a lazy smile. "I think you've hypnotized me, Hannah. I make it a habit never to spend the night with a woman, but with you? I want to be able to see you and touch you every minute, and not because you're in danger. It's a lot more than that. Something's going on here, something that shocked the shit out of me, and in a way scares me to death. But I want it, so how about sliding over so I can crawl in here, too?"

She moved over to make room for him. He stretched out on his side and adjusted her body so they were spooning. His long, thick cock, shockingly semi-hard again, nestled between the cheeks of her ass. She wondered if her own hormones would be able to resist the intimacy. Then she wondered why it mattered. Why she was fighting it? Her whole life was crap right now and yet, in the midst of it, here was this terrific guy. *Maybe there's a ray of hope after all.*

Chapter Eleven

Diesel had not slept well and he was pissed. He resented the fuck out of his life being upended and his peace of mind destroyed. Well, he guessed that was what happened when he had to deal with fucking idiots. And Henry was the worst of them all. Him and his goddamn political career. Okay, so his ass was hanging over the edge of a bridge with rushing water below it. But that was the kind of game he was in and had been for years.

"This is his chance to win the pot of gold," the man sitting opposite him in his den said. "The one he's been salivating for. If he gets it, we own him, and we can do anything we want."

The other man had given himself the code name of 'Conductor'. They always used code names when the two of them were involved in conversations, even if no one else was around. It established a pattern and prevented their real names from slipping out of someone's mouth at the wrong time and in the wrong place.

"Like assassinate people?" Diesel snorted. "Somehow, when we planned all of this, it sounded so smooth and simple. I didn't see complications like this."

"This one just blew up in our faces. We had our story ready, our asses covered, then Modell somehow just disappears. We better find her before this blows up any more."

"I'm worried about Henry. He's worse than an old woman with this shit."

"He's getting exactly what he wants. Give him another drink and tell him to shut up. Don't tell me you're getting cold feet."

"Not even for a damn second. We spent too much time putting this together, and we have too much on the table for the future." At that moment, his cell rang. He looked at the screen. Ed Fletcher. "This could be good news," he told the Conductor.

"Let's hope so."

"Yeah, Ed?"

"We had to be lowkey about this, you know, because…"

"Yeah, yeah, because we didn't want to send off any warning signal. Let's have it."

"We sort of hit pay dirt in a bar not far from the hotel where we had the woman stashed."

"What do you mean sort of?"

"We finally connected with the bartender who was on duty that night, He thinks he recognizes Modell. Said she was sitting next to someone he'd never seen before and he thought they'd just met there in the bar."

"And?" Diesel hated it when people strung out bits of information.

"And after a few minutes of chitchat, they shared what he called a hot kiss."

"A hot kiss? I'm not interest in their sex life. Did she know him? Did the bartender tell you that?" Diesel ground his teeth. *Jesus. What is it with people?* And Ed Fletcher was one of their best.

"Said it looked to him as if they'd just met when she came in. But then, a few minutes after the kiss, she left with him."

Diesel rubbed his head. "Unbelievable, but she found someone who, for whatever reason, decided to help her. Do you think she told him what was going on?" That would be a barrel of shit.

"Hard to say. The bartender said she was only in there for fifteen minutes or so. Maybe she's a lot hotter than you think and she got the guy to take her to a motel."

"I don't think sex was what she had on her mind," he snapped.

"Even if it got her out of the area and maybe a willing helper?"

Diesel thought for a moment. Men often thought with their dicks, so that was possible. He couldn't afford to ignore it.

"That's it?" *It's fuck all.* That didn't get them anything. They had to find this guy. "Didn't anyone know his name? What about a credit card receipt?"

"Nada. Paid cash."

"Well, hell." That couldn't be the end of it. "And he'd never been in there before?"

"Uh uh. But there may be something."

"You stringing me along here, Fletcher?" He was getting so frustrated with the man that he wanted to pound nails. *Or maybe pound him.*

"Nope. Just telling it like it happened. Like I said, I did manage to get one clue."

"Well, fuck, Fletcher. Talk about burying the lede." He took a swallow of his now cooling coffee and made a face at the bitter taste. "So give."

"The bartender said he did overhear him chatting with another person at the bar before our problem showed up. He thinks the guy is a pilot. That he flew into Houston for some kind of quickie job and now he's gone back to base, wherever that is."

"You got a description of him?"

"I did. My team and I are going to start hitting the Fixed Base Operations. There are seven airports in the Houston area, so we'll get to it."

"Don't forget to show her picture around."

"What am I, stupid?" Fletcher snapped. "How long have I been doing this?"

"Yeah, yeah. Sorry. A little uptight here, you know? Get going."

"Already on the way. We've split up to cover more at one time. I hope to have something by late tonight, depending on how many flights left in that time period from Fixed Base Operations. I hope we hit pay dirt, because it's a lot simpler than trying to figure if someone snuck onto a commercial flight. Okay. I'll be back to you."

When Diesel disconnected the call, he relayed the information to the Conductor.

"Well," the other man drawled, "at least it looks like we're getting somewhere. I realize it's still a big haystack where we're searching for the needle, but at least it has more of a focus."

"Yeah." Diesel snorted. "It's smaller all right, but I bet the list of cities to check is still pretty damn long."

"Wonder what she told the guy she met at the bar to get him to leave with her? Maybe she just offered a night of hot sex in exchange for getting her out of there."

Diesel barked a laugh. "Not Hannah Modell. I'd bet an ice cube is warmer than she is. She probably sleeps with her drones."

"You'd better hope not. We've made some adjustments in them that no way in hell do I want her to figure out."

"Like the changes in the GPS programming."

"Exactly." The Conductor rubbed his jaw. "This is the last time we'll be able to do something like this exactly this way. That's the risk in taking a high-profile contract and trying to dump the blame. It'll take a damn long while for the media buzz to die down."

Diesel shrugged. "We didn't have a choice. There was too much on the line here."

"I'm well aware of that. The key now is to clean up the mess before the committee elects a new chairman. And without leaving any trace."

"We can do it." *I hope.*

* * * *

Hannah was glad that Peyton had come over in the afternoon and talked her into hanging out on the dock again.

"Don't leave the property," Viper ordered, after giving her a hot kiss.

"Not to worry." Hannah actually laughed. "I have no desire to go anywhere while I still have a target on my back."

"That was some kiss," Peyton said in a low voice. "I guess I don't have to ask how things are with you guys."

"I'm almost afraid to accept how good they are. What if—" She stopped.

"What if what? Hannah, you can *What If* yourself to death, but let me tell you. When one of these guys makes a commitment, even in a very short time, it's a done deal."

"I hope so, because he's…incredible."

"And it's obvious he's staked his claim on you," she teased. "That's how Blaze was."

"Well, thanks for coming over today. I'm going stir-crazy in the house. All the guys are busy, Viper included, digging into Lowden Tactical to see what threads they can pull. I've told them everything I know, which isn't a lot. I guess I must have been deaf and blind working there. I just thought it was a great company that had interesting contracts both from the government and private industry. It was exciting and energizing, especially when I discovered I had a real aptitude for programing and flying the drones."

"And I want to hear all about it. I am so jealous."

"Jealous? You? The famous author?"

"Well, maybe sort of semi-famous," Peyton joked.

"Well, I do need to get out of Viper's way for a while. Leave him alone so I'm not distracting him."

"I don't think that plays too well with him." Peyton grinned.

"Oh, I know." She smoothed back her ponytail. "He'd be happy if I sat glued beside him every minute

I'm not sleeping, but I can't do that. For one thing, he has work to do, digging into my stuff. For another, I'm too itchy to sit still and do nothing. I know those guys are looking for me, and I promise you, they don't give up."

"And I promise *you* Galaxy is working to make sure that doesn't happen. But I know where you're coming from." Peyton heaved a little sigh. "I get that. Been there, done that. At least while they were out doing their thing, I was sitting with my sister. Focusing on her." A shadow swept across her face.

"You said she's doing well?" Hannah asked.

A smile replaced the shadow. "So well. Better every day. She's struggling to deal with Dane's death, but she's determined to honor him by living life as he wanted her to. On that note, she's really getting back to her photography again." She studied Hannah, head tilted. "I know she'd love to do some shots of you. How about if I bring her over here tomorrow, in the afternoon? I mean, if that works out."

"I don't know about that." Hannah blew out a breath. "Lots of tension in the air right now. And I'd hate it if seeing what the guys are doing brought back memories of her own tragedy."

Peyton shook her head. "She's spent some time with them off and on, and if anything, she's especially grateful to them for finding Dane's killer and the person who nearly took *her* life. Besides, this will be a good way to ease that tension, especially for you. I hate to say it, but you could use a little light-hearted diversion. I mean, besides hanging out on the dock with me."

Hannah nibbled her bottom lip. "I guess."

"Come on. It's impossible for you to get away from the house right now, but this could certainly take your mind off things. I know she'd get some great shots down by the water."

"Anyway, I'm sure she has other things to do," Hannah protested. "So do you. Aren't you working on a book? By the way, I downloaded one this morning. It looks great. I can't wait to wade into it."

"Oh! Thank you. That's really nice of you. But I am happy to send you the files."

"You work hard on your books. You deserve to get paid."

"Anyway, no, I'm not currently working on one. My most recent one is with my editor, so I have a little break."

Hannah shook her head. "I am so in awe of you for being able to do that. What talent."

Peyton laughed. "Talent? Oh, Hannah, you're the one with the talent. I couldn't begin to understand what goes on in that fantastic brain of yours."

"Yeah. So talented I let myself be set up to take a fall for something I didn't do."

"Listen." Peyton took both of her hands. "You never saw it coming. How could you? And it could happen to any one of us. You know all about the crazy lady who killed my brother-in-law and almost killed my sister. I guarantee neither of them saw it coming. So, no finger pointing allowed. Come on. Let's get some cold drinks and go sit where we can enjoy the scenery."

* * * *

Diesel was in his office when his cell phone rang. He saw Ed Fletcher's name on the screen and hurried to close his door. Only one other person — the Conductor — knew that he'd had the room soundproofed. There were things he discussed inside the room, both in person and on his cell, that he did not want anyone else to hear. This was one of those times.

"This better be good news. We're running out of time."

That was the fucking truth. Henry had called an hour ago to let him know they had a deadline with the upcoming appointment of a new chair for the Senate Armed Service Committee. And again, all the maneuvering they'd done to make sure Henry was at the top of the list and practically a shoe-in could not be allowed to go to waste.

"We've got three possibilities," Fletcher told him. "And before you complain about three being too many, let me tell you it took a fucking lot of work to get to that point. People do not like to give out information about customers or clients or whatever they hell they are."

"But you got them to tell you this. How do you know they aren't lying?"

"Is this the first time I'm doing this?" Ed snapped. "We've been working our asses off on this, by the way, and narrowing things down faster than I thought we'd be able to. We managed to eliminate all the FBOs except the one at Hobby. But then getting anyone there to give us info proved to be the hardest. They are very protective of who flies in and out of there and we nearly came up dry."

"But you got it?" Diesel snapped. "Tell me you did. Christ, Fletcher, we need a lead."

"Of course we did. Do I ever give up?"

"No, you don't." *And thank god for that.* "So what's the result?"

"Okay, then. Here's where we are. We have narrowed it down on good information to three target cities. New Orleans, Atlanta and Tampa. These are the three locations which information we pried out of people indicates as the logical destinations. We eliminated all the others listed at the FBO, and let me tell you again, it was next to impossible. These people do not like to give out information, no matter what."

"So how did you get it?"

"One of my guys knew a mechanic who works there who'd do anything for money. But even with cash in hand, it took some coaxing. He could easily get in trouble with the FAA, and the people who run the FBO at Hobby practically demand confidentiality. They'd lose a lot of business if they gossiped about their customers. But this guy did identify the picture of your drone engineer. Sort of."

"What the fuck does that mean?"

"It means there were three women who all resemble her. He couldn't decide which one, so we got the names of the cities the three of them flew to. One of them will bring us the jackpot. I'm telling you, they could be triplets, they looked so much alike."

"I just hope this isn't a fucking wild goose chase," Diesel grumbled. "We're about out of time."

"I'm telling you," Ed insisted, "it's one of them."

"At least they're all in the same general area of the country," Diesel pointed out grudgingly. "Not that it matters much, I guess. But, Ed? Those are damn big cities. How the everlovin' fuck are you going to find her, especially if she's hidden away somewhere? And who could be hiding her, anyway? The guy from the bar? Would he get this involved with a stranger?"

Ed sorted. "If she's a hot piece of ass, he might."

"Except everything we have on her says she has no contacts or connections outside of Houston. And no personal relationships."

"Well, somehow she talked this guy — or someone — into giving her a ride out of here, and I got a description of each of the planes. I can't get to the specific plane without the registration number, which I can't get without other information. But I am working every angle I can. We'll even hack the manufacturers to see who bought the plane, but that will take time."

"Which we don't have," Diesel pointed out. "So how are you going to find it, for god's sake?"

"I've got the model of each plane that our target might be on. I'm confident it's one of the three the guy told us about. He swears this is Hannah Modell and that she definitely got on one of these three planes. Once we get to those cities and check the FBOs there, find where it's hangared, we'll be in better shape."

"And the tail registration numbers?"

There was silence for a moment.

"I'll have to dig a little harder for those. Once I manage to locate the plane, we'll find out who owns it. I've got enough info to make a visual identification once we locate it. I know it sounds complicated, Diesel, but we can do it. Just keep your britches on."

"Easy for you to say. It's not your ass on the line."

"Yeah, well, like I said, keep your britches on and your ass will be covered. Let us do our job."

Diesel ground his teeth as he reached for control. "So when do you head out?"

"Tomorrow. I'm spending some more of your money to field three teams instead of one. That way we hit all the cities at the same time."

Diesel nodded to himself. "Smart. Okay, get going. And check in regularly."

"Will do."

He disconnected the call then punched the speed dial for the Conductor.

"We have a possible lead," he told the man.

"Only possible?"

"Jesus fucking Christ. We're lucky we have anything, under the situation." He gave the other man what he'd learned from Ed. "We've got three teams on it."

"It's still like looking for a needle in a haystack," the Conductor reminded him. "And time is getting short."

"Yeah, I know. Henry says others on the committee are doing exactly what we expected—pushing for the president of the Senate to appoint a new chairman right away. We have to get all the other loose ends tied up before that happens or Henry could drop to the bottom of the list and fuck everything up."

"Then get your damn ass busy. And tell Ed there's a fat bonus if they find the woman within the next forty-eight hours."

"Will do, although I think they're already highly motivated."

"Just keep me in the loop."

Diesel disconnected the call and sat back in his chair. How the fuck had he misjudged Hannah Modell so badly? He'd been positive she'd be cowed by the whole incident and easy to handle. Stash her in the hotel, convincing her they were protecting her. Then tell her they were moving her to a secure location until the rest of the dust settled. Then make her disappear forever. They could blame everything on her because she'd never be around to defend herself.

But everything had gone wrong because some macho flyboy had decided to play hero. Well, they'd get rid of him, too. Meanwhile, he had work to do here, managing this mess and still running the operation.

Chapter Twelve

Viper could tell that Hannah was exhausted, emotionally more than physically. Being with Peyton was good for her, but the uncertainty and danger hanging over her were taking their toll. He was amazed at the strength that had kept her together so far, but everyone had their limits. He certainly knew that. What she needed was some TLC that would help her relax and hopefully get a good night's sleep.

Peyton was staying in touch with Senator Franz, Rocket was plugged in to what Tom Hernandez was doing, and Eagle and Blaze were monitoring everything else. He knew he had things to be working on, but Hannah's state of mind was more important. He figured a full body massage would be just the thing to soothe her frazzled nerves.

Remember. This is therapy, not sex, so keep your dick in your pants.

That would be the hardest thing. Next to said dick, of course. But he had years of discipline he could use to keep his shit together. The important thing was to get Hannah to relax so she didn't shatter. She wasn't a weak person, by any means, or she would never have survived the past two weeks, especially the last couple of days. But this kind of stress would affect anyone.

He finished resetting the security system after everyone had left, then went to find Hannah. She had wandered out to the patio, where she stood looking out at the water. The sun was just setting and cast a golden glow on the water. Boats were cruising the surface of the bay, people out for an evening ride. It was such a peaceful picture compared to the shitstorm they were caught up in.

He came up behind her and wrapped his arms around her, pulling her back against him.

"I need to get you out on my boat," he told her. "When this is over, we'll get out there and cruise around. You'll love it."

"I glanced at it when Peyton and I were sitting out here. I'm embarrassed to say I know nothing about boats at all."

"Don't be. Most people don't unless they're boat owners or fishermen. This is what's called a deck boat. Good for just cruising the surface of the water."

"No big cabin cruiser?" she teased.

He shook his head. "Not my style. I can take this out for an hour or so without any complications and unwind. Of course, right now staying off the water is our best bet. Too much exposure out there."

"You think they'd attack me from a boat? Shoot me? Try to grab me?"

"Darlin', the more I learn about the situation, the more I think everything's on the table. They have a lot to protect and desperation makes men do crazy things." He squeezed her shoulders. "But I'm not going to let anything happen to you. And when this is over, when we get rid of this shit, I'll take you for a nice long boat ride."

She turned in his arms and looked up at him. "Will we be able to do that? I mean, really, Viper?"

He cupped her cheeks. "Galaxy always gets it done, whatever it is. Our logo says we're your last resort, so, yeah, we can handle what no one else can. And yes, we are going to resolve this mess and get you out of it free and clear." He brushed a kiss over her sweet, soft lips. "Meanwhile, I think you could use a very relaxing massage. What do you think?"

"I think that sounds wonderful. I could use something to get this stuff out of my mind."

"Come on, then."

Taking her hand, he led her through the house to his bedroom, where he began to slowly undress her. The sight of her breasts when he removed her bra, the pink nipples hardening, made his mouth water. He couldn't help sprinkling kisses across the upper curves of each before taking a soft bite of each nipple.

Slow, he kept telling himself. *Very slow. Then ease her down to the bed so you can massage the tension from her body.*

"Hold on," he told her, taking a minute to neatly pull back the covers on the bed. Then he finished removing her clothing, forcing himself to be as objective as possible, which was a hard thing for him to do. He wanted to lick every luscious curve of her body. Stroke his hands over her, and not in an objective way. Squeeze the nicely rounded curves of her breasts and slide his fingers down over her stomach until he reached the wet folds of her sex.

Jesus, Roman. Put a pin in it. She's had a rough day and all you can think of is fucking her brains out.

When she was fully naked, he stretched her out on her stomach, head nestled on her arms.

"Close your eyes, darlin'. Just relax."

"I'll try." She murmured the words into the pillow.

He knew he should keep all his clothes on. There'd be plenty of time for sex after he'd worked the tension out of her body. He couldn't, however, seem to make himself comfortable fully dressed, so against his better judgment he stripped down to his boxer briefs and straddled her body. And swallowed. Hard. Then, gritting his teeth, he began to knead the muscles in her neck, her arms, her back. Again, he admired the excellent condition she was in. Supple, toned, but softened by the sexiness of her curves.

Of course, he guessed she had to be for the work she did. He'd done some reading up on avionics and drones while working at the table with his team. A person had to be fit to handle the long hours and the demands of her job. Whatever else she did, she obviously took time to keep herself in shape. Of course, he shouldn't be surprised. He'd learned by talking with her over the past three days exactly how focused she was. He just hoped she kept that focus on him when this was resolved, because he had no intention of letting her walk away.

He'd been with a lot of women in his life, maybe even more than his share. He'd enjoyed almost every one of them, liked them, given and received pleasure. But he'd never had the instant connection with any of them that would make him jump into their lives like this. But for whatever reason, the minute she'd slipped onto that bar stool next to him, he'd been hooked. That kiss, which was supposed to have been just for effect, had sealed the deal. Whatever she'd needed, he was hooked.

"Are you falling asleep there?" she murmured, a touch of humor in her voice.

"Oh." He realized he'd gotten lost in his thoughts. "Sorry about that. I'll just—"

"No, *I'll* just. Let me show you what I really need." She rolled over onto her back so fast she took him by surprise, sat up and grabbed his face in her hand. "I need this."

She planted her lips on his in a hot, open-mouthed kiss, thrusting her tongue inside and licking every inch of the surface. He found himself unable to do anything except hold her head in place so he could tangle his tongue with hers and fall into the kiss. When she finally broke the connection, they were both breathing heavily.

He stared at her, nearly singed by the heat in her eyes, and his lips curved in a half-smile.

"So no massage today?"

The look on her face was anything but humorous. It was hungry and needy and desperate.

"Not today. Today we have this."

Only because she caught him off guard was she able to twist around, push him onto his back and straddle him. She sat with her sex planted firmly on his chest, the slick lips hot on his skin and sending electric charges through his body. Then she leaned forward and began to devour him.

She planted a string of slow kisses along his jawline and down the side of his neck. He tried to put his arms around her, to hold her close to him, but she pushed them aside. In fact, she gripped his wrists and dragged his hands over his head.

"Keep them there."

Not a question. Okay, then. This was interesting.

She licked the side of his neck, punctuating the kisses with little nips with her teeth before licking the hollow of his throat and sucking it. Hard. Then she paid attention to the other side of his neck before trailing her lips over to his chest. She tugged on the soft hair with her teeth, each little pull like a sharp flash of heat right to his cock and balls.

He started to move his hands to cup her head and direct it, but she bit one of his nipples.

"Ow! Damn it!"

When she looked up at him, he couldn't miss the hunger and heat in her eyes, the desire that was like a living thing. A pulse throbbed in his cock.

"I said, keep those hands there. I'll tell you when to move them."

Their first night together, he'd seen some of this in her, but not this intense. He loved it. It stunned him, but he wanted more.

She went back to his chest, licking each nipple before giving little nips to them. He couldn't help groaning at the sensations racing through his body. He had to resist the urge to grab her, lift her and lower her onto his cock. But she'd made it obvious this was her show. She wanted the control and he was going to let her have it.

She worked her way slowly down his body, her soft lips sprinkling kisses, grazing her teeth over them. When she swirled her tongue in his navel then took a little bite of the curled flesh, he felt it everywhere in his body. Heat consumed him and every nerve sparked and flared. *God!* He wanted to just lift her up and slide her onto his cock right now.

She eased further down his body, sliding her fingers into the waistband of his boxer briefs and rising to her knees as she tugged them down toward his feet. His cock sprang free as if it had been locked in a closet, swollen and throbbing, the head a deep purple. Hannah straddled his thighs, bent down and licked the tiny drop of cum from the soft skin. Electricity shot through him and he had to grit his teeth to control himself.

"Jesus, Hannah."

She didn't say a word, just looked up at him and licked her lips. Then she lowered her head again to move her tongue the length of his shaft in slow strokes from tip to root, before reaching between his thighs to cup his balls. The touch of her hands was so erotic, the feel of her lips electrifying. Viper wanted to come in the worst way and she'd hardly even touched his cock.

Hannah left his boxer briefs at his ankles like a restraint so he couldn't move his legs, and when she slid past his dick to lap the inside of his thighs, fire surged through him. He wanted nothing more than to bury himself in her heat, to feel her mouth close around him or the touch of her fingers squeezing his balls. But again, he dug down for his hard-earned SEAL control. He clenched his fists and gritted his teeth, but staying still was one of the hardest things he'd ever done.

Those soft lips traveled downward, the sensation making every muscle in his body clench. Her warm breath feathered over his already heated skin, the combined sensations testing his willpower.

At last she reached for the nest of hair surrounding his dick. She sifted her fingers through it, tugging lightly, sending another burst of fire through him before finally — finally — taking him in her mouth and sliding her lips all the way down to the root. Then, gripping him with her fingers, she began the steady up and down movement, filling her mouth with him then slowly releasing him.

She did it again. And again. He was hard as a rock, the blood pulsing through the thick vein that wrapped around his shaft, and still she kept teasing him. Several strokes with her mouth, a hard, sucking motion, then she'd slow down again. He was losing his mind. He'd had a lot of women go down on him, but none this good, this natural, at the same time with an innocence that made it even hotter.

"Please, Hannah," he begged

She looked up at him, the little smile flirting with her lips again. "Please what?"

"You know." He ground out the words.

"Tell me," she teased. "Say it."

Damn! Hotter and hotter!

"Make me come." He practically bit off the words.

Hannah did one of those slow lick things, then wrapped her fingers around the base of his shaft, took him in her mouth and began to stroke and suck the life out of him.

Jesus, Jesus, Jesus.

He was so turned on that it took very little time before his orgasm rolled up from deep inside him. At the last moment, she eased her hand between his thighs and squeezed his balls, milking him. His dick pulsed and throbbed as he filled her mouth with his cum. She swallowed and sucked until she'd taken in every single drop. Then she slid her mouth slowly from root to tip, let her tongue slide over the head and released him.

Then she sat back on her heels, and in the hottest thing she'd done yet, she wiped her mouth with the back of her hand.

Okay, that was it. A man could only stand so much.

He pushed himself to a sitting position, lifted her so he could move his legs and kick off his boxer briefs, then turned them both over so she was flat on her back. Now it was his turn.

Hannah ran her tongue over her lower lip, the gesture unbelievably making his worn-out cock flex. *Jesus!* This woman might be the death of him. She affected him in a way no other woman ever had. It might have terrified him, except he saw how well things had worked out for Blaze and Peyton. Plus, no way in hell was he giving her up.

He bracketed her with his thighs and took a long moment to study her face. She did that thing with her tongue again, and damn! He felt himself getting hard once more.

"My turn," he growled, but he wasn't as soft and light as she'd been.

With his hands buried in the thick silk of her hair, he took her mouth in a hungry kiss, swirling his tongue inside over every inch and scraping her tongue with his teeth. He even nipped the tip of it a little before doing it all over again. He was ravenous to taste every inch of her. He concentrated on her jawline and the slender column of her neck, peppering it with little bites and laving them with his tongue.

He sucked the tender flesh at the hollow of her throat, pressing the tip of his tongue against the beating of her pulse there. He felt the throbbing of it all the way through his body to the tip of his awakening dick. *God!* Everything about her turned him on. No woman had ever affected him the way Hannah Modell did. He could devour her on a daily basis and never tire of it.

He brushed his mouth over her soft skin, trailing the line of her shoulders and the upper swell of her breasts. Bracing himself on his elbows, he drew circles around her breasts with his tongue before pulling one firm nipple into his mouth. He sucked on it, hard, then closed his teeth gently over it. When he'd tormented one until it was rosy and firm, he switched to the other one. He thought he could suck on them forever, except there were other parts of her body he wanted to get to.

Hannah was moving beneath him, those sexy little moans drifting from her mouth as he attempted to devour her. The shifting of her body sent a message straight to his hungry dick. The more she moved the hotter he got. He strung kisses over her stomach, pausing the same way she had to pay attention to her navel.

She was writhing under his body now, the sounds she was making driving him crazy. He'd wanted to take more time doing this, but he was suddenly gripped with a craving to taste the sweetness of her juices. Spreading her legs wide and lifting them so they were draped over his shoulders, he opened the lips of her sex with his fingers, took a moment to inhale her scent then lapped the sweet pink flesh from top to bottom.

"Mmmmm." The soft sound drifted from as she pushed her hips upward toward his mouth.

He did it again and again, savoring every inch of her, loving the taste that was uniquely Hannah. When he bit down gently on her swollen clit, she lifted her hips to push herself harder against his mouth. Tasting how ready she was, he slid two fingers inside her hot channel. *Jesus!* He thought he could come just from touching her, and how was that even possible when he'd barely had time to recover from before?

As he drew his fingers in and out in a slow, steady rhythm, Hannah clenched the walls of her sex around them, squeezing as if she were squeezing his cock. And *that* thought made him now completely hard and ready to go again.

Adding a third finger, he increased the pace of his strokes. Hannah dug her heels on the bed and rode his hand, those delicious moans drifting from her mouth. The spasms in her hot sex were harder and stronger now. He knew she was close, so he clamped his lips over her clit and sucked hard on it.

And just like that, she exploded, riding both his hand and his mouth as he sucked and pulled and stroked, her inner walls gripping his fingers, her sweet liquid flooding his palm. He never slowed his pace or lifted his mouth, or stopped sucking, until the last tremor rippled through her and the tension eased from her body. Her legs relaxed, her entire body in a state of lassitude. He looked up at her face, her features as relaxed as her body.

He kissed his way up from her thighs, trailing his lips up her skin until he reached her mouth.

"Good?" he asked, then ran the tip of his tongue along the line of her jaw.

"Mmm." Her face was flushed and her eyes held a languid look.

He grinned. "Sleepy?"

"I could nap." She breathed a soft laugh. "But not for long. Just so you know."

He kissed her again. "Where did this wild woman come from?"

She shrugged. "I don't know. Shall I send her away?"

"Not on your life."

In an instant, he changed the kiss from gentle to fierce, thrusting his tongue deep then sucking on hers. Sliding his hands down to her breasts, he cupped them, squeezed them, molding them with his fingers. He pinched her nipples, gently at first, then harder, loving the little moans of pleasure they drew from her. He wanted her good and hot for what he had in mind.

Then, giving her no warning, he shifted and flipped her over so she was lying face down on the bed. Palming her hips, he tugged at her body until she was on her knees, braced on her hands. Had she done it this way before? He had no idea about her sexual experience except that his instincts told him it had been sparse and probably not inventive, no matter how hot she'd been that first night, and since then. He wasn't holding back, not with all the signals she kept sending him, especially tonight.

The curve of that luscious ass was so tempting that he bent his head and showered kisses on the soft skin. It was hard to miss the shiver that raced through her, so tempting that he did it again. He was surprised when she wiggled her hips at him, but she continued to be full of all kinds of surprises.

"Like that, darlin'?"

"Yes," she whispered, and wiggled again.

"Lots of men kiss that sweet ass?"

She froze for a moment then shook her head.

Good!

He wanted to shout the word. Beneath that disciplined exterior, Hannah Modell was an explosive firecracker and he had the satisfied feeling that he was the only one who'd been able to unlock it. He palmed her ass, squeezing the soft flesh. *God!* He wanted to slip his dick right into that hot, tight little channel, and he planned to, before too long. Just the thought made his balls ache.

"I don't care about that. Any of that. This between us started the night we met and it's been full heat from the beginning. I love it. The hotter with you the better, so don't hold anything back."

He waited for a long moment to see what she would say.

She let out a breath. "Good. That's good. Really good. Because I have to tell you…I don't want to stop."

Thank god!

"And that's not usually me," she went on.

He delicately bit shoulder. "I don't care what you did or didn't do before or who you did or didn't do it with. We have something special here. I knew it that first night."

He slid his fingers into her wet slit and stroked them up through the crease between the cheeks of her ass. He loved the tremors that raced through her.

"Me, too. I think that's why I practically threw myself at you."

"And thank god you did. You can be sure I'm not throwing you back."

He shifted slightly so he could reach the drawer of the nightstand and pulled out a couple of condoms. With an ease borne of too many years of practice, he unwrapped one and slid it onto his now very achy cock. He tested her readiness, thrilled that she was still soaked from her orgasm.

"Hang on, darlin'," he told her.

Gripping his dick with one hand and positioning the head of it at her entrance, he eased it slowly inside. Heat flashed through him as her inner walls gripped him tightly, flexing and squeezing him. *Shit!* He hoped he lasted long enough to give her yet another orgasm. Her pleasure was more important to him than his own.

Gripping her hips to hold her in place, he began a steady in-and-out movement, slow at first then increasing in speed. She rocked on her hands and knees, pushing back at him in a measured rhythm. In seconds they were rocking together, her movements as strong as his. Sliding in and out of that hot channel nearly blew his mind. He wasn't sure how long he'd last, so he reached around with one hand to her sex, finding her clit and pinching and stroking it.

"Oohhh." The long sound slid from her mouth.

The harder he drove into her, the more he teased that hot nub of flesh. He felt the spasms coming to life in her inner walls, grabbing and squeezing his cock, so he picked up the pace. Faster. Harder. More and more and more. The moment he felt her orgasm begin, he let go, pulsing into the condom. She rocked back into him again and again, the muscles of her sex clenching and tightening, milking him.

It went on for so long, he wondered if they'd both survive. Then, after an explosion that shook them both, the spasms subsided, leaving them sated but exhausted. He eased her onto the pillow face down, stretching her body out beneath him. His cock nestled perfectly in the crevice between the cheeks of her ass. He was so tempted, but for one thing, he had already worn her out pretty good, and for another, when he got to it, he wanted it to be the main event. Cataclysmic. Earth-shattering for both of them.

Besides, right now they were both spent and languid.

"I think I can't move," she murmured into the pillow.

"Good. I don't want you to." He pressed a line of kisses from shoulder to shoulder. "Listen to me. Galaxy is going to clean up this shit as fast as we can so you and I can get on with our lives. Together."

"Now it's my turn to say good." She paused and looked back over her shoulder. "But do you really think you can? Fix this? It's a huge mess."

"Darlin', there's nothing we can't do. Count on it." He gave her another light kiss, this one on her neck. "Don't move. I'll be right back."

He disposed of the condom in the bathroom and hurried back to the bedroom. Hannah was lying exactly where and how he'd left her. He turned onto his side and adjusted her so she was molded to his body, one arm wrapped around her waist. Again, the way they were lying together, his dick found a home just between the cheeks of her ass. He banded her with his arm when she wriggled against him.

"You better stop that. We're both too tired right now, and when I get to that I want plenty of energy and plenty of time."

She shivered and squeezed his arm.

"If you can fix this, you can have any kind of celebration you want."

He kissed her cheek and thought how lucky he was that he'd decided to have a drink in that particular bar on that particular night. He was damn sure going to get this mess cleaned up, because he wanted them to get on with their life together.

Chapter Thirteen

Diesel had been in his office since six o'clock, doing his best to dig through the shitstorm that seemed to just continue to grow. Henry and the Conductor were all over his ass. Investors were screaming that if he didn't fix this, they wanted their money back and they'd take their plans somewhere else. But it would also be the end of Lowden Tactical, and a lot of people would be after his ass if that happened.

Diesel was barely at his desk in his office, with his perfectly brewed mug of coffee, when his cell phone rang. He looked at the screen and thumbed the Accept button.

"Go," he said to Ed Fletcher, who was on the other end of the call. "And it better be good news."

"Better than before."

"Okay." Diesel ground his teeth in impatience. "Let me have it."

"I put extra men on this, so don't throw a shit fit when you get my bill."

"If you can find this bitch and bring her to me, I don't care what the fuck it costs. Now let's have it."

"We eliminated Atlanta and New Orleans, so I brought everyone to Tampa. I've got four of my guys sitting with laptops searching for every place that fits the description we got within a hundred-mile radius of the city." A pause. "We're slowly narrowing it down. We have to break into databases because no one is going to answer the questions we need to ask."

Diesel frowned. "They won't tell you if a plane is hangared at their facility? Or if they know where you might find one?"

Ed's sigh could be heard over the connection. "I'm telling you, it's a bitch. No one gives out information about anything, unless you're the police or the Feds and have a warrant. They protect the privacy of clients like you wouldn't believe."

Diesel resisted the urge to yell at Ed. The man was doing his job. Diesel knew that.

"Ed, this is not some cheap little dinky plane we're talking about here," Diesel reminded him. "The purchase price is anywhere from eighteen to twenty-one million. How many could there be in that area, for fuck's sake?"

"You'd be surprised. There's a lot of money in this area. Plus you have northerners who spend half their time here and fly back and forth. So even if the plane we're looking for flew here from Houston, it could have left to go back up north already."

Shit. Just damn shit.

"So where are we, then? We're running out of time."

"You think I don't know that?" the other man snapped. "I just wanted to give you an update. We'll get it done. At least we're in the right city."

Diesel damn sure hoped so.

"All right. Keep me in the loop. I want regular reports."

"Of course."

"And, Ed?"

"Yeah?"

"Money is no object. If you can't actually get to her, destroy her and everyone with her. You know how. You're good at leaving no clues to follow."

There was a short pause.

"That urgent?"

"Yes." Diesel's answer was short and clipped.

"Fine. Consider it taken care of."

He'd no sooner disconnected the call from Ed when the phone rang again. When he looked at the screen, he wanted to throw the thing out of the window. *Henry. For fuck's sake, will the man just keep his shirt on and let us take care of things?*

"Yes, Henry. We're taking care of things."

"You'd damn well better be," the man snapped. "If you want to continue your glory ride, that is. The announcement of the new committee chair is next Monday."

"Plenty of time," Diesel assured him, hoping to hell he was right. "I have an expanded team on it right now and we're closing in."

"I want regular updates," Henry insisted. "The others are getting antsy, too. And you know what happens when they're displeased."

Diesel knew all too well. "I'll call you later."

That was about all of Henry he could take at the moment. He leaned back in his chair and thought of that first meeting that had taken place and everything that had moved forward from there. They'd all, the core group, been coincidentally at a gathering on a remote Caribbean island. Somehow, five of them had gravitated together for drinks at the bar. Then they'd moved to the Conductor's suite.

As people loved to say, 'liquor is often the key that unlocks many doors'. The Conductor, dissatisfied with so many things on the world stage, had had a plan he'd been hatching for a long time. All he'd needed were like-minded people in key positions around the world and heavy financial backing. He'd take it from there. And it has all fallen into place.

Diesel had to admire the man. There was no doubt he played his role brilliantly. No one outside their circle meeting him would have a clue that this was the mastermind behind their growing program. Sometimes he had to swallow a smile at the way people reacted to him, as if he was just another guy, albeit a smart one.

But Diesel was well aware that the sum of his future lay with the Conductor. If he fucked this up, if he didn't get his hands on Hannah Modell and dispose of her, if he didn't clean up this mess, everything could blow up in his face and there wouldn't be a hole deep enough for him to hide in.

Fuck it all, anyway. How had he misjudged the woman so badly?

He busied himself with work during the morning, the cell phone sitting in painful, tantalizing silence. Maybe he should have shot the woman himself. He could have planned it like any other operation. Let out the word she was a traitor. That they had brought her back for a debrief and she'd managed to get away, and they had not seen her since. He could kill her and bury the body where no one but an archeologist could find her.

That was what the Conductor wanted him to do. But he'd hedged his bet. He was worried that there was something, some small thing they might need her for. *Then* they could dispose of her.

Stupid, stupid, stupid.

If they didn't find her before she did any damage to their plans, it might easily be his body that people would find generations from now.

Coffee. He needed coffee. Not that he wasn't already enough on edge, but coffee was his drug of choice, and right now he needed it. A lot.

Then he forced himself to go back to work, hoping the tasks ahead of him could make the day pass fast enough. And that before the end his problem would be solved.

* * * *

Rocket accepted the drink Tom Hernandez handed him then followed the man out to the back patio.

"You want to tell me why we're meeting at your house instead of your office?" he asked, sitting in one of the chairs. "I didn't think this was a social occasion."

"No, it's not."

"I take it you learned something too hot to share in your office."

Tom nodded. "That's the damn truth. Holy shit, Rocket. You guys keep getting yourselves wrapped up in political chicken wire. You're lucky you don't have a big target on your backs. Or that you all haven't just disappeared off the face of the earth."

Rocket lifted an eyebrow. "What the hell is that supposed to mean?"

For a long moment, Tom said nothing else. Then he sipped from his own drink, set the glass down and shoved his hands into his pockets. When he began to pace the tiled surface, Rocket knew this was more than just relaying information. When Tom had called to set up the meeting, it had been obvious from the tone of his voice that something big was up.

"It means the more you get into dirty politics, the greater the risk, and you guys are really stepping into it now." He rubbed his jaw. "This is more than just some people trying to cover their asses. This wasn't a mistake. This was planned in careful detail, driven by politics."

"Well, shit, Tom. You'd better explain yourself. I didn't think this had to do with any kind of politics, dirty or otherwise. What's the deal, anyway? Why don't you just spit it out, whatever it is? Since when do you have trouble telling me anything?"

Tom swallowed more of his drink. That in itself was a signal of trouble to Rocket. The other man was not much of a drinker, especially in the daytime, so this must really have been off the charts. Every muscle in Rocket's body tensed up, but he did his best to keep a calm expression on his face.

"First of all," Tom began, "you need to know that getting you the information on this stuff is very tricky. This all revolves around the Senate Armed Services Committee. They control a lot of stuff that provides very lucrative contracts for private firms, depending on the project."

"I can smell trouble already."

"Uh huh. Among many things the committee has oversight for is the Pentagon and their contract bids. Also approval for projects that create those contracts.

And the committee chair has the ability to manipulate things." He raked his fingers through his hair, an unusual nervous gesture for a man who for the most part stayed calm and unruffled. "You guys are stepping into some deep shit here and we've barely gotten started asking questions."

"Exactly what does that mean?" Rocket was doing his best not to show signs of the tension creeping through him. "What kind of deep shit?"

"They don't like people roadblocking them or interfering in their business. Not even a little. This is a hell of a lot more than a mistake in programming a drone. This was a deliberate kill. There are people who are part of this that can bury you if you don't get your nose out of their business. I'm not kidding, Rocket. I am stunned at the powerful names that keep sliding into the conversations I'm having." He paused. "You sure you want to do this?"

"I'm sure that Viper is in all the way, and if he is, so are we. So let's have it already, for fuck's sake. What else can you tell me and what do we need to do? Who do we need to watch out for?"

"When you guys were investigating that attorney, Peter Kendrick, and his dirty former senator friend, Warren Sulzberger, did you ever come across or hear the name Henry Baumann?"

Rocket frowned. "I don't believe so. And I try to stay away from politics unless I have to. Too many people like Sulzberger. What's the deal with Baumann?"

"He's been in the Senate a long time and is a big deal on the Senate Armed Services Committee. Second-longest-serving member, as a matter of fact. Survives no matter which party is calling the shots."

"That's really saying something." Rocket snorted. "He's either very good or very crooked. What's his involvement in this?"

"My sources tell me he's been angling to chair the committee every time his party is in control. He's always been outdone by someone with more connections and more power, although Henry's no slouch."

"Must be pretty pissed off," Rocket commented.

"He hasn't been happy, that's for sure," Tom agreed. "He was ripe for something like this and he's been building his power base. Promising things if he were the chair. From what little I have been able to glean so far, Baumann works hard to portray the image of the politician with all the connections who can solve all your problems. He spouts patriotic platitudes, which is one reason why he keeps his position on the Senate Armed Services Committee. But—"

"But what?"

"But there is a lot going on beneath the surface. The Armed Services Committee has a lot of power where the military is concerned, and can influence contracts. Hell, they can even propose changes to legislation that affect the way the Pentagon does business. People manipulating events for their own personal gain."

"That's not really anything new," Rocket pointed out.

"But it's the force of the people involved. They can destroy small countries. Gossip behind closed doors says Baumann has gathered some pretty formidable people behind him who want this to happen. Hegman was a stumbling block. Besides being unwilling to manipulate what the committee does to the benefit of the rich and powerful, he liked investigating companies that he felt screwed the military or had improper contracts. They needed a way to get rid of him that wouldn't come back on them and Viper's woman became the fall guy."

"Shit, Tom. Are you kidding me? What a fucking mess."

Tom nodded. "Baumann was ripe for this. He wanted the power. Lusted for it. They courted him, helped put him in the position he's in now, and as chairman, he could manipulate things so the people backing him profited."

"But how does that affect Hannah Modell?"

"Like I said, Hegman had to be eliminated so Baumann could move up. Someone came up with the idea of using a drone and saying the payload for an off-the-books government contract was delivered to the wrong place. They chose Hannah for the project because they decided she could be sacrificed for this. As far as they knew, she was pretty much alone in the world."

"Which she was," Rocket pointed out, "before she met Viper."

"The word is they were planning to stash her away until they had all their ducks in a row. Then they'd announce she either screwed up or had been paid off or something, show her off to the public, then get rid of her and tell people she'd escaped and they had no idea where she was. Of course, they'd bury her body where it wouldn't be found in this millennium."

"I'm sure the last thing they expected was for her to hook up with someone like Viper."

Tom nodded. "No shit."

"I'm guessing all this is the reason you had me come sneaking into your house."

The other man actually laughed, breaking the tension a little. "Sneaking into my house?"

"Yeah. What else would you call it? We usually hook up at your office or over lunch. Or dinner."

"Yeah, well. I didn't want to leave any trail for someone to follow and have you lead them back to Viper and thus to Hannah. I'm pretty damn sure, since I started asking questions, there have been eyes on me."

"Good thought. You know they're doing their best to find her as it is."

Tom rubbed his jaw. "Rocket, this is bigger than I even imagined. I'm sensing it everywhere I turn. It's so big no one even wants to touch on it. Almost as if they're running away from something. Hegman's murder — let's call it what it is — was just the first step."

"We have to find out what's next."

"Yes, we do, and very carefully. And listen to this. Two of my sources very quietly told me one of the top people pulling the strings has a code name. The Conductor."

"The Conductor?" Rocket frowned. "Sounds like some spy game. A black ops operation."

"Well, it's no game, that's for sure. None of them know who this Conductor is, just that he carries a lot of the power. I also learned there's someone nicknamed Diesel who I guess partners with him, but he didn't have any other information."

"Or didn't want to give it to you," Rocket pointed out.

Tom nodded. "That, too. My sources are pretty tough people, in many ways. There's not a lot that scares them, but I had to pry and cajole every nugget out of every one of them."

"I'm not liking the sound of this at all."

"Join the crowd. We have to get to the heart of this, my friend, and find out who is behind it all. Then find a way to just shut it down, because more than just Hannah Modell's life is involved. And knowing who in the government is involved is going to take a whole lot of digging."

"You know Lowden Tactical has to be right in the thick of this to play such a key role in Hegman's murder. I'd love to know exactly what their role is. A lot of people told me they wondered where the huge amount of startup money came from. Someone needs to look at their other activities, because having a drone company under your control gives you a big edge in a lot of things. Viper better be on the alert where his woman is concerned."

"His woman." He stared at Tom, then nodded. "Guess that's right. Damn. It sure happened with him just the way it did with Blaze."

"You guys must have something contagious." Then he sobered. "No sweat. It's what you do. What all of us do. And if the people who are after Hannah think they've got all the power, we'll just show them they're wrong. But without letting them know where Hannah is so you all can keep her safe."

"If these people are as powerful as you seem to think, they have ways to find things out." Rocket hated to think about that. "There's always that chance, no matter how farfetched. People like you're talking about have far-reaching power. And they use it no matter who gets hurt, as long as it isn't them."

"But Galaxy is good," Tom reminded him. "Better than good. That's why people come to you. You do what others can't. If my life was in danger and I needed someone to save me and get the bad guys, the Galaxy crew is the only team I'd turn to."

"We like to think so. We just have to be better than these people. Which we can be. Okay, I'd better call Viper to round everyone up so we can put an action plan together. We'll also do some digging and see what we can find. Our amazing software that Zander designed can do just about anything."

"I'll keep digging, too," Tom assured him, "but I have to do it carefully."

"Just don't get your dick caught in a wringer."

"Believe me, I plan to be very careful. And keep in mind, Hannah may not even be safe in Viper's house," Tom pointed out. "These people are capable of anything."

"We'll be alert," he acknowledged.

"Good. And I'll let you know when I find out something else."

The minute Rocket was back in his car, he called Viper.

"Better gather the troops," he told him.

"Why? What did Tom have to say?"

"This isn't stuff to discuss over the phone. Just get everyone to your house. And I mean ASAP."

All he could think as he drove was, *what a shitstorm.* The likelihood that Hannah Modell would find herself in the middle of an international conspiracy had been slim to none, yet here she was. And Galaxy right with her. Not that any of this was her fault. *Hell, no.* What scared him was that could happen to any unsuspecting person and they might not have Galaxy to help them.

Chapter Fourteen

Hannah stared at the faces of the men seated around the table in the dining area and a chill raced the length of her spine. She had seen them serious when they'd first gathered to begin their work on her situation, but this was more than that. They wore the hard faces of men going into battle, a 'take no prisoners' look. It was not lessened by the presence of their guns on the table next to their laptops. It gave her a real sense of why SEALs were considered the world's fiercest Special Forces.

"I know I asked this the other day," she said, "but do you guys always have those guns with you? Even at a meal?"

"Darlin'," Viper drawled, "it's who we are. Always prepared."

"And a good indication of how seriously we take protecting you," Rocket added.

She could get on board with that. It had become more and more obvious to her, as information unfolded, that if Lowden got its hands on her, she'd be dead before she could blink.

"It's hard to make a plan," Eagle told everyone as he looked around the table, "when you have no idea what your enemy's plan is. Hell, we don't even know who specifically is after Hannah or who the head guy is. Maybe there's even more than one. And now Tom says even this house may not be safe. Talk about a goatfuck."

Listening to them talk, Hannah was seized with a sudden fear she hadn't felt up until now. She must have a guardian angel that had connected her with Viper just when she was in desperate need. If she were still on her own, she'd be a sitting duck for these people, with no help, no resources and no place to hide. She'd been lucky. Nobody could protect her better than these four battle-hardened former SEALs.

"We'll take care of things here at the house," Eagle pointed out. "We've been in worse situations before."

"Do you think this Conductor is in charge of everything?" she asked.

"Possibly," Rocket told her. "But he may not be powerful enough. But let me tell you, this is the first time I've seen Tom Hernandez uneasy about anything."

Blaze raked his fingers through his hair. "Which makes me uneasy."

"But it will also make us twice as alert," Eagle pointed out. "So where are we here? And please don't tell me no place."

"You don't need me to say we need to find a way to go after these guys. That's what we do. But we need to have the other names and the details of what's on their agenda next so we can put a tight plan together."

"We need a starting point," Blaze told them. "We have Baumann's name, so let's begin there and trace back every day of his life beginning with today. Eagle, how about coordinating everything on our all-powerful search engine? We'll divide up Baumann's life among the rest of us, and every time we come up with a name, we'll throw it at you and you can slide it into the machine."

"Sounds good. Okay, here we go." Eagle tapped the keyboard to access the program. "A program called Stargaze was designed exclusively for Lowden by a computer whiz they'd known for years. One of the first contracts Lowden took was to find his sister who everyone had insisted had just left home on her own. Lowden turned the world upside down, following leads everyone else had said were just indications of the prevailing theory."

He paused while he typed something.

"They rescued her just in time from a sex trade group, and Zander French had promised them anything they wanted or needed computer-wise for the rest of their lives. He'd set everything up on their laptops and on the plane, and had everything feed into a very secure cloud that he monitored for them. Plus, with every new innovation, he was always tweaking their setup."

"Okay," Viper nodded. "We've got that much, Let's start digging.

Hannah knew that the more people were working on this, the more information they'd be able to dig up. She'd insisted on participating, so once again Viper set her up with his secondary laptop. Because she knew more about Lowden and the people there, they gave her that assignment. The hope was that she'd find some place where Baumann and Eric Lowden had hooked up.

Sitting next to Viper, she felt the heat from his body and the scent of the aftershave he'd slapped on after his shower drifted across her nose. Even this many hours since the previous night, she could still feel the touch of his hands on her skin, his mouth on her nipples, his fingers inside her. His *cock* inside her.

She'd heard about the kind of sex she had with Viper—even read about it when she isolated herself with her growing collection of romance novels, her secret vice. She'd had hard sex and fast sex and unsatisfying sex, but nothing had even come close to what she shared with Viper. There was an intense connection that made what was happening to them way more than physical.

She hoped it wasn't just the hyperintensity of the situation. She was smart enough to know that that could escalate things beyond reality. But while her analytical brain told her there was a good chance of that, her intuition told her this was real. She just hoped she got out of this alive so they could make a life together.

She methodically fed in the names of everyone she knew at Lowden from Eric Lowden down and including the executive veep, Greg Kingsley. It was a long, tedious task, even with the super-duper system Zander had created, and most of it was exactly what she expected. Dull and useless.

She tried using different key words and groups of words, searching the media. She tuned everything out, ignoring the back and forth between the guys so she could focus on what she was doing. Every so often, Viper would reach for her hand and give it a squeeze, and her nerves would settle. She'd been at it a while when an article in an obscure newspaper caught her eye.

"Hey, guys." She cleared her throat.

Everyone stopped what they were doing to look at her.

"What's up?" Viper asked. "Did you find something?"

"I think so. Maybe." She clicked her mouse. "I almost missed it because it's so off the beaten path. It's an article in this magazine about a party weekend on someone's yacht. Baumann's front and center, but standing off to the side is Eric Lowden."

"Let's see that. Can you turn your computer?"

"I can do better than that. I'll send the link for this to all of you." In seconds, it was done.

"Shit." Rocket was staring at his screen. "Did anyone ever hear of this gossip rag?"

"If you look them up," Hannah told him, "they have a very low subscriber rate. Even their Twitter account doesn't have a huge number of followers."

"So this says the party was held on Aaron Jacobs' yacht. I'm not into this stuff, so anyone know who he is?"

"Got it," Eagle told them. "It's one of the largest aerospace and defense contractors in the world by revenue and market capitalization. Their products include missiles, air defense systems and…get this…drones."

"Drones?" Hannah narrowed her eyes. "Is that Eric Lowden's connection to them?"

"Looking it up right now." Viper's computer keys clicked away. "Okay, Lowden worked for Jacobs before he got the job at Bright Star. But this party happened between him leaving Bright Star and starting Lowden Tactical."

"There's gotta be a real thread there somewhere. This is not just coincidence." Rocket looked around the table. "We need to dig into it more."

"And if Baumann is at a party on Jacobs' yacht," Eagle mused, "there's a good chance Jacobs is funding his campaigns and wants something big in return."

Hannah stared at the picture on her screen. "They targeted me, didn't they?"

It wasn't even a question, and the realization of it made her nauseous. How stupid she'd been, so flattered she'd been offered the primo job with Lowden.

"Hannah," Viper began.

She held up a hand to stop him. "Don't bother. I'm not sure anyone could have foreseen this, so I'll only beat myself up a little. But it makes me realize how long they've been planning whatever this is. I wonder how many so-called candidates they checked out before they decided I'd make the best patsy."

"You can't give yourself shit over this," Eagle said in his soft drawl. "Trust me when I say no one would have seen this coming."

"You had two forces at work here," Viper told her. "Military contractors who wanted a bigger share of defense spending and who also didn't want to be called on Mark Hegman's hot seat. They played to Baumann's ego and manipulated him, then did what they had to for him to move into the position as chairman of that committee. You can't decipher people who are that devious unless you are expecting it. Trust me."

"But—"

"But nothing. Just read your own resume, Hannah. Talk to yourself for a while. You are not a stupid woman, so please give yourself a break."

She was still trying to digest it all when they finally quit at the end of the day. All of them were shocked at what they'd pulled from the list of party attendees — the connections between military contractors, private security and Henry Baumann.

"The thing is to take them down before they can find Hannah," Viper reminded them, "and I don't have a lot of time. We need to reach out to our own military contacts and see what they hear."

Eagle slapped Viper on the arm and gave Hannah a hug. "We'll get it done. We always do."

Hannah said goodbye to the men and watched as Viper reset the security codes.

"It's a good thing you have a backup generator in place," she told him, "because using an EMP is going to be the first thing they'll do. They'll want to knock out your security system before they do anything else. Give themselves whatever edge they can, like we already discussed."

"Yup. And besides the backup generator, I've got a shielding system in place, but I also know nothing is perfect."

"So what happens if you're actually attacked?" She shook her head. "Listen to me. Attacked."

"Not so farfetched, as a matter of fact, especially after what Tom passed along. In that case, my entire system signals me, and I get out my fire power. And call in the troops. We're all hooked up in a way that we can alert each other at once." He brushed a kiss over her forehead. "Not to worry. We've got things under control."

"I believe you. Don't get a big head over this, but I've felt safe with you since you kissed me in the bar in Houston."

He chuckled. "I didn't realize my kisses were that powerful."

"I think I could use some now."

She wrapped her arms around his waist and leaned into him. Her brain was frazzled from trying to decipher all the information they'd pulled together and she wanted nothing more than to shut out the world and be locked up with Viper.

He leaned down and brushed a light kiss on her forehead.

"And I think that can be arranged." He nipped the edge of her ear. "All my kisses belong to you now."

"Good. I need them."

"Tired?" He studied her face. "Learning all this stuff made for a stressful day."

"I think part of it was just realizing how blind I'd been to everything."

"Don't beat yourself up about it," he insisted. "Everybody's been there at one time or another."

She buried her face against his solid chest. "I just feel like such an idiot."

"Well, you're not. You're the smartest woman I have ever met." He tilted up her face and his mouth curved in a grin. "But don't tell Peyton I said that. Or Blaze. He's convinced he's got the prize, which is the way it should be." He brushed his thumb over her bottom lip. "But the real winner is me."

He lowered his head and pressed his mouth to hers, his lips firm and warm. Tingles sizzled through her just from the contact, and, as with every touch, heat streaked straight to her core. Her nipples hardened and ached and her panties dampened. When he opened his lips over hers, she thrust her tongue deep into his mouth. The heat ratcheted up about twenty notches.

Viper thrust his fingers into her hair, holding her head steady as he fucked her mouth with his tongue. She sucked on it hungrily, scraped it with her teeth then bit down gently. He moaned, the sound vibrating along her nerve endings.

He slid his hand down her back until he reached her ass, squeezing and kneading it, the movement of his fingers making the inner muscles of her core automatically flex and liquid gather at her center. *Lord!* It seemed as if all the man had to do was touch her and she heated up.

Viper cupped her chin, tipping her head so he could touch his mouth to hers. The moment their lips connected, she opened her mouth to invite his tongue. He swept it inside, licking the entire surface and dancing his own tongue over hers. Her inner pulse throbbed harder, enough that she had to squeeze her legs together or she thought she'd explode.

The kiss went on, tongues twisting together, his one hand continuing to knead and caress her ass. When he moved his hand and wriggled it inside her jeans and panties, she moaned and pushed herself against him. He slid two fingers into the crease between the cheeks of her ass, rubbing them up and down before teasing her opening with the tip of one.

"Soon, Hannah. Soon I'm going to take you right here. Then every bit of you will be mine."

She wanted to tell him to do it now, tonight, but she wasn't sure she was ready. Almost, and just the thought of it sent a dark thrill racing through her.

"Soon," he growled again and clutched her body more tightly to his.

Even with the thickness of his jeans, she could feel the hard, swollen outline of his cock, and she rubbed herself against it.

"Jesus, Hannah," he breathed, tearing his mouth from hers.

"I want you inside me."

She wasn't a shy flower by any means when it came to sex, but it seemed with Viper there was a connection that made her bolder and more aggressive. She'd liked the slow, delicious sex, but right now she wanted hard and fast. She wanted to lose herself in him completely and forget about this mess she was in simply because she'd been recruited for an exciting job.

He skewered her with the heat in his eyes. "You sure you're up for this? It's been a draining day, absorbing and researching all this stuff."

"I need it more than ever. I need *you* more than ever. Do you want me to beg?"

"Fuck, no," he growled.

He cradled her ass, lifting her, and she wound her legs around his waist, pushing her breasts to his chest.

"I want you, Viper. I *need* you."

"I want you, too."

He walked them into his bedroom, where he grabbed the bed covers and yanked them back. He was just as rough when he placed her on the mattress and began pulling off her clothes. Shoes, jeans, T-shirt, bra. He took a moment to pinch each nipple, squeezing them hard enough to send delicious shivers of pain spearing through her. Then he yanked off her panties, crumpling them in his big fist. When he held them up to his face to inhale her scent, her inner walls spasmed.

"Jesus, Hannah. Your scent is…incredible."

Then he tossed the panties aside, knelt between her thighs and placed her legs over his shoulders. When he used his thumbs to open her sex wide, electricity shot through her. He licked the soft inner skin before pulling her clit into his mouth. The rasp of his tongue against her sensitive flesh nearly made her come right then and there. When he did it again and again, she had to clench her fists to maintain some semblance of control.

"Please," she begged.

He looked up from his place between her thighs. "Please what, darlin'?"

"Please…fuck me. Now."

The strain of everything seemed to coalesce into a hard ball that only his thick cock inside her could relieve.

"I live to serve," he told her, before rising to his feet.

She'd never seen a man undress so fast. He tossed his clothes everywhere, grabbed a condom from the nightstand drawer and rolled it on. Then, taking her legs and pushing them back to open her wider, he poised for one moment at her entrance before thrusting inside.

Oh, god!

He filled her completely, his thickness taking up every inch of space and then some, and it aroused her beyond her imagination. She wrapped her legs around him to lock his body to hers and managed to flex her inner muscles to clamp down on him. He lowered his head and took one aching nipple in his mouth, sucking on it.

"Bite me," she begged. "Bite my nipple."

He clamped his teeth over the tight bud and bit down just hard enough to send pleasure shooting through her. When he moved his mouth and focused on the other one, she arched up to press her breasts against his lips. He'd learned she didn't hold back anything as far as sex was concerned, but where was this really aggressive female coming from? She'd never been like this, hot and hungry and demanding, with anyone until Viper and it raised her need even more.

Viper drew in a deep breath, let it out slowly and kept his gaze still locked with her as he drove into her again and again. His strokes were hard and swift, his dick filling every inch of her. With her legs wrapped around his waist, she pressed her heels into the small of his back, nearly lifting her body to his. He thrust harder and faster, his eyes never leaving hers.

"Pinch your nipples," he ordered.

She palmed her breasts and squeezed the hard tips, matching the thrusts of her body with her own. The orgasm spiraled up from deep inside her — then there it was, the explosion, only a second behind his. They shuddered together, his cock throbbing against the walls of her sex, his hips pushing again and again, her inner walls squeezing him. She didn't know whose heart was beating harder, hers or his.

At some point, the intensity subsided, finally leaving her weak and depleted. She could tell Viper was the same. He braced himself on his elbows, arms shaking slightly, catching his weight, then slid his mouth over hers. He licked the edges of her lips before giving her a soft kiss.

"I don't know what lucky star sent you my way," he told her, "but I'll be forever grateful. I'm going to take care of you and protect you — *we're* going to do that, the whole team — so you and I can get on with our lives."

She smiled at him, her body soft and liquid, all her important places happy. She flexed the muscles in her core, squeezing his dick and eliciting a small groan from him.

"You'll be the death of me, Hannah, but what a way to go." He grinned at her. "Let's get up and shower and we'll talk about dinner. Then we can go over what we all dug up today and match it with what Tom Rodriguez told Rocket. How about if I fix us some drinks? We can sit on the patio and dissect it. Then dinner." He wiggled his eyebrows. "And after, I think we can find some way to spend the rest of the evening."

"I think that would be great." She squeezed her thighs against his hips. "If only you didn't have to get up to do it."

His laugh was low and sexy and rough. "All I need is a little rest to recharge and I'll be happy to be of service again." A serious expression washed over his face. "Hannah, I know it's been less than a week, and I'm not given to saying shit like this. However, what we've got going here, I've never had with any other woman. I hope you've never had it with anyone else, either, because once we get this shit taken care of, I want us to build a future together."

"I'd like that, too."

She could hardly believe she was saying this. Her personality had never clicked with anyone else's and she'd resigned herself to never having anything permanent with anyone, at least someone who meant something to her and who *got* her. Viper was turning out to be a real gift in many ways.

"Okay. Let's get crackin'." He gave her another soft brush of his lips. "But next time we're taking it slow and easy." Heat flared in his eyes. "And maybe we'll be a little adventurous."

Every pulse point throbbed in response to his words. She wet her lips.

"I'm ready."

He stared into her eyes for a long time. "Me, too."

Chapter Fifteen

Diesel had just poured himself a drink to settle his edginess when his cell rang. When he saw Ed Fletcher's name in the readout, a tiny thread of hope wriggled through him.

"If you're calling this late," he told Fletcher, "I'm going to hope it's with good news."

"Almost."

"Almost? Jesus Christ, Fletcher." He wanted to throw the damn phone out the window. "Either you located the plane or you didn't."

"Calm down, will you? We're doing the best we can. This is not a simple situation."

"What's so fucking complicated about it? Did you find it?"

"It took a lot of work to narrow it down to what we have," he growled. "Let me tell it my way."

Diesel tossed back a healthy swallow of his drink. Before this was all over, he might turn into a full-fledged alcoholic.

"So give."

"We went down the list we compiled and eliminated all but one. Good thing I had a bigger crew with me, because it was a pain in the ass."

"It'll be more than a pain in the ass," Diesel snapped, "if we don't find this woman and get rid of her. So you found it?"

"We've eliminated it down to one. But you won't like this. It belongs to some phantom company called Galaxy, which is owned by four former SEALs."

Diesel's stomach knotted. He'd been in both sides of this business long enough to know that SEALs were total badasses. If Hannah Modell were involved with former SEALs, getting to her was going to be a much bigger problem than they'd imagined. *How the fuck did she hook up with them, anyway?*

"What do they do with the goddamn plane? Run a charter service?"

"Worse than that," Fletcher told him. "I got this information from someone who knows a good friend of theirs and had to swear in blood I would never let anyone know who told me. They run a dark security and black ops agency, taking jobs no one else will or can handle. Kind of like a last-resort operation, which is how they refer to themselves. They don't hangar the plane at any airport, either."

Diesel frowned. "Where do they keep it?"

"They bought a large piece of property outside the city limits, and built a hangar and a runway."

"And the city doesn't object?"

"If you've got enough money, you can get anything done."

"But this still doesn't tell us where the Modell woman is," Diesel pointed out. "Do you at least have the names of the SEALs?"

"I'm not a total dumbass," Fletcher snapped. "I wanted to have everything I could get before I called you. Four friends, former SEALs, own it. I'm in the process of identifying where they all live. We'll go from there. Plus I have a team heading out to where they hangar the plane. Spend enough money and you can get at least some of the information you need."

"Just don't get caught."

"You think I'm stupid?" Fletcher's tone was edgy. "After all this time? It's dark, and we've got sophisticated equipment that can detect security sensors."

"Hurry," he snapped, and disconnected the call.

Of all the things that puzzled him, the question of how Hannah Modell had hooked up with these people was still at the top of the list. He almost dreaded another call from Henry asking for an update, because this really changed the situation. This was a lot more than getting their security people to bust into someone's house, tell whoever was there that Hannah was wanted for murder and treason, and grab her.

As if the thought had conjured the man up, his cell buzzed again and Henry's name appeared in the window.

"We're making progress," he said by way of greeting.

"I damn sure hope so. The word is I am a shoo-in for the chairmanship. If that gets fucked, not only will a lot of people be pissed, and there's a ton of money they'll lose, but our lives won't be worth ten cents. These are not nice people, Diesel. They don't take defeat or screwups at all. They'll kill you as soon as pour you a cup of coffee."

"No one is more aware of that than I am," he reminded the other man. "But trust me. We have a lead on her and expect to have her in less than twenty-four hours."

"Don't expect. Do it. Period. We need the announcement that she's been apprehended and will be brought to justice at once. And in the next two days."

Diesel's entire body tensed with a combination of anger and irritation. He didn't need Henry to keep pounding that home. He was as aware of it as everyone else. Before he could say something that would set the other man off even more, he disconnected the call, and decided he needed another drink.

* * * *

Viper woke to the sound of an alarm coming in short bursts. At first, he thought it was the house system going off. But then he blinked and realized it was one of two satellite phones he kept on his nightstand. He picked it up, pushed a button and said, "Who's on?"

Four voices answered.

"It's the hangar," Eagle said. "I'm on my way right now."

The hangar? What the fuck?

"Me, too." Saint's voice.

"And me," Rocket added.

They all had satellite phones that allowed them to communicate as one group. The cell phones were great but did not have the same facility. Many times, like now, it was a very important element of what was happening.

The alarm setup at the hangar was pretty sophisticated and had more than one level of security. Like the house, even an EMP couldn't take it out completely. It connected to the homes of all four partners, plus Saint. And it was soundless and dark, so it gave no warning to intruders. It only fed to their satellite phones.

They also had an understanding with the county sheriff's department, since it was located outside the city limits. Viper knew that Saint was calling them even as he headed for the hangar.

"Viper." Blaze's voice came through the sat phone. "You stay put. If they're after the plane, they probably identified all of us by now and know where we live. People like this can find out anything. Although I have no idea why they are targeting the plane."

"Maybe to blow it up," Rocket suggested. "So we can't beat a hasty retreat out of town."

"Fuck." Viper sat up and ran his fingers through his hair.

"You and I have something to protect besides property," Rocket reminded him. "We need to stay back and do that."

"No shit." 'No shit' was right.

"Can Hannah shoot?" Blaze asked.

Viper frowned. "I have no idea."

"If we get past tonight—no, *when* we get past tonight—you need to take her out to the range at the hangar."

"Ten-four on that."

"All right, everyone." This was Blaze. "The line is open. Waiting for a report from the others."

Viper wanted to smash something. This definitely had to do with Lowden and the political crap that was going on. No one else would try to break into their property. They had finished with their last client before Hannah had blown into their lives and they didn't have any disgruntled holdovers from other cases. They were very careful to make sure that never happened.

The question was, what did these people want with the plane? What could they do with it? Stealing it under these circumstances was next to impossible. How would it get them closer to finding and grabbing Hannah? Surely they didn't think she'd be one of the people showing up at the hangar. He knew he needed to stay here with Hannah and not leave her unprotected, but he really wanted to be out there grabbing these guys and beating the information out of them.

As Viper rose from the bed to tug on his boxer briefs and jeans, Hannah rolled over.

"What time is it?" she mumbled, her voice heavy with sleep.

"Three-thirty."

She sat bolt upright. "In the morning?"

"Yes, ma'am." He pulled on a T-shirt, then grabbed his gun from the nightstand drawer.

"What's happening, Viper? Why do you need your gun? Where are you going?"

"The gun is for insurance. Same reason I keep it next to me when we're working. No situation is perfect and I leave nothing to chance. And where I'm going is to get a cup of coffee. Come with me so I can tell you what's going on."

"Absolutely."

He could tell she was wide awake now. She was right behind him in the kitchen, pulling out mugs while he took out the pods for the single-serving brewer.

When they both had full mugs, they carried them to the counter and sat on the high stools, where he filled her in on what was happening.

She stared at him. "They're at the hangar? How did they even find it? It's not like there's a sign or anything. Plus they'd have to know it's yours, right?"

"Unless they were checking out all the Gulfstream 550s in the Tampa Bay area." He swallowed some coffee. "Hannah, you've read the stuff we keep digging up. These people can find out anything about anyone. At least for the most part. And if they have our names but don't know where we live, maybe they thought there was some information out there."

"But how would they even know what kind of plane to look for?"

"When you have enough money, which they do, you can find out anything. You just have to—"

Before he could finish his sentence, he was interrupted by Saint's voice on the sat phone.

"I'm here, and I've got a present for you guys. One got away, but we've got the other two. Sheriff's deputies are hauling them to be booked."

"Plus," Rocket added, "we have the car they drove in and we're running it through Zander's Stargazer to see if we come up with anything."

"We're tagging along with the deputies." This from Eagle. "They said we could watch the questioning, but I don't think they'll get much out of these guys."

"Why not?" That was Blaze's voice.

"These guys are tougher than rubber boots. They remind me of the enemies we came up against in some of our missions. They'll die before they give anything up."

Blaze was shocked. "But this isn't religious zeal or a commitment to a cause, like those guys."

"Maybe in a way it is," Rocket told them. "Anyway, stay ready and one of us will call after the questioning. Saint put in a call to the two guys we've used before. Told them to get their asses out here and watch the premises. Doesn't hurt to have live bodies if we've got a target on our backs. Meanwhile, Viper, be sure and check everywhere around your house. Check for strange cars."

"Yeah, yeah, yeah," Viper broke in. "I've done this a time or two before. On it. But, Blaze? Your setup's a little more dicey. People could be checking you out and you might not know it."

Blaze lived in a townhouse, a situation that could allow people to use the adjoining homes to mask what they were doing.

"Oh, I'll know it," he assured them. "I know everything about my neighbors, including where their freckles are. I'm good here. You guys just check your situations and one of us will call after the cops finish questioning these assholes. Leave your sat phones on."

"Okay, going to check outside." Viper drained his mug and carried it to the sink.

"I'm gonna check the exterior and see if anything's going on. Hannah, have you ever fired a gun?"

For a moment, she just stared at him. "A gun?"

"Yes. It wouldn't be a bad idea for you to know how. I don't expect you'll need it, but I'd feel a lot better."

Her lips curved in a tiny grin. "No, but I've always had a secret urge to learn. Just never had anyone to teach me."

He couldn't help laughing. "Well, aren't you just full of surprises? Okay, we'll put it on the list and get to it as quick as we can. I'll feel a lot better if we do. We built an indoor range at the hangar that we use for practice. It's a good place to learn. Anyway, I'm going to check the outside. Please stay right here in the kitchen. I don't think anyone can get it in, but let's play it safe."

"I trust you to take care of me," she told him.

Those were the best words he'd heard in a long time.

"Thank you." He had to take a minute to give her a quick squeeze and a soft kiss before heading for the security panel. "I'm taking the remote with me so I can reset it and unlock it from outside. I'll be quick about it."

"Take your time. I want you to be sure you check absolutely everything out there."

"No worries there. Remember. Stay in the kitchen."

First, he needed to gather his equipment. He tucked his gun into the waist of his jeans at the small of his back, turned off the alarm so he could get outside and grabbed the remote. He also picked up the small but powerful binoculars he kept at the end of the breakfast bar. Like everything, else, just in case. Finally he shoved his cell phone into a pocket of his jeans.

He placed the sat phone on the breakfast bar where Hannah was sitting.

"If someone speaks," he told her, "just press this red button, tell them what I'm doing and that you have the phone."

"It's okay for me to do that?"

"Yes. In fact, I'll let them know." He pressed the button. "Everyone who's listening? I'm checking the area outside. Hannah has the phone. Feel free to pass anything along to her."

As soon as everyone acknowledged, he set the phone back on the bar.

"Okay. You're good to go."

"Be careful, please," she urged.

"Careful's my middle name." He gave her a light kiss on her lips. "See you soon."

The minute he was outside, he pressed the remote to set the security codes. As he began his scouting, it occurred to him for the first time that all the windows that he loved in his house, the windows that gave the place such an open feel, weren't the best for protecting anyone. He'd taken pains to set up safeguards to keep people from breaking in, but not to keep them from seeing him.

Of course, he hadn't expected, when he'd bought the house, to have a beautiful woman with a target on her back hiding there, either. When this was over, if the house was still standing, he should have the regular glass replaced with bulletproof and the blinds changed out for the solar ones he could see through from the inside but that blocked anyone's view from the outside.

Okay, time to get to work. He headed across the patio and beyond the pool. There was a three-quarter moon tonight, lighting up the backyard. Viper crept along the side of the house and down one high wall, alert for anything that might be moving or look out of place.

So far, so good.

He eased back up to the patio and slipped over to the other side of the yard, doing the same thing. *No one there either, thank the lord.* He pulled up the binocs and scanned every inch of the yard, wishing he'd taken the time to get his night vision goggles. But the moon lit up the backyard area enough, along with where the bay lapped at the shoreline, to let him see almost everything. There were no boats out there at this time of night, so that was one less thing to worry about.

When he was confident no one was lying in wait in the back, he crept along the wall to the gate set in the concrete. Viper entered the code and slid the gate open, then eased it closed behind him. He used the landscaping to hide his body as he moved toward the front of the house, crouching by a tree and scanning the street with the binocs.

There was no one moving at this time of night, not at his house or any of the others on this curve of the street. Most of the houses had outside night lights to discourage people from sneaking around. Viper swept both left and right with the binoculars and was about to head back into the house when his gaze paused on a driveway four houses down across the street.

He stopped and adjusted the glasses to get a better look. He'd made it his business to memorize all the cars the homeowners drove so he could tell when there were strangers in the neighborhood. Not only was the car in the driveway unfamiliar, but the house itself was for sale, an off-market listing. The owners had already moved. Viper knew it because he kept up with things like that. Every single thing that happened in his neighborhood could affect him and he needed to be on the alert for it.

And he was definitely on the alert where this car was concerned.

The moon was bright enough that he could see the license plate, so he pulled out his cell and jotted it down in the Notes section. When he got back inside, he'd run it through Zander's super-duper Stargazer system, although he was sure it would come back to a rental place. Then it would be a matter of tracking the information on whoever had rented it.

It was hard to tell for sure with the ambient light if there was anyone in the car. If there was, he was sure they were watching the house, but why be so obvious about it? Didn't they think he'd be suspicious? Or were they stupid enough to think... *Think what?* He couldn't imagine.

He waited a good fifteen minutes to see if there was any action, but nobody approached the car and no one got out of it. Finally, he headed back into the house, using the remote to shut off the security system. Back inside, he reset the code then turned toward the kitchen. What he saw made him grin.

Hannah was standing at the end of the breakfast bar, holding the fireplace poker like a baseball bat.

"Do I look so ridiculous?" she snapped.

He took the poker from her and laid it on the bar.

"Not at all. You look adorable. And fierce. And smart that you figured out some kind of weapon to use, although I'm not sure bullets could bounce off it."

"Well, Mister Smart Ass," she spat at him. "I figured they wouldn't shoot me before asking questions and trying to drag me out of here. This way at least I could do some damage while they made the attempt."

Viper's chest swelled with pride, along with his cock, which seemed to be in a perpetually engorged state around her.

"That's my girl." He wrapped his arms around her and held her tightly to his body. Only then did he realize she was shaking. "Hannah?" He rubbed her back, trying to ease her tension. "It's okay, darlin'. It's fine. I've got you. And I'm damn proud of you for your quick thinking."

She shook her head. "But I hate that I was scared like that. It's not me. But worse than that, Viper. Think about all the things we all dug up about these people. They have a lot at stake. They aren't going to let your security setup deter them. If they want in, they'll plan an assault and carry it out. The more I think about it, abut Lowden and the people and the whole situation, and what information Tom Hernandez passed along, the more I'm convinced that's what they'd do. What did you find outside?"

"Nothing on the water side, although they could still bring a boat close. Or use scuba divers. Anyway, across the street, though, there's a car in the driveway of an empty house that's for sale. I can't imagine they'd be stupid enough to think I wouldn't know it was out of place. I make sure I know everything about my neighbors, for my own protection."

"But I'm telling you," she insisted. "Look at what's at stake for them. These people thought nothing of killing a high-profile, high-ranking senator. Look at the money and power behind them. And what's at stake here. They can't afford to have me pop up and answer questions that the Feds are dying to ask me."

"You're right." Viper frowned. "According to Tom Hernandez, he had trouble getting anyone to give him anything at all, and not because they didn't know it."

"Maybe you should arrange for me to tell my story to someone. I'm not sure who, but you guys would know and could set it up, right?"

"Yes, but we'd have to do it carefully. For all we know, Baumann and his crew have ears in all the federal agencies."

She started to shake again, "Listen. I wouldn't put it past them to try to blow up this house once they confirm I'm in it. Or even if they only suspect. They even tried to break into your plane."

"Yeah, that's a puzzle. I guess they were hoping to find information there. Shit." He cradled her face. "Let's wait to hear how the questioning goes. Then I'm going to get Rocket and Eagle over here so we can make some plans." He pressed a soft kiss to her lips. "No more sleep tonight for any of us. Let's have some fresh coffee while we wait for the guys to call again."

Another hour passed before the sat phone beeped.

"Yeah, go ahead," Viper said.

"This is Rocket. Fun time's over for tonight. Neither of those guys said a word except to ask for their phone call. The sheriff ran them through all the databases but their names don't appear anywhere except for a driver's license and voter registration. How do people stay totally off the radar like that?"

"Because whoever is running this entire show has the power to make it happen. And that scares the shit out of me."

"Tom was right when he said there was a lot of power and money behind this. And get this." Rocket's voice had an edge to it. "A little while ago, not one but two attorneys showed up. I checked them out with Tom. Apologized for waking him up, but asked him about these guys. He said they cost more than a mortgage and the people who retain them are located in the stratosphere, politically and socially. He said even judges try to avoid having them in their courtrooms."

"Shit. So I'm assuming these guys are gone?"

"Unfortunately. The sheriff—not too happy about being dragged into this at that hour of the day—managed to get a bail hearing. The attorneys posted bail and took their clients with them. And, Viper? Get this. Bail was set at one million each and they paid in cash. These are not your average bad guys here."

"Holy motherfucker."

"Uh huh. These people want Hannah and they'll do anything to grab her. And they have the money and power to make it happen."

"Okay." Viper gave Hannah a smile he hoped was reassuring. "Blaze is going to have to stay put with Peyton. He needs to keep her as far away from this as possible. I'd move Hannah someplace, except—no offense—I feel a lot better keeping her with me."

"Understood."

"However, you and Eagle get over here so we can make some plans. Thinking about everything Tom Hernandez told us, these people may be getting ready to make a move. I wouldn't put it past whoever this is to just attack the house and try to grab her."

"After watching these two guys and getting a sense of them, I can't say you're wrong. See you shortly."

He set the sat phone on the counter and pulled Hannah into his arms again.

"I am not going to let these people get their hands on you," he promised. "I want you to believe me when I say that."

"I do." She pressed against him. "I just still can't get my head around how I happened to be the one they decided to make the sacrificial lamb for this."

He held her tightly against him, loving the feel of her body against his, the soft swell of her breasts. He cupped her chin and tilted her face up to his.

"I don't know how you did it, Hannah Modell, but you found the key to me when no other woman has been able to do it. And I'm glad of it. Is it quick? Without a doubt. Would I go back to my life before you? Hell, no. Please tell me you have nothing that would drag you back to Houston. Or anywhere else."

Her laugh had a slightly hysterical twinge.

"Well, I live in a rental apartment with no personality and I sure won't have a job to go back to. No friends to speak of, just acquaintances. Both my parents are dead. No brothers or sisters. So can I start a new life with no problems? Without a doubt. Does that answer your questions?"

"In spades. That's good, because I planned to beg you to stay here when this is all over." He grinned. "And I'm not the begging kind."

He pressed his mouth to hers, desperate for a taste of her, plunging his tongue inside. She tasted like seven kinds of sin, but she also tasted like home, like a woman he could freely commit to for the rest of his life. He had no idea how the fuck he'd gotten so lucky, but when this was all over, he might have to send a big thank-you note to the bartender in Houston who, for whatever reason, had given them the heads-up when the scumbags had barged into the bar looking for her.

He slid his hand down her back and over the sweet curve of her ass, and despite the critical situation they were in, would have forgotten everything and dragged her not the bedroom if the sat phone had not beeped just then.

"We're about a minute out," came Eagle's voice. "Open the gate, please."

Saved by the phone!

Reluctantly he released Hannah, with a brief kiss.

"I have to go let them in."

"And I have to put on some clothes. I—" She paused. "I'm all in, Viper."

He swallowed a smile as he went to the panel and punched in the code. Then he opened the front door.

Chapter Sixteen

The sound of his cell phone woke Diesel, although his sleep had been restless and edgy. There was so much shit going on that he considered himself lucky to get any sleep at all. If this was Henry, he might have to kill the man — then none of this would matter. No, Ed Fletcher.

"Tell me the first step is done."

"Not exactly." Ed's voice was flat. "You won't be happy."

Diesel sat up and turned on the bedside light. "What the hell happened? We'd finally gotten a break about these four guys, their plane and their addresses."

"And not without spending a lot of money," Ed reminded him.

"Fuck that. I thought we were moving forward."

"Sometimes I think this whole setup is cursed," Ed growled. "It's been nothing but a disaster from start to finish. These guys had some kind of sophisticated silent alarm system setup. Sheriff's deputies were there before they could finish getting the hangar door open."

"Crap."

"That's not the worst part. Two of the Galaxy SEALs showed up before long, and let me tell you, my friend, you don't ever want to tangle with these guys."

"What's the problem? We can handle them."

"Don't bet on it," Ed told him. "These guys are former SEALs. The whole world is afraid of them."

How the fuck did Hannah Modell get hooked up with these guys?

"So what happened?"

"The two Galaxy guys went along when the deputies hauled our guys off. I called two of the attorneys on our list and they just hustled their asses right down there. They said our guys kept their mouths shut and we bailed them out."

"You'd better stash them someplace where no one will find them," Diesel warned. "People are not going to be pleased they were caught. Didn't the EMP work?"

"Believe it or not," Ed told him in a tired voice, "there are pieces of equipment you can use to defend against it. It's not failsafe."

"Well, disabling the plane won't matter anymore. That cat's out of the bag, so to speak. Now the thing is to grab that woman and stash her where she'll never be found again."

"Easier said than done," Ed told him. "We have to get into the house where she is and do a snatch and grab."

"Right in your wheelhouse," Diesel pointed out. "Scope it out, let me know what you need and get it done. And I mean now."

"I've got people covering their homes as best we can."

"What the fuck does that mean?" Diesel bit off.

"It means they all live in the kind of neighborhoods where we'd stick out like sore thumbs if we used the usual surveillance tactics. We're doing drive-bys using alternating vehicles. And every other technique we can make work."

"You need eyes on them at all times." Diesel wanted to punch something. Or someone. How had this become so difficult?

Because we aren't dealing with the kind of people we usually do.

"Hold on a second. I have a call coming in."

Diesel waited impatiently until he heard Ed's voice again. "Well? What was so important it interrupted our call?"

"We know which house the woman is at. That important enough for you?"

Yes!

Diesel wanted to raise his fist in triumph. "Which house?"

"The one on the water that belongs to Matt Roman. I understand his call sign is Viper."

"Better hope he doesn't strike you first."

"Don't worry. We've got it covered."

Diesel snorted. "I've heard that too many times before the hammer fell."

"Well, this time it's true. As soon as we hang up," Ed told him, "I'll go over the info with all my men and see what they need. This needs to be a coordinated attack, but keep in mind this could cause a big mess. If we have to kill these guys, there'll be hell to pay. How do you plan to cover it up?"

"Maybe we'll blame Hegman's death on them and tell the media we were grabbing the girl to get the truth out of her. They fought us and we had no choice."

Diesel barked a humorless laugh. "Not a bad story. Remind me to give you a raise if you and your men can pull it off."

"Don't worry. We'll be earning every penny."

"Remember," Diesel warned. "You're good, but these guys? I don't think there's anyone more dangerous."

"You might have other Special Forces argue that point with you, but yeah, I'd probably have to agree with you. But the men I've gathered are tough and well-trained too, and don't care what they have to do to get a job done."

"What's next? You planning to just barge into the house where the Modell woman is?"

"Do we have a choice?" Ed asked. "It's not as if they're taking her out anywhere."

"So what's the outline?"

"We can't do it until tonight. We have a boat to arrange for and some of my guys will need scuba gear. We'll hit them from both sides."

"Hope your EMP works better this time," Diesel complained.

"Won't matter. They'll be ready for us anyway, but we'll be more prepared."

"You'd better be right. We'll only have one chance," Diesel reminded him, "so there's no room for mistakes. Call me when you get ready to launch."

He disconnected the call and pulled on sweatpants and a T-shirt. There'd be no more sleeping for him tonight. First, he'd fix coffee. Then he'd wake the Conductor. The man was in charge, so it was time for him to act like it. *Do something besides just bark orders.* Everything was coming down to this. If they screwed up tonight, they could all look for someplace to hide, because the fallout would be astronomical.

Coffee in hand, he dialed the Conductor. If he, Diesel, wasn't getting any sleep, then neither was the man running this whole thing that had now turned into a shitshow of the first order.

* * * *

The man known as the Conductor wasn't getting much sleep himself, but for a different reason. The last week had just been a fucking mess. For the past five years, he'd led an effort from the background to put military contractors in a position to get a lock on contracts. To build a group where there was no limit to the money they could make. Where no one suspected what they were doing, what influence they paid for in Washington and elsewhere. Where they wielded influence from the background with a powerful fist.

Lowden Tactical was the lynchpin for their setup. The drones could go anywhere, do anything. Drop explosives. Videotape facilities, meetings, private activities. He thought he'd been so smart, burying his money in numbered accounts, changing his name and altering his appearance. Taking a position that people looked at as secondary, so the focus would never be on him.

The only person who knew where the funds for Lowden had come from was Eric himself, a man smart enough to know that all his power and even his life would go away if he opened his mouth. But there wasn't much danger of that. He'd made the man rich, and in turn Lowden kept quiet and followed orders when he should.

Mark Hegman had been in a position to blow it all up. Whatever had caught his attention had caused him to call for investigations by his committee of some of the contractors in their group. And not just here in the States. Hegman wasn't all that happy about using foreign companies to manufacture goods for America's military. He also had begun to question some of Lowden's contracts, although Eric always managed to disguise the details. While Hegman's decision had come out of the blue, the Conductor was sure he'd spent months gathering information.

Shit. Just plain shit. That overly righteous man could have fucked up a wet dream, so he'd had to go. And it had to be done right. First, they'd needed a replacement, one they could engineer into the position who could bend to their will. Baumann, bitter and disgruntled for so many years, had been a perfect choice. The groundwork had been laid and a subtle bill of goods sold to the president of the Senate. With Hegman's death, they were ready to move forward.

He'd had a bad feeling about picking Hannah Modell to be the fall guy. Yeah, it had seemed simple. A lone wolf, absorbed in her job, no friends, few acquaintances, no family to speak of. No resources. Stash her away while the groundwork for laying it at her feet was set. Then trot her out long enough to announce she was the culprit, whisk her away and bury her body where it would never be found. How easy to tell people she'd escaped and they had no idea where she was.

Then it had all gone to shit, because apparently Hannah Modell's smarts were not all about drone engineering. She'd turned out to be sharp, resourceful and fortunate. A microscopic search had not turned up any prior connection to the men of Galaxy, so it made her the luckiest piece of ass that she'd run into one of the partners when she'd escaped the hotel and he'd chosen to help her.

Now they were in the soup. Information about Galaxy had been close to impossible to come by, and when they did get some, the Conductor had known they had big trouble. These guys didn't play around and getting to her would be next to impossible. They had to be smart and figure out the best story. Putting out there that Galaxy had turned bad and was keeping her prisoner seemed the best option. She had to be rescued, and too bad people had gotten killed in the process.

He'd have to monitor the situation carefully, though. There had been too many screwups not to, starting with Paul Santos, who'd let the little bitch bop him on the head and get away. Then he'd have to pull the right strings to make sure Baumann's appointment came off in time and without a hitch. He filled a mug with coffee and decided that even though the night was just beginning to fade, it wasn't too early to add a little alcohol to it. Not with what he'd been through and what was to come.

* * * *

While Hannah took a quick shower then threw on jeans and a top, Viper called Tom Hernandez.

"Sorry for waking you, buddy, but I knew you'd want an update on what was happening."

"I can't say I'm surprised," Tom said when Viper finished telling him what he knew. "I told you these were powerful people who operate in the shadows and believe they can do whatever they want."

"I was shocked that the judge set a bail hearing so fast, and in the middle of the night."

"Yeah, well, you can believe some mighty hands twisted some arms for that. These are people who can make anything happen."

"Well, you were damn right about that."

"Listen, Viper." Tom cleared his throat. "You guys better be prepared. If they were bold enough to try to get to the plane and disable it, I wouldn't put it past them to launch a full-out invasion on your house with the excuse they were 'rescuing' Hannah so they could turn her over to the police."

"Don't worry. We'll keep her locked up tight. And we'll make sure you're in the loop on whatever goes on. Thanks for all your help. We'll get these guys."

"I'm counting on it."

He was just disconnecting the call when Hannah tugged his arm.

"I have an idea that will give us eyes on what's happening."

"What kind of idea?"

When she told him, he actually laughed, even in their critical situation.

"I love a smart woman."

He made a phone call then checked his watch. If this all worked, they'd have pretty good eyes on the situation. Thirty minutes later, the speaker sounded on their security system.

Viper pushed the button. "Who's there?"

"Pizza delivery."

Then Tom Hernandez was inside, carrying a grocery tote from a pizzeria — only it didn't carry any food.

"Thank you so much for doing this," Hannah told him as she grabbed the bag.

"You must be the famous Hannah Modell." He held out his hand.

She shook her head. "Maybe infamous. And I'm happy to meet you. Thank you again."

"These guys are like my brothers," he told her. "I'd do anything for them."

She looked inside the bag. "I can't believe you were able to get such a high-end version at this hour of the night. Or morning. Or whatever."

"I have a client who owns a specialty electronics store and was happy to do me a favor. Although I can tell he was biting his tongue not to ask questions."

"Well, when this is over, please thank him for us. And thanks to you, for doing this."

Hannah grabbed the box, pulled out the large box inside and began to assemble the drone it contained. Tom looked at her and Viper couldn't help grinning.

"Beautiful *and* smart," he bragged.

"Well," she pointed out, "neither of us could exactly walk into a store and buy one with who knows how many sets of eyes on us. Certainly not me. They'd find a way to grab me for sure."

Tom nodded his agreement. "Still, it's the edge you need."

"Well," she reminded him, "it's what and who I am."

"And Viper is damn lucky," he told her.

"You bet," Viper agreed. "Okay, let's get to work."

Before he could do anything, however, his phone rang again.

"Punch the buttons for the alarm and the garage," Blaze growled. "I'm five seconds away."

"Okay."

Well. That was a shock. Surely Blaze hadn't left Peyton alone and unguarded? He did as his friend asked, and in seconds the gate to the driveway swung open just as the door to the third bay in the garage rolled up.

Hannah came back into the hallway just as he was resetting the codes.

"What's going on?"

"Damned if I know, but I'm sure gonna find out."

He opened the door from the garage into the house in time to see Blaze climb out of his truck, carrying a case Viper knew held a rifle, and Peyton unfold herself from beneath a blanket on the back seat. *What the hell?* He was just about to ask when his phone rang again, this time with a text from Eagle.

We're heading down your street.

He pressed in the code to open the gate, and in moments Eagle and Rocket walked through the door, each carrying their own gun cases. They stared at Blaze and Peyton, exactly as Viper was doing.

"You were told to stay put at your place," he growled at Blaze.

"Yeah, right." He snickered. "You try arguing with a woman who threatens to cut off your balls if you don't do what she says."

Eagle burst out laughing.

"I think this is the first time I've ever seen you afraid of someone," he told Blaze. "And you must weigh twice as much as she does."

"Gimme a break." One corner of Blaze's mouth quirked up. "You know who wears the pants in our house."

Peyton planted her fists on her hips and huffed a breath.

"You guys are mentally deficient if you think he's going to just sit this out when all the action is here and he'll be chewing his knuckles. We got me here without anyone seeing, right?" When they all just stared at her, she repeated, "Right?"

"She knows it's always all hands on deck," Blaze told them. "She said she'd never forgive herself if anything happened to any of you and one more person could have made the difference. That we operate as a team. That if we can't protect Hannah here, we can't protect her. And besides, she's a crack shot with a new toy. Show 'em, honey."

Peyton's lips quirked as she reached into her purse and drew out a Glock 19, the special favorite and familiar weapon of SEALs. Although Viper knew Blaze had been training her at the hangar, he was still surprised at the assurance and dexterity with which she handled the weapon.

"I'm ready to do my part." She stashed the gun at the small of her back and walked over to give Hannah a quick hug. "Besides, I have to take care of my friend."

Viper saw the quick flash of emotion in Hannah's eyes, a hint of hesitation, then she hugged back.

"Thank you." Her voice was thick with emotion. "Thank you very much."

Peyton winked. "We have to stick together. The guys have each other, Now we have our own two-man crew."

"What all else is going on here?" Rocket asked. "Tom, what the hell are you doing here this time of night? Or early morning."

"Delivering pizza," he joked.

Eagle lifted an eyebrow. "Excuse me?"

Viper tilted his head to where Hannah was assembling the drone on the counter. "Hannah's idea. Both the drone and how to deliver it."

Admiration washed over Eagle's face. "Damn smart, Hannah. Good thinking."

Her faint blush told Viper she might not be used to compliments, and he wondered why the hell not. The woman was obviously hella smart.

"Let's let her get it assembled, then we can discuss the best possible uses for it."

"And we need to sit down and plan this whole thing out," Rocket reminded them. "Tom, we can use your input on this if you can hang around."

"I would, but if these people have eyes on your house — which we're sure they do — they'll wonder why the pizza guy is still here. But I am only a phone call away for anything you need or any questions I can try to answer."

Viper lifted an eyebrow. "A two-pronged attack?"

"Uh huh. It might end up being noisy and messy, but in their way of thinking it will get the job done. And they have a ready story, just as we discussed."

"Then let's sit down and figure out how to stop them."

Viper set the blinds on the glass doors and big windows at an angle, so light filtered in but no one could get a clear image of anyone inside. The other three men lifted their cases to the counters and removed the weapons inside. While they were doing that, Viper fetched his own from his bedroom. For the next fifteen minutes the women watched silently as the men carefully checked their weapons, made sure they were loaded and stuck extra ammo in their pockets.

Then, as before, they sat at the dining room table, each of them with a full mug of coffee and their handguns on the table in front of them.

"Okay." Viper looked around the table. "They won't approach the house until after dark and they'll probably hit the front and back at the same time. We need to keep an eye out for boats on the water. Although...."

"Although what?"

He tapped his tablet and searched for a particular page. When he found it, he put it on the table where everyone could see it.

"They could actually slip into the water over here at Seaside Beach and swim over to where we are. The beach closes at nine and there's no one around to see them. Scuba gear is black, so hard to see at night. Once they're in the water, they'll slip beneath the surface and be really invisible. And with the proper gear, weapons aren't a problem."

"Also," Eagle added, looking at his digital watch, "there's no moon tonight. That could be both good and bad, for them as well as us. Your sea wall is low enough that they can climb over it."

"They'll probably bring an EMP gizmo to kill the security system," Rocket pointed out.

"That's okay," Viper assured them. "There are sensors in the water side of the sea wall that will catch them before they try to do that."

"Plus," Blaze added, "we'll be watching for them with night vision goggles. Both front and back."

"And we'll have Hannah's secret weapon," Viper reminded them. "Moonlight or not, it won't matter. This drone is infrared-capable, so we'll have eyes on them regardless of what they do."

"And they won't be expecting it," Rocket pointed out.

"What I'd like to know," Peyton said, "is how they expect to get away with a home invasion without calling attention to it."

"It's dark," Blaze reminded her. "While they probably think we're expecting them, I believe they underestimate our abilities. They probably figure that with no moon, they have an edge. Plus I'm sure this isn't their first assignment like this. They're experienced and believe they'll have the element of surprise to a degree."

"And," Eagle added, "they're probably arrogant enough to believe they're better than we are."

"We'll be expecting them to attack us from the rear," Blaze explained, "while another team climbs over the front wall and breaks in from there. But you can bet they believe the EMP killing our security system will give them the edge they need. They must know the one at the hangar had a backup system, so I don't understand why they'd count on it working here."

"Maybe they have a different one with a stronger bolt of electricity. Either way, we'll be ready."

"Pardon my stupidity," Hannah said, "but even as good as you guys are, won't it take more than the four of you if they have two groups attacking at the same time?"

Viper's lips curved in a savage grin. "Not with the preparations we'll make."

She frowned. "Preparations?"

"Uh huh. Just watch."

Although for the most part she was occupied with fine-tuning the drone, she was still fascinated watching the men doing their thing. They spent most of the morning at the table with their tablets, planning logistics.

"It's like getting ready for a mission," Peyton whispered at one point.

Blaze overheard her. "That's exactly what it is. We plan it down to the tiniest detail, so we don't get caught with our pants down."

"What I'd like to know," Peyton said, "is how they expect to handle the media fallout from this. A home attacked in this expensive neighborhood. Maybe dead bodies?"

"There's enough power in whatever this group is," Rocket answered her, "at least according to Tom, that they can cover up and squash anything."

She shivered. "That kind of power scares me to death."

"Me, too," he agreed. "Which is why we have to stop this whole thing."

Hannah and Peyton fed everyone during the day, but by the time it began to get dark again, no one was interested in food. Viper worked with his partners on their plan, trying to allow for every contingency. Blaze and Eagle had slid out of the back and slithered their way to the front, laying traps for intruders, lying on their stomachs to avoid detection. Even if whoever was watching had infrared glasses, the stone wall that rose five feet from the ground across the front of the house concealed them very well.

They placed the drone on a little table at the side of the patio. It was active but not moving, its 'eyes' focused on the bay.

Then, at midnight, in the dark, they began the watch.

Chapter Seventeen

Hannah had stationed herself in a chair just to the side of the big sliding glass doors, holding the controls for the drone. Every so often she would send it out over the water for a recon run, then bring it back. Shortly after one o'clock, the drone picked up movement.

"I see people slowly easing from the water," she told Viper. "Finally. They're wearing scuba suits and gear and moving slowly."

"Have they reached the wall yet?" he asked.

"No, not yet."

"Don't move the drone until I tell you. What are they doing now?"

"One of them is pulling something from what I assume is a waterproof pouch around his waist. He's pointing it toward the house."

"The EMP."

They'd left a nightlight on at the breakfast bar so they could tell when the electricity died. Ten seconds later, it went out.

"Here they come," Hannah told them. "They're over the wall and past the pool. Approaching the house."

"Send the drone. Have it check the front of the house."

Hannah fiddled with the controls. "You called it. Three bodies creeping up to the wall in front."

Viper pressed his throat mic. "Everyone stand by. Breach is imminent. Blaze, three tangoes on your horizon. Be alert."

"On it," came the answer.

"Hannah, fly the drone over the water and back again," Viper told her. "Let's see if we can get some action out of them and kill their stealth."

He watched as she manipulated the controls. The night vision goggles he wore allowed him to see the men approach, the drone lift off then fly straight at them and around them. One of the men aimed a handgun and shot it directly at the drone, which they had expected.

Viper signaled Hannah to get the hell out of the room. They didn't need anyone laying eyes on her, no matter what happened. She slipped into the hallway toward the bedrooms where Peyton was waiting before they could see her.

When she was safely out of sight, he and Rocket watched as the men outside turned to each other, one of them nodded, then they were all at the sliding doors.

He was sure they'd planned to use a glass cutter to reach in for the lock, but with the drone inserted into the situation, they instead smashed the glass with a gun. Then they were inside, four of them, handguns drawn. As soon as that happened, Viper and Rocket, who had been waiting to the side out of sight, stepped up to the two at the rear and placed the barrels of their rifles on their necks.

"Tell your friends to drop their guns," Viper ordered, "or two of you will have holes in your neck in six seconds."

"Go fuck yourself," the man next to him said.

"You first," Viper told him and pulled the trigger. He'd learned in his first year as a SEAL not to screw around with guys like this.

"Who's next?" Rocket asked.

One of the other two men shot at Rocket, but the bullet lodged in the vest he was wearing. All the Galaxy men had put them on when they'd begun the countdown. Viper shifted the barrel of his rifle and shot the man through the arm. He cried out and dropped his gun, which Rocket kicked to the side.

"Anyone else?" Viper asked. "One body, four bodies, doesn't matter to us."

At that moment, he heard Blaze's voice in his ear.

"Three tangoes down out front. We're hauling them into the garage."

"Good copy," Viper acknowledged. Then he looked at the men still alive. "Your friends have run into a little problem. They won't be socializing any more. I think it's time for you to join them."

One of the two men still standing and holding a gun made a move with his pistol.

"Do it," Rocket said. "My trigger finger's real itchy right now."

The man looked at both Viper and Rocket, then at his friends, and finally bent and placed his gun on the floor.

"Smart decision."

All the men were wearing throat mics and earphones, just like the Galaxy team.

"Better collect these," Rocket said. "Someone might know how to track them back."

In minutes, they had all the men — including the dead body — in the garage, gagged and stretched out on the floor, hands tied behind their backs.

"What's next?" Eagle asked.

"They all have to have cell phones. Let's check them and see if we can find any numbers."

"Good idea," Viper agreed. "While you do that, I'll check on the women."

He found them in his bedroom — or his and Hannah's, as he preferred to think of it.

"Thank god you're still in one piece," Hannah breathed.

"Is Blaze okay, too?" Peyton wanted to know.

"Everyone in Galaxy is fine," Viper assured them. "I can't say as much for the idiots that thought they could get away with a successful home invasion."

"Where are they?" Hannah asked.

"Restrained in the garage. Rocket's on the horn with Tom Hernandez to figure out the best thing to do with them. There's still a whole lot riding on this and we're running out of time. One of us will keep you in the loop, but we think it's safer, just in case, if the two of you stay in this room until we know for sure what's going down next."

"We understand where you're coming from," Peyton assured him. "And we don't want to add to the stress of the situation, but don't leave us out. Okay?"

"We'll do our best."

He answered the rest of their questions as best he could, but he was antsy to get back to the garage. He walked in to see Rocket grinning.

"What's up?" Viper asked. "I didn't think there was much to smile about."

"We took pictures of each of these guys, woke Zander and shot them over to him. He can run them through facial rec with his machines a thousand times faster than we can."

"And?" he prompted.

"The guy you shot in the shoulder is named Ed Fletcher. We've had a lot of people awakened tonight to give us answers, Viper, including Tom Hernandez. Who woke up *his* friend, and..."

"Jesus, Rocket. Get to the fucking point."

"Yeah, we're trying to get answers, too," Eagle snarled. "Come on, Rock."

"Yeah, sorry. I'm just trying to wrap my head around this." He blew out a breath. "Okay, Ed Fletcher has a full-time job as troubleshooter mopping up problems. And get this. He works for none less than Eric Lowden at Lowden Tactical. Who, by the way, has the code name of Diesel."

There was dead silence in the garage, heavy and thick. The men all looked at each other, stunned.

"Fucking shit," Viper said at last.

"Amen to that," Eagle added.

"What the fuck?" This from Blaze.

"Tom says we need more than local law on this one. This is probably hooked up to this whole business with Senator Baumann and the death of Senator Hegman."

Viper stared at Rocket. "So Lowden's not the innocent bystander in Hegman's death they pretend to be?"

Rocket shook his head. "Not even a little. This looks like it's all part of the plan to make Baumann chair of the Senate Armed Services Committee. And who knows what else we'll find when we open the lid?"

Eagle nodded. "All that stuff Tom's friend was telling him about."

They had been watching the men on the floor as they talked. Mostly they sat immobile, even the guy with the bullet wound. But an expression of *oh shit* briefly crossed the face of the one identified as Ed Fletcher.

Oh, yeah, Viper thought. *He knows they're in deep doo doo.*

"So what's our best move now?" he asked.

"Tom says we need to call in the Feds," Rocket answered. "I took the liberty of asking him to make that happen for us and he said he would."

"Good. We owe him big thanks on this one."

Rocket's phone rang and he punched the button to answer.

"Yeah, how did it go? Uh huh. Uh huh. Okay, thanks. We're really in your debt on this one and we plan to make good on that. Thanks again. Yeah, I'll be looking for it."

"Tom?" Viper asked.

"Uh huh. There's a team of Feds on the way from the Tampa office. Tom asked them for photos of whoever's coming so we know for sure it's them."

"Good move." He looked around. "So we wait, right?"

They all nodded.

"I'm gonna check on Peyton," Blaze said, "but I'll be right back."

It was close to an hour later by the time the FBI arrived. Jason Halliwell introduced himself as the SAC — Special Agent in Charge — of the Tampa office.

"I'll be running point on this," he told Viper after all the introductions were made. "This is too sensitive to hand it over to regular agents, although everyone on my team is top notch. In fact, all we're doing is transporting them to an airfield. A helo's coming from Washington to pick them up. This one's above even my pay grade, and I'm happy to hand it over."

"Thanks for responding so quickly," Viper told him.

"We like to wipe out scum like this as fast as we can."

"One of the tangoes is injured and one of them is dead," Rocket pointed out.

Halliwell snorted. "Good riddance. Maybe they'll just dump his body out of the helo. And it won't hurt the one who's wounded to suffer a while. Not after the kind of shit they do."

It didn't take long for the agents to load everyone, including the body, into the vans they'd arrived in. The guys helped Viper block the hole in the glass doors. Then everyone split to their own places.

"Tomorrow," Blaze said as he left with Peyton. "We need to go over all of this, because you can be damn sure the Feds will be all over us about it."

"And I want to protect Hannah as much as possible," Viper added.

"Understood." He looked at the others. "Let's touch base in the morning and set a time to meet."

Everyone agreed, then headed out of the door.

Viper set the security system then reached out to Hannah to pull her close to his body.

"Almost over, darlin'."

She pressed her face to his chest. "I can hardly believe it. A week ago, I thought I was either going to jail or about to be killed. And now..." Her voice trailed off.

"And now you can look at what the future holds for you." He cupped her cheek and tilted up her face. "Hopefully with me."

She wet her lips. "If you're still sure you want me."

"Hannah, honey, I was sure I wanted you the minute you sat down next to me in that bar. That feeling only keeps getting stronger." He studied her face. "What about you? What do you want?"

"I want you."

She said the words without hesitation, which made the tight band around his chest loosen.

"Thank fuck for that."

"I googled the Tampa Bay area and there are a couple of companies that really intrigue me. Of course, it depends on whether this thing with Lowden has tainted me."

"I think we can get the FBI to give you a sterling recommendation. After all, without you, none of this would have come to light."

"I'll hold you to that."

"How about holding me to something else? I need to bury myself deep inside you so I know for sure this is a done deal."

He was so hungry for her that he hoped he could make himself wait until they got to the bedroom before stripping off her clothes. He wanted to imprint himself on this woman. *In* her. Make sure she knew that he loved her fiercely and wanted her with him forever.

Her mouth curved into a sexy little smile. "I can get on board with that."

He swung her up in his arms and carried her to his bedroom, No, *their* bedroom. He stood her on her feet only long enough to remove every stitch of her clothing. Then he knelt in front of her and ran his hands from her breasts over the curve of her stomach to her sex, sliding his palms between her thighs.

He pressed his face to her mound and inhaled deeply, her scent making his balls ache and his cock swell even more than it already was. Separating the lips with his thumb, he drew a long line in her slit with his tongue, lapping from top to bottom and back again. She shivered at the sensations and a little moan eased from her mouth, so he did it again.

He rose to his feet and stripped off his clothing. Then he reached into the nightstand drawer and took out some condoms and one other item, tossing them on the bed. He stripped back the coverlet and stretched them both out full length. Positioning himself between Hannah's legs, he began to kiss every inch of her body in earnest.

Her breasts received focused attention, especially her rosy nipples which he alternately sucked and nibbled. She shifted beneath him, running her hands down his back and urging him to do more. He knew part of this was the easing of the tension that had gripped them for the past twenty-four hours, but he couldn't think of a better way to relieve it or anyone he'd rather do this with.

From her breasts, he trailed his tongue down to her navel, tracing the curled flesh again and again before moving even lower. Again he dragged his tongue between the lips of her sex, flicking her engorged clit and nipping it gently with his teeth. Hannah was already writhing and moaning and begging for more, but he had a plan.

"I want to touch you," she pleaded.

"If you do, I'll go off in your hand before you can close your fingers around me once. This is my show, darlin'." He glanced up at her face. "Hannah, tonight I'm really going to make you mine."

He continued stringing kisses up one leg and down the other, teasing the swollen nub of her clit and licking the walls of her sex. Before long, she was shivering in anticipation and he could tell her orgasm was starting to rise inside her. His own anticipation was at the 'explosive' level.

"I'm so ready," she moaned and tried to wrap her legs around him, pulling him against her.

"Not yet," he told her as he continued to tease her in every sensitive place. "Tonight, I'm going to make sure you know that you're mine. That I'm going to love you forever and that everyone in the world will know it."

He turned her over onto her stomach and pulled her gently to her knees.

"Stop me if you don't want this. I'm good with whatever." He wanted to make absolutely sure.

"I've never…"

"If this is too much for you…"

"No." There was no hesitation in her voice. "I'm glad you'll be the first." She paused a moment. "And only. Forever."

Thank you, god.

She was trembling beneath his touch and begging him for more. He placed kisses on the cheeks of her ass as she continued to shiver with need. When he separated those luscious cheeks and ran the tip of a finger down that crease, she moaned in obvious pleasure. When he pressed a fingertip against the opening, she groaned even louder.

Oh, yeah, he thought. *This is what I want. Forever.*

When he tested her sex, she was soaked, so he used some of her own liquid to lubricate her delicious rear channel.

"Doing all right?" he asked.

"Yes. Please, Please, please, please."

She was ready. He could feel it. With one hand, he rolled on the condom. Then he covered it with the special lubricating cream he had, because he didn't want her to suffer a moment's discomfort. He pressed the head of his dick at her opening and began to slowly enter her.

"Still okay?" he asked, pausing when he was half inside her.

Shit, he hoped she was because he was on the edge of the ledge himself.

"Yes, yes, yes. Don't stop."

She wriggled her ass back against him, a movement which nearly made him lose it right there and then.

Slowly, slowly, slowly he pushed forward until he was inside her all the way.

"Still good?" he asked, taking a nip of her shoulder.

"I will be if you get moving in the next second," she told him in a breathless voice.

Okay, then.

He began the familiar in-and-out movement, only this time he was in a channel so tight that her flesh squeezed him. He increased the pace, faster and faster, holding her hip with one hand and using the fingers of the other to stroke her clit and the wet flesh surrounding it. He would have loved for this to go on forever, but he could tell she was as aroused as he was because of the release of the night's tension and the need for each other. It brought them to the edge of climax way too quickly.

"I can't hold on much longer," he told her, gritting his teeth.

"Me, either. Do it, Viper. Make me come."

He drove into her one last time, pinched her clit very hard and exploded just as her orgasm shook her body. They shuddered together with spasm after spasm, her body thrusting back against his. It seemed to go on forever until, at last, their bodies were trembling but quiet. He lay there on top of her, his dick clutched by her hot channel, unwilling to move. But then he realized he might be making her uncomfortable, so he eased from her body. Disposing of the condom, he flopped to the side, turned her over and pulled her into his arms.

"Did I hurt you?"

She gave a giddy little laugh. "Only the kind of pain that gives pleasure." She nibbled on her bottom lip. "I know I said this already, but you're the first...I mean..."

"Good." He ducked his head and kissed her shoulder. "Nobody before me, and nobody else ever. That makes you mine, darlin'. Forever."

"We still have a mess to get through," she reminded him. "You sure you want to be hooked up with that?"

"I wouldn't have it any other way. Hannah, stay. Forever. Make a life with me here. Please."

She smiled at him. "If you can handle it, I'm in for the long haul." Then all evidence of humor left her face and she studied his expression. "I love you, Viper. I never thought I'd find someone to say that to."

"Same goes both ways. We'll get past this mess and the rest will be a piece of cake."

He fell into the kiss with her, giving thanks for that night in Houston.

* * * *

They were still wrapped up in each other the next morning when they were eating at the breakfast bar and watching the national news.

"It's a scandal of epic proportions," the reporter was saying. *"Eric Lowden, head of Lowden Tactical, which has many government contracts for some questionable missions for its sophisticated drones, has been revealed as code name Diesel, a man who used his company to kill for power and money. But the shocker was the revelation that Gregory Kingsley, Lowden's vice president, was actually the head of a shadowy organization that took contracts to manipulate politics not just here in the United States but in other countries.*

Known as the Conductor, it has been revealed that he is the money man behind Lowden. He's the man who took the contract to kill Senator Mark Hegman to make way for a new chair of the Senate Armed Services Committee, someone who would be more friendly to Lowden and the things the Conductor wanted. That someone was to be Senator Baumann, who has gone into seclusion and is unavailable for comment.

Drone engineer Hannah Modell, who was first accused of misdirecting the drone and killing Hegman, has been exonerated. She has yet to…"

Viper switched off the television.

"Enough of that shit. The whole thing makes me sick. And they didn't mind one bit making you the scapegoat."

"But it's over. I don't have to hide or look over my shoulder any more or be afraid of each day." She leaned across and kissed him. "Thanks to you."

"I'll just be glad when it finally all fades away."

She slid off the stool and carried their dishes to the sink. "Don't forget to call Blaze and find out what time everyone wants to gather here today."

"Couldn't I just tell them I'd rather spend the day in bed with you?"

"Sounds good to me, but you guys do have business to attend to."

He reached out to grab her and pulled her close to him. "But we'll get rid of them early, okay?"

She laughed. "Okay."

He cradled her chin in his palm. "I love you, Hannah. I'll never get tired of telling you that."

"Right back atcha."

He pulled her in for a deep kiss. When they broke apart, she smiled at him.

"I think you're right. We owe that bartender in Houston a big thank you."

"We'll discuss it," he agreed and lifted her in his arms. "Right after I finish fucking your brains out."

She laughed all the way to the bedroom.

Want to see more from this author? Here's a taster for you to enjoy!

Galaxy: Supernova
Desiree Holt

Excerpt

Fuck, it was hot.

John "Rocket" Hardin thought that in the mountains it should at least be cooler, especially out of the sun in this little cave. But no, the heat invaded the space and made it into a warm, wet towel. He was sweaty and streaked with dirt that had blown against him as they'd climbed the rocky trails. He used the tail of his shirt to wipe as much off his face as he could, but only a shower was going to attack this mess.

He'd been fucking pissed off when his SEAL team had been told they were being sent to rescue a writer — rescue from the Taliban. Ten years in the service and he had to waste his time because some wacky writer thought it would be great to hang out with terrorists and interview them. And, oh, yeah, write books. *Stupid idiot.*

But they'd executed the extraction just as night had begun to fall, hoping to take advantage of the cover of darkness. But hadn't been cloudy or overcast, damn it, the stars bright in the sky and the moon like a big spotlight. The team had done its best to stay concealed but without help from nature, someone had discovered their captive was gone before the SEALs were fully away. Rocket had broken off with Mallory, radioed Command to let them know, and taken off with her in the mountains so their enemies wouldn't find her. She hadn't complained, just followed him, despite what she'd been through already and the severity of the landscape.

Getting them out of that terrorist camp hadn't been a picnic, for sure, but his team was experienced and it had almost gone off without a hitch. But then things had gotten very hairy. His stated job was to get Mallory to safety above all else. He hated splitting from the rest of his team, but he had his marching orders. Their job was containment so he and Mallory could get the fuck out of there. The orders had come straight from their commanding officer.

She was a trooper, he'd give her that, moving at his direction until they were far enough away from the camp and could find a place to hide. Using his satellite radio, he'd informed Command where they were and had been told to wait for extraction. Once the chopper arrived and landed on the plateau near their cave, they'd be out of there. And he'd probably never see her again.

Damn!

He glanced over at her and saw she was in almost the same condition he was. Her hair was wild, and she'd managed to push it behind her ears. But her skin looked about like his, sweaty and streaked with dirt, not to mention the bruises on her wrists from the rope that had tied them.

He'd been shocked at his reaction when he'd first seen her in the hut where she was being held. In jeans and a T-shirt, hair wild and mussed, hands tied behind her back and smears of dirt on her cheeks and arms, she was still the sexiest woman he recalled ever laying eyes on.

But danger, it seemed, was an aphrodisiac, ramping up everything in his system well past the boiling point. This place was certainly as uninviting as any he'd ever been in, as far as sex was concerned. Despite that, he was so horny his dick hurt and his brain was filling with very un-SEAL-like thoughts. Mallory Kane was every man's wet dream, with her lush, toned body, her curly auburn hair and green eyes that blazed like emeralds.

Maybe it was the aftereffect of all that tension. Maybe it was a need to reaffirm life after escaping from a lethal situation. Or maybe he felt that she needed something to erase the aftereffects of her captivity.

Whatever it was, he wanted her more than he wanted to breathe. And wasn't that just a damn shock for someone with his discipline? This was no place for sex to intrude. Life was fucking not fair. At all. But maybe after…

Business first, asshole.

Now they sat side by side, leaning against the wall of the cave, Mallory pulling herself together.

"Thank you," she told him when her breathing finally evened out.

Her voice was soft and rich, almost musical, even with the stress she was going through. He thought he could listen to it every day. The only problem was it went straight to his dick which was doing its best to break the zipper of his camos.

"You're welcome." He slid a glance at her and grinned. "All in a day's work."

"Those must be some days, then."

"It's part of our motto," he told her. "The only easy day was yesterday."

She snorted. "If this is an example, then you guys deserve a ton of awards for that you do. I didn't think I would leave there with my head still attached."

"You should try and get a little rest," he told her. "It will be a while until the helo gets here. I radioed that we were secure here."

"Rest?" Her laugh had a tinge of hysteria. "I almost rested permanently. I am just so grateful that you came to rescue me. I know those people were going to kill me. And soon."

Rocket studied her for a moment. "Can I ask you something?"

"Sure." She shrugged. "You saved my life, so I guess you can ask me anything."

"So, just out of curiosity, you had to have known how dangerous this whole thing was. I mean, you might as well have committed suicide. What made you set this up to begin with?"

When she didn't answer at once, he glanced over at her and saw she was frowning.

"Is that question a problem?" Rocket pushed.

"No. Not a problem. I just..." She swallowed. "I guess I was just focused on getting the story and writing the book. The last one I did was very successful and I have a great contract for this one."

"But that's not all of it, is it?" he asked.

"The main part."

He waited but when she didn't say any more, his curiosity got the better of him.

"Is it so exciting that you're willing to risk your life for it?" When she didn't answer he turned sightly and reached over to cup her chin. "Mallory?"

She sighed. "It's a long story that you wouldn't be interested in. But it's a way to prove myself and I really don't want to discuss it now. Okay? Please?"

"Sure." He could understand that, although that didn't kill his curiosity by a long shot.

"But…" She nibbled her lower lip. "I do want you to know I realize that I owe you my life."

She raised her eyes to his and he saw a whirlpool of emotions swirling there. Okay. There was more than just following a story here and writing a book. But how did he find out what it was? She was the first woman to pierce the emotional shell he kept himself locked in and he wanted to know more about her. No, he wanted to know *all* about her.

"And this may be inappropriate, but I'm doing it anyway, because I really want to thank you for what you did." She knelt beside him, cradled his face in her hands and pressed her mouth to his.

Holy shit! His dick tried again to escape the pressure of his fly and he was sure his temperature went up. It shocked him because he'd sure had enough sex in his life to be able to control his reactions when he needed to.

He was not prepared for this. He was supposed to be rescuing and protecting her, not thinking about sex. He thrust his fingers into her disheveled hair to hold her head in place, pressed his tongue against her lips and, when they parted slightly, thrust his tongue inside. She tasted like ten kinds of sin. When he licked the inner surfaces of her mouth, she brushed her tongue against his and before he realized what he was doing, he slipped his hands around to the front and cupped her breasts, gently squeezing them. He felt a tear in the fabric of one cup and anger gripped him. Had the barbaric terrorists molested her?

"It's okay," she whispered against his lips, as if she knew what he was thinking. "They didn't rape me. I swear. Just tried to demoralize me. Break my spirit. But it didn't work."

"Good. I can see that."

"But I need to get it all out of my mind. You can see that, right?"

Oh, yeah. And it might be against the rules but he was all on board with this. "I just don't want you to think I expect—"

She moved until she was straddling him, her hot center pressing hard against his aching dick. "I don't just *want* this. I *need* this, to celebrate the fact I'm still alive."

At some point he'd get the details of what happened out of her but not now. Right now he could tell what she wanted was to wipe the worst of it out of her mind and he was glad to help her. They had another hour at least before the helicopter coming to extract them would be here and he intended to make good use of every single minute. He had never done anything like this before. Business was always…all business. But there was such electricity between them. And they'd just come through a harrowing situation and needed reaffirmation of life.

"If you're sure, then, damn it, yes. I want this, too."

He took her mouth in another kiss, moving his hands to lightly pinch her nipples. She moaned, sliding her hands beneath his shirt and dragging her fingernails across his back. Heat filled his body. *Jesus!* Although he sure never had trouble responding to a woman, he didn't ever remember reacting this way before. Or this fast.

Rocket eased her T-shirt up so he could touch the smooth skin of her abdomen. Before he could even think about it, he had unfastened her bra and pushed it up so he could palm her bare breasts. Rubbing his thumbs over the taut nipples made them bead beneath his touch. Temptation was too much for him, so he pushed her top up even higher, bent his head just enough and took one of those nipples into his mouth. When he sucked it, hard, she moaned and leaned into him.

He didn't know if she'd object or smack him but he yanked off the shirt and the bra and tossed them to the side. Then he went after her breasts with a vengeance, licking and sucking and squeezing. Mallory threw her head back, more little moans drifting from her mouth, the sound of them heating him up even more. He didn't even stop to think about what he was doing, or the trouble he could get into because of it. He knew he wanted this woman and that hunger was driving him forward.

Mallory arched up to him, her nails scraping his back, the sensation shooting straight to his cock and his balls. He was afraid he'd come just from sucking her breasts and miss the best part of the fun. He lifted his mouth and slid it to the hollow of her throat where he swirled the tip of his tongue before dusting kisses along her neck.

Realizing at last they were in a somewhat uncomfortable position, he lifted Mallory and moved her body so she was straddling him. She sat pressing against him so his cock was nestled right at the vee of her thighs, right at the heat of her sex. He was sure she could feel how hard and thick his dick had become. He had to restrain himself from ripping her clothes off and plunging into her fast and quick. But that wasn't him. It was bad enough that he was probably breaking a million rules. He needed to treat her with respect. She was a strong woman who had survived an ordeal that would have destroyed a lot of people. He might never see her again (although he pushed that aside) but he wasn't going to go at her like a rutting pig, either, despite how he started out. And he wanted to make sure she knew that.

He lifted his head, cradled her face in his palms and looked directly into her eyes.

"Before we go any further, I don't want you to feel you have to do this," he told her. "You've been through an ordeal and I want to respect that. The fact that I want you, bad, shouldn't come into consideration."

She smiled, raked her fingers through her hair and her disheveled look only made her appear sweeter and sexier.

"I don't do anything I don't want to," she told him, her breathing accelerated. "And I want this, too." Her lips curved in a very sexy smile. "What better way to celebrate the fact that I'm alive and not with my head rolling on the floor in some barbarian's camp? And who better to celebrate with than the man who rescued me?" She gave him a tiny smile. "I do want this, Rocket. And it's not an obligation for saving me. Okay?"

She grabbed his head and pressed her lips to his, sliding her tongue into his mouth.

Holy shit! Even her kisses were off the charts.

"Okay. Good to know." He cupped her chin. "We've got most of an hour before the helo gets here. I think I know a good way to pass the time, right?"

"Yes." She wriggled against his cock. "I want this. With you."

He locked his gaze with hers for a long moment, but he felt a little better about this now. "Good. I want this, too."

The time for talking was over. Rocket set Mallory aside so he could strip off his fatigues and lay them on the floor to give her as much protection from the dirt as possible. He thought about leaving his boxer briefs on then figured, what for?

When he turned around, Mallory had kicked off her shoes and stripped off her jeans. She looked at him as she eased her bikini panties down her legs, giving a sexy wiggle. Was it possible for him to get any harder? If he did, his dick might just break off. But he couldn't tear his eyes away from her toned legs, her nicely rounded butt and the trimmed patch of auburn hair that covered her sex. His mouth watered as he imagined the sweet taste of her.

They were lying on the floor, naked bodies pressed together, the heat of her sex scorching him when his brain kicked into gear.

Shit!

"Mallory?"

"I thought we were done talking." She wriggled beneath him.

"Yeah, well, I have to tell you this."

She frowned up at him. "A confession? Now?"

"Uh-huh. I, uh, don't have any condoms with me."

She burst out laughing. "I already figured that. You're on a mission, not a night out., No sweat. I'm on birth control."

"And I'm clean," he assured her. "I get tested regularly."

He didn't want to tell her it was a leftover from his days as an extreme horndog. He waited for her to say something, but instead she pulled his head down to hers and licked his lips. Her tongue was like a hot flame, scorching him clear to his balls. He held her head in place as he licked every inch of her mouth before trailing his tongue along her chin and down her neck. He pressed the tip of his tongue against the hollow of her throat, feeling the strong beat of her pulse, before moving down the smooth skin between her breasts. He loved the feel of them against his hands as he palmed them and rolled the nipples between thumb and forefinger.

Mallory moaned, a soft, sensuous sound as he trailed his mouth down over the slight curve of her stomach until he reached that gorgeous thatch of auburn hair. He slid his arms beneath her thighs so he could place them over his shoulders and used his thumbs to separate the plump lips of her sex. The pink bud of her clit peeped out at him and he couldn't resist stroking it with his tongue.

Mallory shivered and lifted her hips, raising herself closer to his mouth. Shit, she tasted like the sweetest sin, a flavor that he had a feeling he could become totally addicted to. He traced the delicate skin on either side of her clit with slow licks, stopping to nibble that little bud every few seconds. Each time he did, she made such a delicious sound that spiked his hunger even more, and tried to lift herself to his mouth. The painful ache in his dick and his balls told him he was closer than he would have liked. He wanted to make sure she got her orgasm before he lost all control.

Nudging her thighs farther apart, he slid two fingers into her soaked channel, humming his satisfaction as her inner walls tightened around them. Her eyes were closed and her face flushed with pleasure, obvious even in the dim light of the cave. The little sounds she made aroused him even more. When he added a third finger, she planted her feet on either side of him and pushed herself into his touch.

"Don't stop," she begged.

He gave a low, throaty chuckle. "Don't worry. I have no intention of stopping."

As he increased the pressure, he curled his fingers slightly, so with each glide, he scraped lightly against her sweet spot. She pushed against his hand harder and harder, riding it, her little moans making him impossible more aroused.

Her orgasm rolled through her, tightening her body, her inner walls fucking his fingers. He thrust again, pinched her clit…and she came, making those delicious little sounds as her liquid coated his hand.

At last the shivers subsided, the groans of pleasure became softer and her body relaxed slightly. But he was almost at the breaking point, drinking in the sight of Mallory lying naked and flushed on the floor. He was so aroused by this time he had to grit his teeth and reach for control.

Then he was on his knees between her thighs, lifting her legs to rest on his shoulders so her hips were raised. She was open to him and he could not wait another minute. With his fingers wrapped around his throbbing dick, he positioned the head at the opening of her sex, drew in a breath and thrust forward. Her hot, wet flesh gripped him like a vise, the electricity of it shooting straight to his balls.

Oh, sweet Jesus!

He didn't remember the last time he'd fucked where his cock was bare. The sweet feel of her skin and her liquid sent him into overdrive. He closed his eyes for a moment to gather himself. Then with his palms beneath the cheeks of her incredible ass, he began the familiar rhythm. It didn't matter that they were in this cave, his clothes spread out as a shield on the dirt floor, or that the light was so dim he couldn't see every inch of her the way he wanted to. All that mattered was this delicious, hot woman was here and he was having the best sex of his life with her.

She grabbed his forearms, digging in her nails as she moved with him. They fell into a rhythm as if they'd been doing this forever, as if their bodies were used to it. Every one of his nerves was on fire. In, out, back, forth...he wanted to make it good for her, but his control was snapping.

"I can't last much longer," he gasped, "although I'm trying, babe. I really am."

"I'm almost—almost—*yes!*"

He felt the surge of her second orgasm and the clenching of her walls just as he exploded. Their bodies throbbed together, spasming, her tight sex pulsing around his shaft. On and on it went, beyond anything he expected, until finally the last tremor faded. He managed to lower her legs to the ground and fell forward, catching himself on his elbows. He studied her face, seeing the satisfied glow and the look in her eyes. His heart was still beating erratically and hers matched the rhythm.

For a long time, they just lay there like that, staring at each other as if exchanging silent conversation. Then he lowered his mouth to hers and indulged in a deep, deep kiss. And when finally, the last of the tension left both their bodies, he eased his cock from her grasp and sat back on his heels. Fishing in the pocket of his pants, he pulled out the bandana he used to wipe sweat from his face and cleaned both of them.

"We'll both need a good shower after this." He chuckled, but then his face sobered. "Mallory, I—"

She reached up a hand to touch his lips with her fingers. "Don't. Do not say a word. Don't ruin it. Please."

"But I should—"

"No." She shook her head. "It was special and let's keep it that way."

Rocket had no idea where the conversation would have gone from there but at that moment his radio squawked. "Rocketman here."

"Helo is four clicks away," came the voice from the command center. "Get ready. How copy?"

"Good copy," He clicked off and looked at Mallory. "Time to get ready."

They dressed in silence, brushing off as much dirt from their bodies and their clothes as they could. Before they left the cave, he pulled her into his arms for one last kiss, as tender as it was erotic.

"Just so you know," he told her when he lifted his mouth from hers, "I'm never going to forget this, Mallory."

"Me neither, Rocket." She brushed her lips against his. "By the way, where did your call sign come from?"

He grinned. "We'll save that for another time. Because I'm sure, no matter how long it takes, there will be one."

"I'll hold you to it."

"And now we'd better get out there so the helo can see us."

He checked the area outside the cave before motioning her forward. Just as she stepped outside, Rocket heard the sound of the rotors and the helo lowered to the plateau just outside the cave. Rocket grabbed Mallory's hand and they ran for the door one of the men inside was just sliding open. Rocket boosted her inside before gabbing for the hands that hauled him up.

Then they were airborne.

As the chopper cut through the night, Rocket quietly studied Mallory. Was she glowing or was that his imagination? Could the others in the helo look at her — or him—and guess what had taken place? As he studied her, as casually as possible, she glanced over at him and their gazes locked. For one moment, heat flashed, then she looked away. He'd broken protocol with her but he couldn't find it in himself to regret it. *What the hell, anyway.* He'd never see her again, and that actually saddened him.

When they finally reached the field camp and Mallory was helped down out of the helo, two men came running forward to hurry her off. Rocket watched and at the last minute before being hustled into a car, she turned and waved.

Then she was gone, and for a long moment, Rocket wondered if the whole thing had even happened at all.